Praise for *Who Slashed Celanire's Throat?*

"Delicious."

—*Contra Costa Times*

"Mystical, magical, riveting, true. All these words apply to Maryse Condé's thought-provoking novel, *Who Slashed Celanire's Throat?*"

—Colin Channer, author of *Passing Through*

"Maryse Condé is one of the most important novelists writing today. Her stories are both historical and present, in the moment, murmuring secrets flavored with a Caribbean language of swishing rhythms, sweet as nectar, and lyrical as the swooshing skirts of the Guadeloupean women who people her new novel."

—Quincy Troupe, author of *Transcircualrities: New and Selected Poems,* and *Miles: The Autobiography*

"With this 'fantastical tale,' Condé claims her place as the most daring of gothic women writers. Enigmatic, obsessive, and fascinating, this novel is the story of a woman goaded into retribution by the scare encircling her neck . . . [The novel] redefines once and for all what has been called 'witchcraft,' conjuring it rather as a core belief, a project of thought working itself through terror."

—Joan Dayan, author of *Haiti, History, and the Gods*

WHO SLASHED CELANIRE'S THROAT?

A FANTASTICAL TALE

MARYSE CONDÉ

This story was inspired by an event that took place in Guadeloupe in 1995, when a baby was found with her throat slashed on a heap of garbage. The incident sparked the imagination of many throughout the island, mine included.

TRANSLATED BY RICHARD PHILCOX

W

WASHINTON SQUARE PRESS
New York   London   Toronto   Sydney

Washington Square Press
1230 Avenue of the Americas
New York, NY 10020

Originally published in France in 2000 as *Célanire cou-coupé*
Translated from the French by Richard Philcox

Published by arrangement with Éditions Robert Laffont

ISBN-13: 978-0-7434-8260-8
ISBN-10:   0-7434-8260-3
ISBN-13: 978-0-7434-8261-5 (Pbk)
ISBN-10:   0-7434-8261-1 (Pbk)

First Washington Square Press trade paperback edition September 2005

10 9 8 7 6 5 4 3 2 1

WASHINGTON SQUARE PRESS and colophon are
registered trademarks of Simon & Schuster, Inc.

Manufactured in the United States of America

For information regarding special discounts for bulk purchases, please
contact Simon & Schuster Special Sales at 1-800-456-6798
or business@simonandschuster.com.

For Raky, who will not take the trouble to read me

Ivory Coast
1901--1906

1

This was not the first time the Reverend Father Huchard, a long-standing member of the African Missionary Society in Lyons, had landed on these shores. He was an old-timer and had already spread the word of God among the natives of Dahomey as well as those in the Lower Congo. So it was of no surprise to him that the land was so flat, the forest beyond so impenetrable, that the rain over his head never let up and the sun up there, way up there, was so hazy. His eye was fixed on one of his flock of six: an oblate who answered to the name of Celanire. Celanire Pinceau. A most unusual name! The priest's gaze, however, did not betray any covetous look. It was simply the fact she stood out from the others. She hardly spoke. She did not seem curious or excited like her traveling companions, who were eager to begin their missionary work. What's more, her color set her apart, that dark skin that clothed her like a garment of deep mourning. Her features were not strictly black—rather, a hybrid of goodness knows how many races. She did not wear religious garb, since she had not yet taken her vows, but wore a somber gray dress and a scarf around her neck tied with a ribbon from which hung a heavy gold cross. Winter come summer, morning, noon, and night, this tightly knotted scarf never left her and matched the color of her clothes. Where did she come from? From Guadeloupe or Martinique. Well, from one of those colonies that are only French by name, where the natives have been baptized yet still run wild, swear like heathens, beat the drum, and drink strong liquor. She was an orphan raised by the Sisters of Charity in Paris whose desire to do missionary work in Africa had made her join the nuns of Our Lady of the Apostles in Lyons the previous year. Reverend Father Huchard, who had kept his eye on her throughout the voyage, was no wiser now than he had been when the *Jean-Bart* first sailed out of the Gironde estuary in a great swirl of muddy water. The fact was that whenever he regaled his audience with stories about the natives, and he had seen some in his time, she had a way of staring at him that made him ill at ease and reduced him to silence. But there was nothing serious to report. She wasn't insolent. She wasn't disobedient. Even so, Reverend Father Huchard didn't trust her and believed she was capable of anything.

The flotilla of small boats bobbed toward the old freighter, braving the wall of waves, jostled each other on reaching its side, and the passengers began to descend, the women standing in large metal baskets, clasping their skirts around their legs, the men gingerly clinging to the rope ladders. As they gradually boarded the boats, the smell of unwashed body parts wafted up.

It was the long rainy season, the one that stretches from April to July. The sun's beacon cast a reluctant glare over the immensity of the ocean's swell. The land remained at a safe distance behind the line of rollers, a land devoid of life and houses dotted among the greenery. It was a grayish, spongy land, in places eaten away by the mangrove swamps, in others wrapped in a shroud of vegetation. The sky was low, smeared by streaks of clouds. The silhouettes of the African porters could be seen fending off the torrential rain as best they could on the wharf while the European officials huddled under black umbrellas as voluminous as church bells.

At the time when this story begins (but is it the beginning? Where in fact does it begin? That's anyone's guess!) they had barely finished burying the dead at Grand-Bassam. An epidemic of yellow fever had laid to rest all that remained of the Europeans in the vicinity, resulting in the decision by the governor, Roberdeau d'Entremont, to transfer the capital to a more salubrious spot, a few miles distant, on the plateau of Adjame-Santey. In response to the barrage of objections regarding the cost of the upheaval, he pointed out that the many springs located beneath the plateau would provide an ample supply of water, which was not the case with the present capital.

Despite its misfortunes, Grand-Bassam proved to be a pleasant surprise. Forty years earlier it had been a stew of fresh and salt water trickling into the bush, emitting deadly miasmas. Now a neat little town had emerged from the sand, white as snow. There were not only the houses in the French district. A grove of coconut palms added a touch of green beside the Governor's Palace and the offices of the Western Telegraph Company. The Governor's Palace, built entirely of prefabricated material shipped from Bordeaux, was a rich example of French technology. Along the banks of the river Comoé stretched the Essante district, or District of the Converted. It was thought the souls of the newly baptized could be saved by herding them into huts made of palm fronds and branches. Life was returning to normal following the latest epidemic. The warehouses piled high with casks of palm oil were reopening. The priests had started working again with a vengeance, setting up outlying missionary stations along the shore like confetti. Since the church was one of the few buildings spared by the fire that had been set to check the epidemic, the apostolic nuncio had declared a miracle. Leading his flock, Father Huchard headed for the mission. Gone was the time when mass was said in the only priest's one-room hut, which had been used as a makeshift place of worship, bedroom, dining room, storehouse, and shop. The mission now numbered three priests bursting with health and two buildings made of bamboo, one of which was the school for thirty-two children. A group of African women catechists, with unflattering gray canvas head scarves pulled tight over their foreheads and blouses of the same color flattening their breasts, had set up a table in the courtyard and heartily served a frugal meal of rice, fried fish, and slices of pineapple.

Unperturbed, Celanire jotted down everything she saw in a notebook. She had already used up two thick ones on board the *Jean-Bart*. The majority of the Sisters of Charity and those of Our Lady of the Apostles disliked this habit of keeping a diary and thought it a sin of pride. But some of the more indulgent among them recalled that Thérèse Martin, in line for canonization, had written her autobiography. The five nuns from Our Lady of the Apostles were destined for a hospital recently opened in Man, way out in the bush. Only Celanire had been appointed to teach at the Home for Half-Castes some thirty miles away in Adjame-Santey. All because of those vows that Celanire had not taken! Since the nuns couldn't very well stop her from wanting to serve in Africa, they were, nevertheless, adamant she would not be allowed to experience the real hardships of Christian work.

Around midday an army of rudimentarily dressed porters turned up carrying *tipoyes*, signaling the farewell ceremony. Father Huchard blessed everyone, repeating his last words of advice:

"Be careful what you eat, what you drink, and what you

breathe. Beware of the water, the air, and especially the heathens. Those fiends can kill you with their magic."

He was going straight back to France on the same *Jean-Bart*. He would pray for them. Celanire bade farewell to her traveling companions as politely and coolly as she had behaved toward them during the voyage. She had never shared their petty enthusiasm, their elation, or their fears. When they told each other secrets, she would cover her ears. Likewise, when they removed their cornets and veils to soap themselves, revealing their pallid skins, she would lower her eyelids out of nausea.

As soon as her *tipoye* left Grand-Bassam, it was sucked into the sticky armpit of the forest. The trees stood like pachyderms. The penumbra of a cathedral, where the strains of Bach's *Magnificat* would not have been out of place, replaced the rain and dismal, murky daylight. Yet all that could be heard was the squelch of the porters' bare feet treading the humus as they raced along. Their load was no heavier than a child, and then they wanted to arrive at Adjame-Santey before dark. At night, too many evil spirits roamed at liberty. From time to time they turned their heads and tried to figure out this odd creature, black of skin but speaking the language of white men, living among them, and dressed like them.

Suddenly, the silence was broken by a cacophony of sounds. Monkeys, bats, and all kinds of invisible insects called and responded to each other amid the tangle of branches. Celanire was not listening and not even looking at this strange landscape. She had not come to Africa to be a tourist and was lost in her daydreams. What was in store for her in the days to come? She went back over the years gone by. She had not liked Lyons, where her color signaled her presence like a beacon wherever she went, and she had constantly to be on her guard. She missed

Paris. The convent of the Sisters of Charity was situated right on the rue de Vaugirard. Once she had closed behind her the heavy door studded with a cross, she found herself bang in the middle of the jungle of a big city—free to do whatever she liked. At night the cars roared and blinded passersby with their lights. Blacks in tuxedos lounged in piano bars. She had never revealed her secret escapades, and she became the Mother Superior's favorite. She never raised her voice, quarreled, or said a wrong word. By no means meek, she abided by the rules. Once the classes in theology and general instruction were over, she took the nuns by surprise. They were expecting her to return straightaway to Guadeloupe. Instead of which she was going to take her time: revenge is a dish best eaten cold. She was sharpening her pretty pointed teeth one against the other.

Briefly passing through the light of a clearing, they plunged back into thick undergrowth. The trees were different. Gone were the ironwoods, the silk cotton kapok and rubber trees. You could sense the heavy hand of man on nature. Rows upon rows of oil palms followed one after the other, as rigid as soldiers marching. At the foot of the trees the carefully weeded soil was bleeding from its wounds. Then the sky reappeared, pricked with stars, and the porters began to run along a rough track.

Lights appeared in the distance, the sight of which seemed to put wings on their heels, and Adjame-Santey came into view. The *tipoye* began to jolt as if buffeted by the ocean's waves. Indifferent to all this, Celanire sank into a semi-slumber until a commotion of excited voices awoke her. A troop of *askaris,* a comical sight with their legs swathed in strips of cotton fleece and tarbooshes askew, had almost collided with the porters. They were running in the opposite direction to announce some terrible news to the authorities in Grand-Bassam. Monsieur Desrussie, the director of the Home for Half-Castes, the very person Celanire had come to assist, had just passed from this life to the next. And how! He was about to make love to his new sixteen-year-old mistress when a giant spider hidden in the bedsheets had bitten him on his penis.

He had died on the spot!

People couldn't get over it. Only the day before he had been roaming the streets of Adjame-Santey, leering at the teenage girls, his cane under his arm as was his habit. There was no doubt his wife, Rose, had had a hand in the matter, and was tired of wearing the horns. She must have finally found a good witch doctor. For there is no such thing as a natural death. Everything is the work of malicious spirits whom the artful know how to subjugate to their own advantage.

Celanire could not understand a word of what was going on around her. Yet she guessed that her destiny had just been given its first nudge in the right direction. She poured out her thanks to her Master.

Karamanlis the Greek was stunned. No later than yesterday morning he had sold three boxes of matches to Monsieur Desrussie. The latter had come in to shelter from the rain, in actual fact to complain about everything as he usually did, and Karamanlis had had to put up with yet another diatribe about the laziness of the Ebriés and their drunken habits.

He was about to mount his bicycle when he saw the porters come charging into town. Everyone knew who they were carrying and who was coming to live in Adjame-Santey. An oblate. In other words, a nun who was not quite a nun and had no right to be called "sister." He craned his neck to get a glimpse of her and had this vision of a lovely face resting against a pillow of black silky hair. An emotion that he had not felt since leaving Athens stung his breast. It was as if the spider that had finished Monsieur Desrussie off had also attacked his heart. Pedaling awkwardly, he left what went by the name of town center, with its shops, the huts of the administrative services, the school, the church, and the bamboo buildings of the mission. He himself lived in a *poto-poto* neighborhood where cowpats looked as though they had been kneaded into huts. He had arrived in the Ivory Coast a few years earlier, drawn by stories of making a quick fortune from ivory and palm kernels that had replaced the slave traffic. Little did he know that the administration reserved its favors for the French companies, and there was no room for foreigners who massacred the language of Descartes. So he had done just about everything, even panning for gold in the kingdom of Assinie. In Adjame-Santey he made do with a small grocery store trading in dark leaf tobacco, loose sugar, sea salt, rock salt, and paraffin. He led a celibate life, since he did not have the means to contract a colonial marriage, lodging in his two rooms a friend who was even more destitute than he was, despite his attribution of "Mr. Philosophizer." Jean Seydou, a monitor of native instruction at the mission, had forbidden any mention of the name Jean and, out of loathing for the French, claimed to be Muslim and renamed himself Hakim. He was very handsome, with his curly hair, the offspring of a Toukolor princess and a high-ranking white administrator of the colonies. One morning his father had left him in a home for half-castes before sailing back to Perigord. Such an act was especially cruel, since Jean, who was not yet Hakim, had accompanied him everywhere for eleven years, following him from post to post in every nook and cranny from Upper Senegal to Niger. Despite this cruel abandonment, Hakim managed to pass the native examination for elementary studies and was hired as a primary-school teacher by the mission in Bamako.

Karamanlis found him lounging on his bed, buried in a magazine on India. The news did not interest him one bit. Monsieur Desrussie was dead? Good riddance! One bastard less! The oblate? She was lovely, was she? He was not attracted to women, in love with and secretly troubled by the bodies of his students and all those boys colonization had produced: kitchen boys, laundry boys, and tailor's apprentices.

Only once had he crossed the line. He had been a student in his last year at a home for half-castes. Bokar was also the son of a senior administrator and a Toukolor, Awa Tall. His father had left for France before he was born. His mother, remarried to a traditional chief, visited him from time to time, carrying on her head a calabash of *pastels* or a jar of *lakh* that sweetened the dull routine at the home. She always brought her other children, all perfectly black, who cast pitying looks at their illegitimate half-brother. Hakim's and Bokar's beds were next to each other. The inevitable had to happen. There followed months of wild, passionate happiness. Then the love nest was discovered. Either they gave the game away, or else the boys in the dormitory guessed something was going on. Hakim was dispatched to the recently pacified territory of Ivory Coast, while Bokar was left to languish in a school way out in the bush on the edge of the desert. It was here he was to commit suicide several years later. Hakim received the news of his death like a slap in the face. Ever since, there had never been a lack of opportunities—mainly French civil servants come to bury their youth under the sun in the colonies. But Hakim had never given in. He knew he would bring death to those who got too close. He cut short Karamanlis's shallow chatter by suggesting they go and listen to some music at the compound of King Koffi Ndizi.

Under the terms of a treaty signed two years earlier, the French had paid King Koffi Ndizi one hundred rolls of assorted fabrics, one hundred barrels of gunpowder, one hundred shotguns, two sacks of tobacco, six two-hundred-liter casks of brandy, five hats, a mirror, an organ, four cases of liqueurs, and three skeins of coral. In exchange for all that, they whittled down his power. Fortunately for Koffi Ndizi, his fetish continued to strike awe in his subjects, who, among other things, made him offerings of concubines, oxen, sheep, and fowl. His compound was a maze of courtyards and huts into which at least one hundred and fifty people were squeezed. Of an evening, his slaves served roast meat and carp fried in palm oil to almost a thousand admirers while his griots delighted the ear with music from *koras* and *balaphons*. On this particular evening nobody was in a mood to listen to them. Nor even badmouth the French, which was normally their favorite occupation. Two subjects dominated the conversation: the sudden death of Monsieur Desrussie and the arrival of the oblate. On the surface, the two events were unconnected. However, on second thought, who gained to profit from this death? Wasn't it the oblate who very likely would be appointed director of the Home? A woman, director of the Home, and a black woman into the bargain? Come now!

Exasperated, Hakim pushed his way to the royal dais. Koffi Ndizi was overweight, susceptible to inexplicable bouts of suffocation that alarmed him a lot. Like Hakim, he was in no mood to listen to the nonsense from his entourage. Three nights in a row, Zokpou, his senior fetish priest, had had dreams of ill-omen. The first night he had seen vultures swooping down on an impala and devouring it raw. On the second night an anthill over fifteen feet tall had suddenly crumbled into dust. On the third night the Ebrié lagoon was dyed red with blood. Zokpou had concluded that a succession of moons, portents of strange events, would be seen in the kingdom. But what would happen, he did not know. He did know, however, that for once it would not be the fault of the French. Besides, what more could they do? They had already turned Koffi Ndizi into a toothless, maneless lion.

Koffi Ndizi motioned to Hakim to approach. He liked the schoolteacher, always ready to run down his enemies, the French. He was well familiar with his tendencies, but was easy-going, having groped a good many boys in his youth. Together with incest, sodomy is a king's privilege. For two years he had been plotting unsuccessfully to overthrow Thomas de Brabant, the governor's deputy, a poker-faced individual who had two obsessions: building roads and railways. Next to the Romans, de Brabant would say, the French were the people who best realized the importance of roads. He was responsible for countless fathers being snatched from their homes to break stones under the sun. Koffi Ndizi and Hakim had tried to hide a mamba in a drawer of his desk and bribe his cook to poison his meals. Once they had buried a doll in his image in the entrails of a black cat. Nothing doing!

Hakim sat down on a corner of the mat he was offered and recounted his latest readings, for the king, however much a king, could neither read nor write. In India, the British did not attack the traditional authorities. They formed alliances and governed hand in hand with the local powers.

Why did the French have to put everything to the fire and the sword?

2

Alix Pol-Roger, the governor, had gone to negotiate a site for installing a French presence in the northern territories, and Thomas de Brabant had replaced him. Given his character, this suited him perfectly. He had the power to decide, resolve, and take the law into his own hands. Cases were no longer referred to the native courts. Thomas meddled in the most sordid family affairs and poked his nose into the most tangled legal issues of land ownership. That very morning he was struggling with a problem. What a piece of bad luck! Monsieur Desrussie was dead! He was an unsavory character. But useful. Who was going to look after the children in the Home now? The officials who had not yet taken their place in the graveyard were overloaded with work. Recruit a director from the *metropole?* Out of the question! The ministry refused to spend a cent on the new colony. He thought he ought to walk over to the Home and settle any remaining business. He donned his pith helmet, grabbed his umbrella, striped in the colors of his country's flag, and headed out.

Thomas de Brabant had been appointed to the Ivory Coast three years ago. Like the bulk of the administration, he had been transferred from Grand-Bassam to Adjame-Santey and missed the ocean breeze and the smell of salt of the former capital. The Ivory Coast had been his first posting on graduating third from the school for senior officials for France's overseas territories. Aged twenty-nine, he was married, but had had to leave his wife behind. The colonies, which are already hard on men, are lethal for women. The females of the species become dried, parched, and finally wilt. Charlotte, then, had remained on the fourth floor of a handsome building on the avenue Henri-Martin in Paris, the Brabant family being extremely well-to-do. During his annual leave, Thomas had returned to perform his conjugal duty, and ever since, with the faraway Charlotte and little Ludivine in his thoughts, he never forgot to take his quinine. His high position prevented him, so he thought, from having affairs with African women. As a result, he slept alone, eaten up with all kinds of desires, for the very women who were off-limits had a certain troubling effect on him.

It had been raining, of course, since morning. At four in the afternoon the sky skimmed so low, it was almost dark. A scarlet stream surged down the middle of the winding track, and Thomas had not walked more than a few yards before his high leather boots were covered in mud. A soaked flag wrapped around a bamboo mast signaled the school next to the church. Despite this patriotic rag, Thomas knew full well what was going on behind the hedge of seccos. His spies had informed him of what Hakim was teaching his older pupils, and the entire mission had him under surveillance. As soon as they had collected enough evidence against him, he would be shooed out! In one clean sweep! Never mind he was an administrator's bastard! At that very moment Hakim emerged from the school, surrounded by a group of young boys. With his jute bag folded into a hood over his head and his crumpled clothes, he looked anything but a scholar with a particular appreciation for the philosophers of the Age of Enlightenment. Thomas and Hakim avoided each other's gaze and continued on their way, one toward the Home, the other walking down to the lagoon and the king's compound.

The Home for Half-Castes on the plateau of Adjame-Santey was a one-story building in a sorry condition. Yet it had been built according to the plans of the famous architect Sebastien

Depelchin, who had set an example by abandoning there a dozen of his café-au-lait offspring. Behind the main building stood the house of the late director and his widow, one of the few converted Ebriés. The living room, transformed into a mortuary, was deserted except for a group of officials' wives feigning affliction. The widow was sobbing noisily on the breast of a young stranger who was very black of skin and whose hair was not crinkled but straight, brushed into a chignon and twisted into a long braid as thick as your arm. Dressed in the European manner, a black silk polka-dot scarf was wrapped around her neck. Her full lips were painted mauve, her eyelids blue. Yet all this makeup was too garish, as if it had been smeared on by the hand of a novice. Thomas was wondering who she could be when she introduced herself: Celanire Pinceau, arrived the day before. He wasn't expecting anything like this. The oblate, who was the talk of Adjame-Santey, looked like a hetaera. She simpered in a French, perfumed here and there with an exotic accent and punctuated with unusual expressions. Anybody would have been struck by her color. For she came from a remote French colony, Guadeloupe. She had lost both her parents, *maman* and papa, when she was small. So she had been taken in by the Sisters of Charity and raised under their care in Paris. She owed her entire education to them: certificate of higher education; diploma for general and religious instruction. And so on. And so on. She had always been at a loss to understand why for three centuries the missionaries had passed Africa by, sailing around the continent, hardly stopping, on their way to the Indies, China, and Japan. Fortunately, the African Missionary Society had been founded and set up a women's branch. She had thus been able to fulfill her dream: to spread the Holy Name of God on this destitute continent. Thomas, doubting by nature, wondered immediately what she could be hiding behind this inane speech. Her eyes, which were burning into him, contradicted the platitudes coming out of her mouth. She couldn't care less about Africa, evangelism, and her vocation! She had everything she needed to obtain whatever she wanted. Her voice turned beseeching: what was to become of her, now that her director had passed on so unfortunately? Was she going to be sent back to Paris? No, of course not, no, no, Thomas hastened to add. She would take over from Monsieur Desrussie. His mind was made up. He had not seen her references, but apparently they were impeccable. He would speak to the governor as soon as he got back. She could put her mind to rest!

Meanwhile, summoned by the king, Hakim was entering Koffi Ndizi's compound. Locked away in his private quarters, the latter was conversing through an interpreter with a man draped in a burnoose, a dress seldom seen in this coastal region: Diamagaram, a Muslim fetish priest, come down from Kong. When Hakim entered, Koffi Ndizi dismissed the interpreter, since the schoolteacher spoke perfect Malinke. Seated with the Holy Book open in front of him, Diamagaram had also made a cabalistic drawing in a tray filled with sand and was deep in concentration. He could see that evil spirits had recently set foot in Adjame-Santey, terribly malevolent spirits who had crossed over from the other side of the ocean. This was particularly surprising, since spirits never travel over water. They are frightened by this moving expanse inhabited by cold-blooded creatures, and you can hear their roars of anger and helplessness from the shore as they watch their prey escaping them. If they had set foot in Adjame-Santey, this meant they had mounted a "horse." That's the word for a human who obeys their every wish and who can be recognized by a sign. The aim therefore is to discover this sign, to find this "horse" and stop it from causing any harm, not an easy task. Diamagaram confessed that he had chased a "horse" in Bondoukou for months bearing a tiny sign on the body: two toes joined together. Getting the better of a "horse" requires extraordinary sacrifices. Not your ordinary chickens. Neither sheep nor even oxen. No, we're talking albinos. Children born with a caul. Twins. Prepubescent girls. Koffi Ndizi made it known he would do anything. He stared at the fetish priest, visibly impressed by his gift of the gab, his heavy string of beads, and his thick Koran.

At that moment Kwame Aniedo, the heir to the throne, a magnificent sixteen-year-old specimen, crawled in on all fours, as was the custom. He begged forgiveness from his father for daring to disturb him. But this too was an urgent matter. Three royal concubines, one leaving behind her an infant still at her breast, had left the compound without the queen mother's permission. They had refused to say where they had spent the afternoon. How many whiplashes should they be given?

At six in the morning, before the sun had opened its lazy eyes, before the women had lit the wood fires and heated the water for the men to wash, a piece of news was flying from mouth to mouth. The oblate, whom Thomas de Brabant had just appointed director of the Home for Half-Castes while awaiting the governor's approval, was recruiting. There was nothing extraordinary about recruiting! The French never stopped. They recruited to build roads, bridges over rivers, railways, wharfs, sawmills, brick factories, and lighthouses. The surprising fact about this new case was that she was recruiting only girls, and what's more, she was paying them. She handed each of them a small sum of money on the spot—enough to buy wrappers and head ties at the CFAO company store, soap, perfume, and talcum powder at Karamanlis's.

There was a rush to the Home.

Standing in the middle of the garden, Celanire was examining each candidate as if she were back in a slave market. From their teeth to the soles of their feet. Then, with the help of Desrussie's widow, turned interpreter, she switched to the interrogation. Did the candidate have a husband? A betrothed? Did she have any children? Girls? Boys? How many? At the end of the inspection, which lasted a full day, she recruited about fifteen girls whom she assembled under the mango trees together with the little half-castes. A nursery, she explained, would be set up for the under-threes, who would now no longer be left to dribble and poop, like they used to be. The one-class school would be enlarged. Pupils would wear khaki cotton uniforms on weekdays and white ones on Sundays. Girls old enough to hold a needle would learn sewing, but this would not constitute the basis of their education. They would learn the same subjects as the boys. However, on Thursdays and Saturdays the boys would clear the wasteland around the Home to make it into palm groves. They would also plant a kitchen garden and grow tomatoes, eggplants, and cabbages. Together with the chickens and sheep they would raise, the Home should be self-sufficient in a year or two at the most. Is that understood? Dismiss!

At day's end Celanire confided in her newfound friend, the widow Desrussie. She had never got over losing her darling little papa, and he was constantly in her thoughts. He was a splendid half-caste, a mulatto as they were called in the Caribbean, as good as he was handsome. A man of duty whose only passion was science. He conducted experiments on animals and had led a lone crusade against the ravages of opium introduced into the island by Chinese laborers. She described Guadeloupe as a paradise perfumed with the scent of vanilla and cinnamon. Despite her naïveté and her love for a good story, the widow Desrussie, like Thomas de Brabant, guessed that Celanire was not telling the truth. This woman was hiding something. They suspected she was more dangerous than a mamba. Her plans for the Home were troubling, for the land around it did in fact belong to someone. It belonged to the Ebriés.

If Karamanlis had not insisted, Hakim would never in his life have accepted Celanire's invitation. The Home for Half-Castes had too many bad memories for him. They spewed up a whole chapter of his childhood. But ever since the Greek had caught sight of the oblate in the depths of her *tipoye,* he raved about her to anyone who entered his store. He who was so miserly would give back the wrong change and could no longer sleep a wink at night. In short, he begged Hakim to strike up an acquaintance with the object of his desire so that he could get closer to her later on. For he knew that as a common trader, and a foreigner into the bargain, he would never be invited to the Home. Hakim therefore brilliantined his hair and slipped on a white caftan.

Within a few weeks the Home had been changed out of all recognition. The wind sang through the branches of a budding bamboo grove. Pink cassias, magnolias, and bushes of croton grew in profusion. In the drawing room downstairs, where a host of oil lamps cast broad daylight over everything, a rather formal reception was in full swing, and Hakim found himself ill dressed for the occasion. Even if nobody was dancing, a phonograph was playing the latest tangos and *paso dobles* from Paris. Every senior civil servant and factory manager whom Adjame-Santey could muster was present—not forgetting a handful of

officers on leave. These men, starved of women, devoured with
their eyes the pretty young African girls serving red wine and
beer. Celanire, extravagant in her makeup and wearing her eternal choker around her neck, was keeping watch over the occasion. She wore a silk dress whose plunging neckline was in
danger of pushing her breasts out into full view. The last straw
for Hakim was the way Thomas de Brabant behaved as the perfect host. He was wearing his ceremonial dress of white cotton
trousers and a jacket of the same color, adorned with epaulettes
and sleeves embroidered with gold facing on a black back-
ground. The sheath of his saber swung against his hips. His thick
hair was brushed back away from the forehead, and he was
drawing on a Havana as he hugged Celanire to his side. What
was going on between those two? Hakim knew that, by order of
the interim governor, land belonging to Koffi Ndizi had been
confiscated for the benefit of the Home. But he had never had
the opportunity of seeing Thomas and Celanire side by side. It
was crystal clear: they were lovers and sleeping together. Thomas
had finally unearthed the black woman educated in the ways of
the West who would allow him to satisfy his desires. Hakim,
stunned by his discovery, suddenly found himself face-to-face
with the woman filling his thoughts. With a smile Celanire
offered him a glass of beer, which he refused with such an abrupt
gesture that he sent it crashing to the floor. By no means
offended, she offered him another glass while her eyes, roughly
smeared with kohl, gave him such an urgent, inviting look that
poor Hakim's blood froze. He was a Muslim, he stammered, and
never drank alcohol. A Muslim, really? She burst out laughing as
if she had heard a good joke. Then she went on to interrogate
him. He was a schoolteacher, wasn't he? How many pupils were
there at the mission? Hakim managed to regain a semblance of

voice. About a dozen, all sons of local chiefs. It was the aim of the administration and its acolytes, the priests, to make hostages out of the dignitaries' children. Hostages? At the word, she laughed again, apparently amused by his barb. Fortunately, Thomas de Brabant came to put an end to this tête-à-tête. Hakim rushed outside. The warm rain and familiar din of the night insects calmed him down. What exactly was he afraid of? This was not the first time a woman had made known her intentions toward him. The life of a homosexual is strewn with these pitfalls. While he was trying to reason with himself, three couples emerged from the drawing room. One of the girls was propping up her escort, who kissed her greedily at the base of her neck. The others were pawing each other unashamedly. They disappeared under the arcaded veranda, reappeared, and mounted the monumental staircase, which enlaced two frangipani trees between its ramps.

Where were they going?

A crazy suspicion burgeoned in Hakim's mind. He dashed up the steps as fast as he could. The staircase came out onto a landing that disappeared into a corridor, plunged into darkness at this hour. The couples had vanished into the night. He opened a door haphazardly, and the inimitable smell of childhood wafted out: a dormitory. That was not what he was looking for. He closed the door behind him, walked around and around on the landing looking foolish, and then went back down to the drawing room. Nobody now was intimidated by the tango and *paso doble*. The African girls were dancing, following the lead of their escorts and laughing at the outrageous music. The only other place of this kind was at Jacqueville, where an African by the name of Latta Ahui had built a hut for dancing. Only those familiar with the white man's amusements were admitted. The others could watch. Celanire and Thomas were whispering cheek to cheek on a sofa. Thomas's hand was impatiently creeping up the oblate's thighs. Panic-stricken once again, Hakim dashed outside and ran home as fast as he could.

Karamanlis refused to believe a word. A bordello? And what next? Just a few embraces and kisses stolen from girls who were generally easygoing. You can think what you like about Thomas de Brabant, the colony knew he was the very model of virtue. As for Celanire, she was merely an oblate. Not a nun. She was entitled to use makeup and rig herself out as she thought fit. In the end Karamanlis became angry, forbidding Hakim to insult the woman he loved.

From that day on, it was nothing but quarrels and insults.

Within a few days, relations between Hakim and Karamanlis had grown so bitter that one afternoon, coming home from school, Hakim found his belongings thrown out under the rain. He gathered them up under the amused look of the houseboy and the neighbors. Where would he go now? The miserable wages of a schoolteacher were not enough to pay for lodgings. After hesitating, he set off for his only refuge: Koffi Ndizi's compound.

The compound was in a state of pandemonium.

Koffi Ndizi had been in a meeting since morning with the queen mother and the counsel of elders. The three royal concubines had not put up with their thrashing by a cat-o'-nine-tails. Refusing to be treated for their wounds, they had fled, once again leaving behind them their young infants. They had not gone back to their families, as abused women usually do. Where in fact had they gone? To the Home for Half-Castes, where the director immediately recruited them. For it was rumored around, in a confused sort of way like all rumors, that the Home was a paradise for women. Up there, it seemed, you didn't wait for happiness in vain. You grabbed armfuls of it. No more smoke from the green wood stinging your eyes! No more fetching water! No more *foutou* to pound! Hakim knew the way they treated women in Koffi Ndizi's compound. Beasts of burden and fodder for pleasure! Only the princesses had the right to remain independent, to choose their husbands and replace them if they were so inclined. So in a way he could understand their escape. Yet he was afraid of what lay in store for the fugitives up at the Home if his intuition were right.

Since he was unable to approach the king, he walked over to Kwame Aniedo's hut. The crown prince was amusing himself with a slave girl, but, good prince that he was, he interrupted his lovemaking and told Hakim he could sleep as many nights as he wanted in his entrance hall.

Kwame Aniedo was not only a handsome specimen. At school he ranked among the most gifted children, and Hakim had tried to persuade his father that he would have no difficulty mastering the secrets of the white man. To no end! The king wouldn't hear of it. School, he believed, was a waste of time. He had removed his son at the age of thirteen so as to keep his prestige as crown prince intact. As a result, for three years Kwame Aniedo had been doing absolutely nothing except eat to his heart's content, yawn at his musicians playing, and terrorize the girls who refused to go to bed with him. He hated the French who had humiliated his father and lent a sympathetic ear to Hakim's anticolonialist diatribes, without realizing that the latter was only interested in keeping him company while Kwame slipped out of his clothes and dived naked into the lagoon.

In the early evening, the usual crowd of brothers and cousins, idle royal princes, streamed into Kwame Aniedo's hut. The evening was spent downing vast quantities of palm wine while palavering over the fate of the royal concubines. The general opinion was that they should be brought back by force and inflicted a punishment which would serve as an example. The cat-o'-nine-tails was not enough. Rather a few days locked up without food or water. It was late when Hakim finally fell asleep and he was still snoring when a messenger came to wake him: Koffi Ndizi was asking for him. His earthenware pipe wedged between his teeth, the king was pacing up and down. He had not slept a wink all night and had been in constant consultation with the queen mother and the elders. They had finally come to a decision. Since the wretched oblate was the protégée of the French, they had to tread lightly. Hakim would write a polite letter on behalf of the king begging her to return the three concubines. He would explain they belonged to the royal family. To keep them would be a serious breach of tradition, an offense. Hakim therefore went back to look for some paper and a pen and wrote down everything they had asked of him.

After two weeks it was obvious that Celanire couldn't care less about the letter Koffi Ndizi had sent her. This was another pretext for deliberation and consultation. The queen mother was outraged. The elders lost their saliva. Some of them called for a punitive raid on the Home, just like in the good old days. But how would they go about it? Nobody knew. As for the fetish priests, they advised on caution as they could not understand who this oblate was. In order to clarify matters, shouldn't they get her to undergo a trial by ordeal? If she passed the test and came out unscathed, they would know she was a normal person with nothing on her conscience. Okay, but how could they approach her?

Finally, Koffi Ndizi entrusted Hakim with a mission that was to be a last resort. This time he would go in person to the

Home and plead on behalf of the kingdom. Hakim obeyed, with heavy heart.

When he arrived at the Home, Celanire was teaching in her classroom. Madame Desrussie showed him into an office on the second floor. The view was magical. Beneath the balcony the garden stretched away like a priceless carpet embellished with freshly planted Madagascar periwinkles, coral hibiscus, and oleander already in full bloom. The long rainy season was drawing to a close. The sky was losing its leaden color. If the place was in fact a bordello, it hid it well under its aspect of a Garden of Eden. When Celanire appeared, Hakim did not recognize her. She was wearing a dress of tiny blue-and-yellow squares, buttoned from top to bottom, with a buttercup-yellow neckerchief. Her hair had been braided into two plaits. Without makeup she looked eighteen at the most. She was no longer the sensual vamp, but poetically poignant. While they drank mint tea, she talked of her passion for Africa. In her opinion there was only one dark side to the beauty of its civilization: the treatment of women. Was he aware that the Africans mutilated the female genitals? They excised the clitoris and the labia. Then they sewed up the folds, leaving a narrow passage for the urine and the menstrual blood. Hakim's imagination had seldom ventured into such places. Ill at ease, he stammered that this practice was the equivalent of male circumcision. But it was an intolerable aggression, she exclaimed indignantly, perpetrated against women in order to control their sexuality. Then she changed the subject and began to describe the great solitude of her life. She had never known her true parents and was nothing but a foster child. Oh, she had nothing against her foster parents, especially her papa. But it was tough not knowing the sperm that fathered her or the womb that carried her. At Adjame-Santey, she felt an outsider. Thomas de Brabant possessed her body but not her heart. Stunned by her candor, Hakim was rendered speechless. She then turned to interrogate him, and he heard himself confiding and revealing all his childhood troubles. He too felt an outsider in Adjame-Santey. Moreover, he had always felt an outsider in Africa. In short, one hour later, furious with himself, he was back on the path taking him home. Not only had he not breathed a word about the mission Koffi Ndizi had entrusted him with, but he had promised Celanire he would pay her many more visits.

Had she bewitched him?

3

The rains had let up now for two weeks. The hedges of croton bordering the houses of the Europeans could finally lift their heads. The clumps of guinea grass sprouted green along the embankments. Behind the fences of secco the animals frolicked for joy. Only Koffi Ndizi's compound remained unaffected by this springlike revival. One night Tanella, a concubine of Mawourou, the king's uncle on his mother's side, had stuck a knife in his heart while he was asleep. Once the deed was done, she had fled.

Two years earlier Tanella had been one of the gifts, together with the fowl, dried fish, and richly woven wrappers, the village of Attonblan had offered Koffi Ndizi. She had never been much to his liking, and he had left her to Kwame Aniedo, who for a time had used her for his pleasure. One day, while she was pounding plantains in one of the courtyards, Mawourou had caught sight of her fifteen-year-old breasts. Mawourou had fathered a dozen sons, already fathers to sons themselves; but he was still so troubled by the desires of the flesh that he employed an army of fetish priests to concoct his aphrodisiacs. Tanella's crime was only discovered the next morning when the blood that had trickled out under the doors of Mawourou's hut coagulated into a red crust in the very middle of the courtyard. Murder was so rare an occurrence in the region that people first attributed the gaping hole in the old man's heart to a fit of anger by the spirits. Then the truth became obvious. The evil deed had been caused by a human hand. Some women who had got up early recalled having seen Tanella running away in blood-soaked clothes and remembered she had complained of Mawourou on many occasions. His breath was fetid. He had trouble getting a hard-on; he beat her. They searched for her throughout the compound, in the vicinity of the lagoon, and even as far as the forest. A few men ran along the road to the village of Attonblan but came back empty-handed. Nobody had seen Tanella. At day's end the rumor spread that she had found refuge at the Home for Half-Castes. So the widows, the children, and the friends of Mawourou, all those who had known him while he was alive and all those who had nothing better to do, assembled into a crowd and marched off to fetch her back from the Home.

The procession slowly wound its way through Adjame-Santey, where the population, struck with horror, commented on the terrible turn of events. Karamanlis watched from his store as he saw Hakim and his pupils bringing up the rear of the cortege. He eyed him scornfully. So there he was a "liberated" young man taking the side of a lascivious old man, abuser of young girls, who after all had only reaped what he sowed. On reaching the Palace of Justice (a fine name for a clay hut), the procession swelled with all the idle bystanders and onlookers who happened to be around. On the outskirts of Adjame-Santey the crowd quickened its pace without really knowing why, perhaps because night was approaching. The sky was growing dark. Soon the spirits would be on the prowl. In fact, much of the crowd did not really want Tanella to be put to death, the punishment for such a crime. They were marching with the others to demonstrate quite simply that it was time, high time, the French and their henchmen, governors, priests and oblates, left them to their customs and went home. Even the women who, deep in their hearts, were sympathetic toward Tanella, understandably tired of surrendering her youth night after night to the fantasies of an old man, were convinced that a shadowy past in its death throes was preferable to the future these foreigners had in store for them. When the crowd came in sight of the Home, they were surprised to find rows of militia from a neighboring camp pointing their guns at them. Why? The crowd hesitated and began to retreat in disorder. The fearful fled, predicting disaster. The more courageous began to throw rocks and stood their ground. With hackles up, the head of the militia barked a number of syllables that nobody could understand. He barked again. Then his men obeyed. And opened fire.

After the shots rang out, three bodies lay on the ground, including two of Hakim's pupils, the ten-year-olds Senanou and Dabla. Plus a dozen wounded.

Thomas de Brabant reread the official telegram he had just received.

On learning of the grave events at Adjame-Santey, the indiscriminate use of force, the high number of casualties, Governor Alix Pol-Roger was cutting short his mission to the north and returning home as quickly as possible. Having offered refuge to a murderer, the oblate Celanire Pinceau, who was the cause of the troubles, must appear before him immediately. The tone of the telegram left no doubt in his mind. Celanire's appointment as director of the Home would not be ratified. As for Thomas, he risked a reprimand or even a demotion. The hypocrisy of these senior colonial officials made him sick. Hundreds of "voluntary workers" were dying of hunger and ill treatment along the railroad. Nobody breathed a word about them, whereas the three wretched corpses of Adjame-Santey would be the talk of all French West Africa. In fact, the administration was mainly concerned about the two school pupils, Senanou and Dabla. As luck would have it, they were the sons of Betti Bouah, one of the richest merchants of the region, of royal blood, related to Koffi Ndizi, but who had the intelligence to be sympathetic to the French. It was now feared he would switch sides. A paltry excuse! What rules was Thomas expected to obey? Perhaps they would have preferred he let the fanatics sack the Home, stone Tanella to death, and beat Celanire and her assistants black and blue. That sort of tragedy was exactly what his firmness had avoided that evening, and law and order had been restored. Celanire had no intention of shielding Tanella from justice. She only meant to protect her from her compatriots. After having kept her overnight at the Home and calmed her down as best she could, she herself had handed her over to the *askaris* who had taken her to the jail at Grand-Bassam. From there she was to leave on the first ship for Dakar and appear before the supreme court that met twice a year. Thomas's legitimate anger at his superiors was mingled with an insidious terror of their discovering something else, too shameful to mention. He no longer understood what madness had let him be convinced by Celanire and made him approve of her plans. It was as if his mistress had bewitched him. At her side, he was powerless and could no longer distinguish right from wrong. It was a fact they only entertained high-ranking officials at the Home. No subalterns, secretaries, or pencil pushers! Even so, they were at the mercy of a tongue loosened by too much drink.

Incapable of staying still, he donned his pith helmet and mounted his bicycle, since the track was now passable again. He wisely made a detour to avoid the house where the wake for Senanou and Dabla was being held. The place had become a rallying point for fanatics making anti-French remarks where, he had been told, Hakim was in his element.

At the end of the year, Adjame-Santey was to be renamed Bingerville at an official ceremony in honor of the colony's first governor. The administrative buildings, however, were far from finished. The governor's palace had scarcely poked its head out from the building site that had once been the cemetery. As Thomas rode around the mission, he saw a cortege approaching. Flanked by the remainder of his guards, sheltering under an umbrella, preceded by his gold-cane bearer, King Koffi Ndizi, tripping on his sandals, was going to pay his final respects to his cousin's children. The procession took up the entire width of the path, for Koffi Ndizi was surrounded by a good dozen sycophants, including the inevitable Hakim. In a flash, Thomas summed up the situation. Either he kept pedaling straight ahead and rode right into the oncoming procession, knocking over two or three, or else he got off his bicycle and stood like a country yokel in the guinea grass on the embankment. Despite his arrogance, he did not think twice. Adjame-Santey had been through enough confrontations in such a short time. He dismounted. The king walked by without turning his head in his direction, joining both hands level with his mouth in an African greeting, while the looks of his entourage cut him like flint stones. He even thought he heard snickers of laughter.

At present the Home was looking so good it would have been the pride of Dakar. Under the late Desrussie, an epidemic of yaws would follow an epidemic of yellow fever. It was better not to count the number of dead. Once they had buried thirty in a single month. Under Celanire's radiating care the children glowed with health and cleanliness. A group of small children under the charge of two assistants was sitting in a circle on the lawn singing "Frère Jacques" in their delightful little voices. Some of the older boys were marching off in manly fashion to the fields, hoe in hand. The bamboo grove, the young palm trees, and the budding orchard were another treat for the eyes. Celanire had taken advantage of the dry season to have the facade repainted in a very pale eggshell tint edged with dark red. Her choice of unusual colors was evidence of her exquisite taste, which made her so precious to Thomas. It was obvious the meager allowance attributed to running the Home couldn't possibly have been enough to cover all these improvements, and going over the colony's accounts with a fine-toothed comb would have turned up quite a few surprises.

Celanire was resting in a boudoir, draped in a kimono of black silk, a color she seemed to like, embroidered with red roses and buttercups. If it hadn't been for her wide, somewhat triangular nose and her very full lips, she could have been mistaken for an Indian from the French trading posts of Pondicherry, Kana Kal, and Manahe. Thomas smothered her with kisses, then got control of himself and pulled the telegram out of his pocket. Celanire shrugged her shoulders and vaguely asked a few questions. Where exactly was Governor Pol-Roger? Thomas explained he was in Felkessekaha among the Niarafolo Senufo natives. As if this was of no interest to her, she changed the subject. She was thinking of going to the wake for Senanou and Dabla as a way of expressing her condolences to the family. What did he think of the idea? Thomas uttered a shrill cry: Was she out of her mind? The Africans hated her. She would be stoned to death.

In fact hostilities had been declared for some time now between Celanire and the Africans. Celanire had proclaimed loud and clear she had no intention of letting the girls in her care be sexually mutilated. Going by what she said, the very fact that the mothers let their offspring be placed in the Home for Half-Castes by their French papas meant they renounced de facto all their rights, and the children became the sole responsibility of the French administration. Obviously, such quibbling had not made the slightest impression. While the innocent six-year-old Marie-Angélique was spending the weekend with her family, they had grabbed the opportunity to put her under the excision knife. She had almost died from a hemorrhage. In a fit of anger, Celanire forbade her boarders to leave the Home from that moment on and only allowed family visits once every three months. Although some families were not bothered by these rules, others, as you can imagine, raised a hue and cry. Half-caste or not, some mothers were fond of their little darlings and accused Celanire of sequestering them. They camped outside the Home in tears. The courts were bombarded with complaints, and Thomas had great trouble getting the fact accepted that his mistress was within her rights.

Thomas had already noticed that Celanire was a stubborn woman who did just what she liked. Without paying the slightest heed to his objections, she drew him close to her.

Making love to Celanire was a delight Thomas could never have imagined even in his wildest dreams. Deep down he called her "my little panther" because he never knew whether her embrace would make him moan with pain or pleasure. When his strength gave out, she asked for more. At the very end she left him exhausted, worn out, deliciously dead.

Betti Bouah's house made the Africans proud and left the Europeans stunned. It had been built by Appolonian workers from Cape Coast in the Gold Coast and comprised an upper floor that was reached by a dual staircase mounted with open fretwork wooden balustrades. The living room where the children's bodies lay was richly furnished in the European style with rugs, sofas, and armchairs. Low tables were covered in crocheted doilies. There were no less than five clocks and four music boxes fixed to the wall, plus portraits of Napoleon at Arcole, Napoleon Bonaparte Emperor, Treich-Laplène, Binger, Queen Victoria, and gilt-framed round mirrors surmounted by an imperial spread eagle. The showpiece was a sideboard with a display of blue-stemmed crystal glasses. Like all rich merchants, Betti Bouah had collected every gift he had received from his European customers in the same room. Owing to his status in society, people had come from the surrounding villages and even as far away as the Alladian shores, draped in their mourning robes. According to custom, the assembly was divided strictly in two. Inside the house, the women, mothers, stepmothers, and aunts of the little victims. Outside on the verandas, the men. The latter were frantically interrogating Hakim on how to rid themselves of the French. But contrary to what Thomas had been told, Hakim had absolutely nothing to offer and stammered out a series of platitudes. So the more the evening dragged on, the angrier they felt in their helplessness and the faster the calabashes of palm wine were passed around. The fact that Tanella had been handed over to the French authorities did not calm them down. The French had no business meddling in this affair. It was a matter for the native courts. Betti Bouah had consulted with his lawyer in Bordeaux, who advised him to lodge a complaint with the governor-general of French West Africa. And he had got nowhere with Koffi Ndizi, who did not understand a thing about "white men's business," as he liked to say.

When around ten o'clock in the evening Celanire made her entrance, the buzz of conversation abruptly stopped. Those who had a cutlass handy thought of using it. But she had such a gentle look about her, they had second thoughts. She avoided making any sign of the cross or genuflection that might shock these heathens and remained standing, head lowered, in front of the children's bodies. Then, using the widow Desrussie as interpreter, she asked to go and join the women. To do so she had to walk past Koffi Ndizi, spilling out of his armchair, and she nodded her head in respect while the king, seeing her for the first time, stared, openmouthed. Hakim was the only one who believed Celanire had come to thumb her nose at them and see how good she was at getting them to change their minds. For those who had quickly badmouthed her behind her back now retracted and spoke highly of her beauty. Koffi Ndizi even declared that the fetish priests had been wrong and such a lovely individual could never be the "horse" of the *aawabo,* the evil spirits. Some daydreamed out loud and wondered whether she would agree to marry an African. After all, she was as black as they were! However hard a group of elders recalled that a woman's beauty is a man's misfortune, nobody paid attention to these sayings of another age. When Celanire emerged from the women's quarters, Koffi Ndizi ordered Hakim to accompany her home, seeing how late it was.

The night crackled with the cries of insects. The moon had hidden her face behind a crepe of clouds. In the darkness

Celanire laid her hand on Hakim's arm, which immediately became burning hot from her touch. It was as if he were standing next to a fire. She spoke to him in a mellow voice: That wake reminded her of Guadeloupe. There too, death was highly respected. At All Saints the flames of the candles stretched over the graves like a diamond necklace. Oh, sometimes she felt like ditching everything and going back home. But did she have a home? A home is a *maman* and a papa waiting for you with open arms. Those who had adopted her now slept in the shade of the casuarinas. And then seven years, seven long years, had elapsed since leaving Guadeloupe. When you're separated from a place for such a long time, you lose it forever: everything changes, nothing is the same. Listening to her sugary words, Hakim thought it was a good thing Governor Alix Pol-Roger was coming back soon. If he had any sense, neither Thomas de Brabant nor Celanire would be welcome much longer in Adjame-Santey.

Back at Betti Bouah's, the racket had grown louder. According to tradition, the wake had to continue for the remainder of the night and part of the following day. When they finally got around to thinking of the burial, Thomas de Brabant's guards rushed in. Governor Alix Pol-Roger was dead!

Dead? From what? How?

On his way back to Adjame-Santey he had stopped at the encampment of Tentona. It was well known for its abundant water supply and cool air, since it was situated on an escarpment fed by two rivers. While he was eating lunch, under the very eyes of his escort, he had been attacked by man-eating lions, those thick-maned black lions from Mourga, the very ones described by Amadou Hampate Ba. They had burst into the camp and without looking left or right had pounced straight on him, knocked him over, trampled and devoured him, leaving nothing behind but a pool of blood, a few bones, and a pair of legs still standing in tall, brown leather boots.

These unfortunate events brought together two men who up till then had had little contact with each other: Betti Bouah and Hakim. Betti Bouah was the opposite of his cousin Koffi Ndizi, as athletic and muscular as the other was potbellied. He spoke French to perfection and could read and write fluently. He was always prepared to discuss the eighteenth-century philosophers, especially Diderot, his favorite. In spite of the saying that the white man's leader is the Englishman, Betti Bouah had sided with the French. He had lent them his support on every occasion; he had lodged Binger under his roof during his 1889 expedition. He hadn't done all that only to have two of his sons mowed down by militia in the pay of the French. Following these dramatic events, he began to think twice about colonization and came to the conclusion that the Africans should join forces to kick the French out as quickly as possible and take their place. During his games of chess with Hakim, he laid out his plans. Since Hakim lent his fervent support, he offered him a job in his factories. The wages he proposed were three times higher than the mission's. Hakim couldn't believe his ears. To be rid of that mud-brick school, suffocating during the dry season, flooded during the rainy season! Of his dim-witted, fingers-all-thumbs pupils! Say good-bye to those hypocritical and finicky missionaries. Moreover, his cohabitation with Kwame Aniedo was becoming unbearable. He could no longer put up with hearing the prince noisily take his pleasure with his mistresses or bumping into him, quite naked, his pipe stuffed with Bahia tobacco wedged between his teeth. And that wasn't the worst of it. Koffi Ndizi seemed to have lapsed into second childhood. Ever since he had set eyes on her at the wake for Senanou and Dabla, he had become infatuated with Celanire. He now only had one idea in his head: to invite her to his house. But when he looked around, he was ashamed at what he saw. He would never dare entertain someone so sophisticated in such a place. So he endeavored to imitate Betti Bouah and ordered armchairs, beds, dishes, glasses, and even a set of kitchen utensils from Grand-Bassam. Since Hakim had spoken highly of the Muslim art of living, he had rugs and wall coverings shipped from Tiassalé. Oh, how he would have liked to speak French, a language that up till then had always stuck in his throat! One afternoon, Hakim paid Koffi Ndizi a visit. The king had just received four crates of dishes from Grand-Bassam. He was inspecting plates and blue-stemmed glasses identical to his cousin's, and frantically inquired of his visitor, What did he think? Would Celanire be impressed? At a time when the atmosphere in the colony was loaded with tension, such fickleness exasperated Hakim. He ran to Kwame Aniedo's, collected his meager belongings, and took his leave without saying good-bye to anyone.

4

Hakim's new life gradually settled into place.

Betti Bouah was in the business of palm oil. He bought it from the Akouri and Alladian villages or even farther afield. His men filled the casks supplied by the companies in Bordeaux and Nantes, and transported them along the Ebrié lagoon with a fleet of dugout canoes. They then rolled them overland and loaded them onto whaling boats that set out for the ships lying offshore behind the line of breakers. He also sold timber for dyes, ivory and skins that he purchased on the markets in the interior in exchange for gunpowder, guns, spirits, leaf tobacco from Virginia, cutlery, and knives. In short, he seemed a treasure trove for anyone who wanted to do business with him. Under his orders, Hakim no longer had time even to think about eating his bellyful. Up before sunrise, the noise of his little outboard would frighten the caymans wallowing lazily in the mud. Standing under the glare of the midday sun, he would quickly swallow a meatball of *akassan* reddened with palm oil. He dashed from one plantation to another, overseeing the loading. At first he did everything possible in the evening to keep up appearances. Once he had shaved and cologned, he went up and joined his host, who as a rule was sitting in a European-style armchair. Betti Bouah was very fond of chocolate and drank it by the cupful. While sipping this newly discovered drink, the two men would comment on what the French called "pacification" and what they themselves called quite simply "the war." There seemed to be no end to the bloody massacres in the northern territories. How many dead had they already buried? How many more were they going to bury? Yes, Africa had got off to a bad start, and the white man's sun illuminated nothing but misfortune. Sometimes, though, their conversation turned to a lighter side. They talked about women. Betti Bouah explained he had not been impressed by Celanire. A real bag of bones! He preferred full-bodied women, like a good Bordeaux wine. Just look at his wives. And then that ribbon tied around her neck terrified him like a small child. No doubt about it, that's where she hid the mark that indicated she was the "horse" of dangerous *aawabo*. He had once known a "horse" with the distinguishing mark of a wart on his chin. It had taken years to find him out. In the meantime, he had killed off a whole village. Deep down, without daring to contradict him, Hakim scoffed at these superstitions, okay for Africans, but which his father's European education had rid him of.

It wasn't long, however, before he ached all over, and in the evening he would throw himself on his bed, fall fast asleep, and snore until morning. This extreme exhaustion naturally gave cause for thought. In fact, what had he gained by leaving the mission school? He was still a subaltern. He no longer had time to open a book. His hair was no longer combed or brilliantined. The people he kept company with were crude, the banknotes he handled were filthy, and he was no longer Mr. Philosophizer, phrasemonger of French French. It was that very moment Kwame Aniedo chose to ask Hakim to help him pass the colonial administration examination. Kwame Aniedo could no longer put up with the life of idleness dictated by Koffi Ndizi, and he could no longer bear to see him lapse into a second childhood because of his ridiculous passion for Celanire. So he had decided to leave the royal compound, which he considered a lost cause. He was prepared to leave the country for Dakar, the city where nobody ever dies. Apparently, the French were recruiting and paying for all sorts of clerks in their offices and administration. Kwame Aniedo could already see himself as a messenger in khaki uniform with gilt epaulettes pedaling his Motobécane. Hakim, never forgetting that Kwame had offered him a roof over his head when he needed one, saw himself obliged to calculate the square of the hypotenuse while in a state of exhaustion. What was worse, Kwame Aniedo's presence still produced the same effect on him and upset him deep down: that smell of sweat and shea butter of his, that way he had of sucking greedily on his wooden penholder, that childlike expression of his when-

ever he no longer understood his lesson. Hakim despondently
predicted that one day he would be unable to control himself
and would throw himself on Kwame Aniedo. And that would be
catastrophic. For the horrified Kwame would take out his
Sheffield steel switchblade deep within the folds of his wrapper
and stab him a fatal blow. Thus Bokar would get his revenge.

On that particular day Hakim had been called to the Home
to buy the harvest of palm kernels. As a precaution he had kept
out of Celanire's way since the day of the burial for Dabla and
Senanou. The new palm groves were curling their hair over several acres plucked from the forest. A mountain of kernels was
waiting under the trees. Celanire could be grateful: thanks to the
Ebriés' free labor and the work of the senior pupils, the harvest
was rich, and it took over three hours to weigh it and load it into
jute sacks that the porters lugged on their backs to the factory.
Once the transaction was finally over, Hakim was about to turn
on his heels when the widow Desrussie held him back. Celanire
was asking for him. However hard he insisted he was in his work
clothes and had been sweating since morning, the widow was so
adamant, he felt obliged to follow her.

Once he left the shade of the palm grove, the heat fell on his
neck like a sharp blade. The sun was high in the sky, cooking the
tall obelisks of the anthills. With persiennes lowered, the Home
was taking its siesta. It had become a real jewel, nestling in its
setting of trees and riot of flowers. Celanire had laid out flower
beds and introduced heavy-scented roses together with tulips
and carnations she had shipped from France. In an aviary dozed
papilios, giant butterflies with yellow velvety wings striped black
and blue. For Hakim, such serenity was deceiving. He imagined
the Home to be like the castle of a Sleeping Beauty, waiting for
the night to begin its life of debauchery. He crossed the bamboo

grove, his feet sinking into the thick carpet of lawn. The widow Desrussie showed him into a boudoir where everything seemed unreal. In the penumbra, the murky eyes of the mirrors gazed back at him. The chimeras on the screens opened wide their jaws to swallow him, swinging their heavy ringed tails in every direction. He was about to beat a retreat when he caught sight of Celanire watching him, lying on a sofa. She was draped in a silk kimono, encrusted with the same chimeras. A kerchief dripped red around her neck. She motioned to him to sit down close to her, and he was overcome with nausea at the pervading smell of female. He managed to pull himself together, however, while she explained her circumstances in a mournful voice. She had been bedridden for days with a bout of fever, and she truly thought she wouldn't make it alive. He asked her unimaginatively if she had forgotten to take her quinine, and she shrugged her shoulders. Quinine? She didn't believe in those miracle remedies for whites. In Guadeloupe, her papa taught her the virtues of poultices and herbs. *Zèb à Fè. Koklaya. Té simen kontran.* Africa had the same pharmacopeia. That's how she had taken care of herself. Why is she always talking about her papa, Hakim thought irritatedly, especially if he's not her real papa? Hakim had not kept his promise, Celanire complained, and had never come to see her. He apologized. He was overworked at Betti Bouah's and spent his time dashing from one village to another. He was endeavoring to embellish his new life with a set of adventures when she cut him short. Did he like that kind of work? He remained speechless. This woman could read him like an open book.

She laid her hand on his knee, burning it like a firebrand, and then lectured him. You must always like what you do. She had a mission: transform this humble Home for Half-Castes into a monument that would go down in people's memories. For the first time in the history of the colony, her school was entering four girls for the native diploma of elementary studies. The Africans subjugated and mutilated their women. The French taught them merely how to thread a needle and use a pair of scissors. Now they were going to see something else. She did not hide the fact that she had ambitious plans. She had given a lot of thought to the reasons why relations between Africans and the French came up against a stumbling block. Because the colonizers, being men, could only think in terms of men. It was the men they invited to share in their projects. It never occurred to them to ask the women. Whereas in Africa, more than anywhere else, the women welcomed change, which could only be to their advantage. They were tired of working themselves to death, tired of being treated as subalterns, tired of being humiliated, beaten, and abused. Only the women could hold colonization in check for one very good reason. Once the colonizer had clasped a black woman in his arms, could he ever be the same again? No, no, and no! Ever since Thomas de Brabant had found happiness with her, he had become another man. He saw Africa through different eyes. He who was once so contemptuous, so convinced that the continent knew nothing of art and civilization, she had persuaded him to open a museum, and he had started collecting those very same masks he used to swear he would burn in an auto-da-fé. The Home for Half-Castes would be that meeting place that was sorely lacking, a privileged place where love between the races would fructify, grow, and multiply. That was its vocation. She proposed he work for her and teach the senior pupils. She would take care of the juniors. The girls she had trained would look after the tots. Hakim hesitated, looking for an answer that would not be taken as an insult, when her little paw, drawing a

trail of fire, began to crawl up the inside of his leg. He sat petri-
fied while she reached her objective. They looked at each other
straight in the eyes, she visibly surprised by his lack of response.
She stroked harder. In vain. Ashamed, he stood up, adjusted his
clothing, and ran for the exit. Outside, the light brought him
back to earth. He sensed that Celanire would never forgive him
such an affront. When he got back home, overcome with nausea, he washed and soaped himself from head to toe. Then he
slipped on a pair of shorts and a freshly starched cotton drill
shirt and went upstairs to join Betti Bouah. The latter frowned
on seeing him home so early, but managed to hide his feelings
and told him the latest gossip. Thomas de Brabant had just had
his appointment confirmed as governor of the colony, and consequently the lucky fellow was going to be the first to occupy the
new palace. A grandiose building. The juicy bit was that his
wife, Charlotte, was arriving from France with their daughter.
Everybody was wondering what would become of his affair with
Celanire, for it was an open secret they slept together. He was so
besotted with her, he blindly obeyed her every wish. He had
recently authorized her to make the Home a refuge for girls running away from husbands and suitors. What next would she do?
Lovesick, Karamanlis the Greek had tried to drown himself in
the lagoon on several occasions. Every time they had dragged
him back to the shore alive. As for Koffi Ndizi, he had repudiated his thirty-nine wives and concubines, keeping only his first
love, Queen Tadjo, provided she too "converted." He was taking
catechism classes and was preparing to become a Christian, to
the great joy of the mission, since conversions by a chief were
exceptionally rare. The Church only attracted wretches lured by
a pair of shorts and an undershirt that the priests gave to the
baptized. What did Koffi Ndizi expect from such a foolish act?

The following morning Hakim was scarcely awake when the widow Desrussie, bundled up in a wrapper against the cool morning mist, brought him a letter from Celanire. It was written on pretty yellow stationery, well phrased and sober given the circumstances. Celanire apologized for having betrayed a fondness for him that he obviously did not share. As for her job offer, it still stood. She was especially keen on having him, as she knew he could work miracles. Wasn't he preparing that good-for-nothing Kwame Aniedo to compete for the French administration examination? Likewise, he would know how to transform the Africans into responsible men of their times. As for the love angle, he could sleep safe and sound, she would no longer bother him. The trivial adventure was over! Hakim retained only one thing from this epistle. It was no coincidence that Celanire had mentioned the name of Kwame Aniedo. She had seen right through him. She knew about his feelings for the prince. In actual fact, this apparently innocuous letter constituted a threat.

In a state of frenzy, he set out for the landing stage on the other side of Bingerville. A mob of small traders carrying calabashes and makeshift basins brimming with unrefined palm oil was already laying siege to the warehouse. The smell of grease mingled with that of the decomposing mud and humus. All around, the banks appeared strewn with bones, in actual fact dead tree trunks bleached by the sun and the brine. Hakim seated himself in the outboard. Bordered by dense foliage, the blackish waters of the lagoon lapped threateningly against the landing stage. He had always been scared of water. As a child, after his papa had left him, he had only to close his eyes to imagine himself slipping slowly into a bottomless lake and drowning. He shivered. Celanire was like the lagoon, cunning and dangerous.

43

But the day turned out to be so busy, he completely forgot about the oblate.

The day before, the vessel *Alexandrie* had fired a cannon shot, indicating that it was ready to trade. While maneuvering along its side, one of Betti Bouah's boats had overturned. Four men had been sucked under the waves and their bodies kept for good by the ocean. Hakim had had to smooth out the accusations and greed of the families and negotiate compensation. The Europeans had introduced a new system. Everything had been calculated. A man who left behind small children was worth so much. A man who left a betrothed, so much. Several wives, so much. It was nighttime before he returned to Bingerville. An invitation was waiting for him. The following Sunday Koffi Ndizi was going to be baptized, and as a token of their former friendship, he was inviting him to the ceremony.

Hakim had never taken Koffi Ndizi's amorous transports very seriously. Like those of Karamanlis, he got the impression they were sheer lunacy that would heal by itself. But when he saw him standing at the foot of the altar, his hands piously crossed over a thick candle, his braids shaved, and his belly cramped into a white chasuble, he realized his mistake. To go to such extremes, he really had to be smitten. Queen Tadjo, sitting in the front row, seemed to be in agony. He had given her three months to become a Christian. Otherwise, despite all her lineage, he would repudiate her as well.

The church, which dated back to the early days of the colony, was a reminder that the missionaries had followed in the steps of the traders. The altar and the pews had been carved out of ironwood. A local artist had sculpted in clay the fourteen stations of the cross. On that particular day there was the usual lot of "converted" natives and French religious crackpots. In addition, a crowd of Africans was bent on seeing with their own two eyes the extraordinary sight of a king turning his back on the traditions of his ancestors. Those who could speak French fervently sang:

> *Je crois en Toi, mon Dieu,*
> *Je crois en Toi,*
> *L'ombre voile mes yeux,*
> *Mais j'ai la foi.*

The others listened, intimidated by the sonority tumbling from their mouths. The father superior, a Knight Templar, was an ascetic, nothing more than skin and bones, once a great friend of Thomas de Brabant, who often used him as an interpreter. For Koffi Ndizi, baptized Felix, he delivered a long homily, stressing his rebirth and his duties as a Christian. Adopting an inspired look, he prosaically exulted in a conversion that compensated for the defection of his former friend Thomas, up to his neck in adultery with a Negress. The new Felix fittingly received the water on his forehead and solemnly ate the salt. After the ceremony the guests gathered at the royal compound where the free-of-charge domestics who had replaced the slaves served lukewarm lemonade in the famous blue-stemmed glasses. Hakim's eyes filled with tears as he found himself back in that place, that theater of so many sweet moments: drinking bouts, never-ending palavers, and anti-French dreams. Now that the Father Templar had asked the learned assembly of *sébékos* and fetish priests to vacate the compound, their courtyard was deserted. The only witnesses to the past were the queen mother, stripped of half of her suite, and a few elders who had nowhere else to go. Poor Kwame Aniedo! His father had ordered him to convert, swearing he would disinherit him if he refused, for his mentors had forbidden him to bequeath his estate to a heathen.

As a consequence, Kwame Aniedo had not attended the ceremony and was locked up in his hut, amusing himself as best he could playing *awalé* with his favorite concubine. At the very moment the cookies and white wine were brought out, Thomas de Brabant arrived in full uniform and delivered a grand-sounding speech. Noblesse oblige! The king's conversion to the True God was an event of paramount importance with promising consequences for the future as well as a productive collaboration for prospective relations between Africa and Europe. It was almost as if Celanire had dictated the words to him, they were so close to her ideas. Exasperated, Hakim was about to take his leave when Celanire herself arrived, accompanied by her inseparable widow Desrussie. Felix Koffi, the new Christian, who could now put together a few words of French, rushed toward her: "Ça wa ben? Ça wa ben?"

It was pathetic!

Celanire was decked all in white—dress, shoes, and hat—as if it had been her baptism. Around her neck, a choker of white velvet embroidered with tiny multicolored flowers. She thus appeared the most virginal of virgins. She gave a discreet nod to Hakim as if, a few days earlier, her hand had not groped around inside his trousers, and lavished Felix Koffi with smiles. What were her plans for the fat lump? What was she hoping to fleece him of?

Hakim did not have to wait long for an answer.

Three days later, Betti Bouah informed him that Felix Koffi had made a gift of his land neighboring the Ebrié lagoon to the Home for Half-Castes—a good dozen acres in all. The gift was especially shocking as the tribe's land did not actually belong to the king. He was merely the guardian on behalf of the community. Which counsel of elders had he consulted for permission? Betti Bouah worked himself into a frenzy and even considered disinheriting his cousin. There was no longer any justice. The native courts under the thumb of Thomas de Brabant did everything the French dictated.

Surprise! Surprise! Kwame Aniedo proved he was a true Akan and had no intention of turning his back on the gods of his ancestors. Refusing to convert, he left the royal compound. Betti Bouah took him in, gave him a room next to Hakim's, and offered him a job. But Kwame Aniedo had no intention of working himself to death, he who already saw himself in a white-collar job in Dakar, and as an excuse said he needed all his time to prepare for his examination. As a result, Hakim's torture started up all over again. Every day he came face-to-face with Kwame Aniedo. He would even come home to find Kwame lying on his bed, leafing through his books and smoking his Virginia tobacco, wearing the bathrobe he had bought at the CFAO company store with his savings. For the prince had no notion of private property and helped himself to anything he pleased. The real torture, however, was to hear him again night after night groaning with pleasure with his female conquests, who were still just as numerous.

5

The year was drawing to a close, and the short rainy season, the one that lasts from October to November, had just begun when the inhabitants of Bingerville debated a subject of conversation of the utmost importance. Charlotte, the wife of Thomas de Brabant, had arrived with her daughter. So the question was who was the loveliest—Celanire or her? Celanire had no particular reason to be jealous of her white rival. Some even dared to prefer her, being of the opinion that Charlotte was melancholic and did not smile enough. Whereas Celanire, vivacious and gracious, was exquisitely polite on the rare occasions they met her in person. The Africans considered that both of them needed filling out, but conceded that Celanire concealed a little more in the places where it was needed. The general opinion was that Charlotte dressed better in the Paris fashion. But Celanire sometimes wore dresses and head ties in the Akan fashion, which the Africans appreciated. In short, opinions differed.

Sitting in her palace, inaugurated the previous month with great pomp, Charlotte had lost all interest in life. In other words, she wanted to lie down and die. She had never experienced anything so depressing as Africa or imagined a place so frightful as Bingerville. Terrified of snakes and red ants, she spent the best part of her time locked in her apartments. There, with persiennes lowered, she struggled against the heat as best she could. Half naked, she showered four to six times a day, much to the anger of the houseboys, who complained she used up all the water in the tank. She fanned herself with large woven osier fans. Sometimes, in her dressing gown, she would walk out onto the balcony and weep as she looked at the encircling shrubs and trees, so different from the chestnut trees on her avenue Henri-Martin. Every day, at four in the afternoon, a house girl brought her Ludivine, her three-year-old daughter. Ludivine would fidget and push her away, now used to the caresses and pidgin of her housemaid. Charlotte did not recognize her either, now that her hair was decorated with cowries and she reeked of shea butter.

Africa therefore had taken away everything she had. Her child. Her husband, whom she virtually never saw. He told her he was working himself to death for France, whereas she knew he was working himself to death making love to a black girl. When he lay down beside her at night, her nostrils were offended by his smell. Why had he made her come to Africa? She loathed the guests he invited to dinner—senior officials drained by diarrhea and preoccupied by their bowel movements, priests never tired of naming the name of God and martyrizing the Africans in the name of the same God. They never had anything interesting to say, since they never opened a book and never listened to Bach or Handel. They drank too much, and gossiped maliciously. Charlotte no longer had the strength to keep up her diary, where since the age of sixteen she had jotted down her innocent adventures as a young girl. She was at a loss for news to send to her *maman*. In any case, letters took months and months to arrive. When they did, the paper smelled all musty.

That particular afternoon, she felt even hotter than usual. However hard she fanned herself, beads of sweat trickled down her back and formed a pool smelling like urine on the bedsheet. Charlotte was propped up against her pillows, obsessed with the idea of whether a black woman can be beautiful. She had never seen her rival, since the woman never came to church (Father Rascasse went up to celebrate mass in the chapel at the Home). She was never to be seen at any dinner, cocktail, or reception, since she kept the third Friday of every month for her own parties. She never paid anyone a visit. In short, she stayed at home like a flesh-eating spider spinning her web. What did she look like? This question tormented Charlotte. Her dreams had become nightmares, her nights torture. She could no longer bear it and got up. At that time of day, everyone was taking their siesta. She ran down the main staircase, dashed across the garden, avoiding the servants' quarters, and cautiously pushed open the south gate of the palace. No tarbooshed guard in sight. She had seldom ventured outside alone and almost asked her way from a passerby. Then she remembered who she was. The governor's wife. Don't talk to anyone. Avoid getting herself noticed by Thomas's spies.

The rain had stopped. Not for long. Clouds black with thunder scudded across the sky skimming the earth. In the little daylight that was left, the wretched faces of the neighborhood shacks stretched out in a line. In which direction was the Home? It must be this way. A path scarred with ruts unrolled beneath her feet. Left and right, the huts got fewer and finally disappeared; the forest, always ready to run riot, rolled greedily on. After less than a mile Charlotte stumbled up against a metal fence hidden behind thick foliage. She was looking for a way in when suddenly an opening gaped onto a driveway lined with dwarf coconut palms. She went in, crossed a bamboo grove, and suddenly the Home loomed up in all its elegance. Nothing had prepared her for such a picture of harmony. At Bingerville the administrative buildings were massive and devoid of grace. Who was the inspired architect who had designed this marvel? What gardener had laid out these flower beds, pruned these bushes, and grafted these trees? At the same time she had the feeling that a thousand pairs of eyes hidden in the nooks and crannies of the doors and windows were watching her. She thought she saw a window open on the second floor. A shape leaned out. A hand motioned to her to come closer. It was her, it was her! Galvanized into action, she ran to the front door and vigorously rang the bell. After a very long wait, the door finally opened.

A search party was organized to look for Charlotte.

In the night soaked with water, torches were lit by the soldiers, the militia, and the *askaris*. Some searched the length and breadth of the treacherous lagoon that had swallowed up so many human lives. Others marched down to the slime of the mangrove and the swamps, stubbing their feet on the mangrove trees and twisting their ankles against the buttress roots. Another group roamed the villages around the lagoon, flattening the huts with their rifle butts, terrifying the inhabitants, who imagined the slave trade had started up again. Some hacked a path through the forest with axes and cutlasses, only to face the sea. Others searched deep into the pale green savanna rippling to infinity.

Racked by remorse, Thomas directed the search operations. His sweet, gentle Charlotte! Why had he neglected her in such a fashion? It was beyond understanding; as if Celanire had bewitched him. The feelings he felt in his heart for his wife were not to blame. It was his body, that wretched shroud of flesh, that had betrayed him.

His eyes brimming with tears, he recalled how they had got carried away dancing to the "Blue Danube" that summer they had first met; how, strolling through the English garden, he had described to her his life in Africa. She was not impressed: she would have preferred a senator or a banker for a husband, somebody more reassuring. But love had won the day, and they got married at the church of Saint-Philippe-du-Roule.

The search lasted for four days and four nights. Despondency had gripped every heart. At the mission, Charlotte was given up for a case of suicide. Africa can give you a nervous breakdown! Especially for women like her who cannot find comfort in God. She was never to be seen at confession or at communion. But in his grief and guilty conscience Thomas refused to give up, fretted and fumed, ran in all directions and gave contradictory orders left and right.

In the end they found Charlotte's body in the semidarkness of the forest not far from the village of Tiegaba. Straight and smooth, a Bassam mahogany tree was watching over her. One wondered how she had managed to travel so many miles without guide or *tipoye* in this impenetrable, stifling vegetation inhabited by monkeys, leopards, and wildcats. Twice she must have crossed rivers infested with caymans and crocodiles, without stepping-stones, bridge, or ferry. The guards who made the macabre discovery backed away to vomit in the mud. The sight was horrible. It was as if wild beasts, eaters of human flesh and drinkers of fresh blood, had done her in. All around the body the earth had been clawed into ruts. Yet no lion had been reported in the region. They covered Charlotte with branches. They loaded her onto a makeshift stretcher, and the cortege set off for Bingerville. Spontaneously, mourners from Tiegaba now switched their tears and vociferations from the deceased scepter bearer, Adueli Kabanlan, and made a terrible din all the way back to the palace. Exhausted, the governor, who had not slept a wink for three nights, was taking an afternoon nap. He emerged in his shirt-sleeves and almost fainted, seeing what was left of his beloved. But his grief made the entire colony shrug its shoulders. What? A cheat, a liar, and an adulterer making all this racket! Keeping to his bed as if he were in agony! Ordering a first-class funeral. Strewing the coffin with natural and artificial flowers. Ordering all flags to be flown at half staff, as if it were a national mourning or the death of a senior French official!

For the second time in a few months Hakim set foot inside the church. Because of Charlotte. He had met her one day, escorted by her *askari,* while she was shopping at the SOCO-PAO company store. She had not yet that zombie look peculiar to the whites in Africa, and she stared him straight in the eye. To think that all her vitality was now reduced to a heap of pummeled flesh at the bottom of a wooden box! The church was filled with a French congregation who had never seen either the front or the back of Charlotte, but were grief-stricken even so. The newspapers in France had given the tragic event wide coverage, as had the *Courrier de l'Ouest Africain,* whose head offices were in Dakar. Standing to the left of her papa, Ludivine was crying because her maid had told her, calamity of calamities, she would never see her *maman* again. Her head ached from all these flowers piled onto the coffin. On behalf of the Home, Celanire had sent an enormous wreath of assorted dahlias, roses, and lilies. But neither she nor her good friend, Madame Desrussie, had come in person to the mortuary at the governor's palace. Those who love a bit of scandal were highly disappointed. For the general opinion held her responsible. How come? Although the Europeans did their best not to give in to superstition, the Africans had no such qualms. There was no doubt about it— Celanire was a "horse." The number of mysterious deaths around her was beginning to mount up. Monsieur Desrussie: one. Alix Pol-Roger: two. Now, Charlotte de Brabant. Who would be the next victim?

The wreaths had not yet wilted on his wife's tomb when Thomas set off again for the Home. Blacks and whites alike saw it coming. Even so, they were shocked. Should a defenseless child be handed over to her *maman*'s murderer?

They say you cannot remember anything before the age of five.

However young she was at the time, Ludivine was never to forget the first time she met Celanire.

She had left the governor's palace midmorning. Her papa had explained to her he worshipped her like the apple of his eye.

But a father cannot take care of his little girl all on his own. He was placing her therefore in the care of a lady who was as good as she was beautiful, who would take charge of her education. She would not live all alone in the palace, lost in a huge mansion. She would have lots of little playmates her own age. He made her say farewell to Ana, her beloved maid. Then they had left. The weather was terrible, of course. To protect her from the rain Ana had dressed her in boots and yellow oilskin, which made her feel too hot. The path up to the Home seemed a difficult climb, pitted with potholes filled with rotten leaves and muddy water. Thinking of Ana, she could not help whining and sobbing, even though her papa kept repeating, somewhat irritatedly; "Stop crying, for goodness sake!"

The Home made her think of a prison with its fence overgrown with thick vegetation barring the sky. As for the garden, the Tuileries and Luxembourg gardens in Paris, where her maid used to take her to play, were far nicer.

Doing her best to keep her head up, she entered the nursery, a huge tiled room, the only adornment being a crucifix nailed to a wall. Here a dozen children of her age—Papa had been right—ranging in skin color from yellowish brown to off-white, boys and girls, all closely cropped, dressed in steel gray smocks, were grouped around a piano. As clean as new pins, even chubby in some cases, they nevertheless had the look of society's rejects, a nobody-wants-me-on-this-earth expression. They were singing with a long face:

> *Baa-baa black sheep*
> *Have you any wool?*
> *Yes sir! Yes sir!*
> *Three bags full!*

This was the music class, which she taught herself, explained the young woman seated at the piano. After giving Thomas a tender kiss, she clapped her hands to indicate class was over and stood up. The children surged to the back of the room, where a group of African women rigged out in blue veils and long white nurse's aprons was waiting for them.

The stranger approached with a smile.

"So you're Ludivine? My name is Celanire. Something tells me we're going to do great things together."

Ludivine was no fool, unlike Thomas, who was staring at Celanire, besotted. This smile clinging lopsided to a set of cruel ivory teeth hung like a piece of frippery on a carnival puppet. It wobbled from side to side. Even so, she was impressed by her beauty. Here too her papa had been right. Not a classical beauty, which Charlotte had bequeathed her—an aquiline nose, a domed forehead, a finely drawn mouth. No, Celanire possessed the beauty of the devil! A thick black braid snaked down her back, as if it had a life of its own. You could not take your eyes off a wide blue ribbon studded with a tiny golden heart wound tight around her throat. What did it conceal underneath? You sensed some terrible, terrifying secret.

"She looks like her mother," Celanire remarked with a semblance of emotion.

Thomas seemed surprised. How could she know? She had never met Charlotte. Celanire was not disconcerted. She explained in a mysterious tone of voice that she had visions and premonitions. In her dreams she could see people who were going to die. Or even those already dead. The day Charlotte disappeared, she thought she saw her standing under her window in the flower beds of dahlias, busy admiring the Home. She was dark, wasn't she? Like an Italian with green eyes. She was wearing a pastel-colored dress, and since she had lost so much weight in Africa, she wore her wedding ring on her middle finger.

Thomas was stunned by the accuracy of her description.

Ludivine went and joined the other children at the back of the room. They made way for her as she approached, then closed in around her, as if to signify they had adopted her. They began halfheartedly to play with modeling clay. The supervising nurses paid scant attention to their charge, talking earnestly among themselves, and never stopped giggling. They were watching Thomas and Celanire, who, shoulder to shoulder, were playing a piece for four hands. For Celanire was an accomplished musician. She sang like a nightingale and was capable of playing Beethoven sonatas to perfection as well as enchanting the listener with her recorder. The nurses seemed to find the sight hilarious. Thomas finally took leave of Celanire, standing to attention and clicking his heels in military fashion before kissing her hand most civilly. Then he lightly brushed his daughter's forehead with his lips and drew the sign of the cross. Ludivine swallowed back her tears, for her papa's was the last familiar face she was to see. When he had disappeared, Celanire signaled to one of the nurses to take her by the hand up to a room on the second floor. A dormitory—rows of identical twin beds tightly stretched with bedspreads in yellow and green African cloth. Beside each bed stood a yellow wardrobe painted with a green number. On the wall, a crucifix like the one on the ground floor.

The nurse assigned her bed and wardrobe number 16. She removed her white chiffon dress and slipped on a smock. Then, armed with a pair of scissors, she began snipping one by one the curls of her mop of black hair until her head was completely shaved. When they went back down, the nurse led her to a table in a refectory as austere as the classroom and the dormitory.

Children and adults alike stood, head lowered, in front of their place. On a platform Celanire was saying grace.

Despite the prayers that tumbled out of her mouth, she looked the very picture of sin. She was so hot she could have set a church font ablaze. Ludivine swallowed back her tears. One of the nurses placed a ball of yam *foutou* on her plate and sprinkled it with chicken *kedjenou*. She realized she was very hungry, and the sight of the chicken *kedjenou* made her mouth water.

Ana had gotten her used to such food, and now she had a natural liking for these spicy dishes and their rough, barbaric taste.

6

In the end Bingerville recovered in next to no time from the death of Charlotte. Too many major events followed the tragedy, one after the other. On the French side, Karamanlis finally managed to commit suicide, by drowning. The Father Templar died from a heart attack. Their beloved Father Rascasse left for the colony of Oubangui-Chari. No sooner had it been built than it was announced that Bingerville was going to lose its rank as capital of the colony to Abidjan-Santey. What had been the point of so much trouble and effort? For the Africans, their concerns were all too clear: *corvée* and taxes had been increased, and then there was the news that Tanella, Mawourou's murderer, had been acquitted by the court in Dakar and was returning to the Ivory Coast. Acquitted! The jury had decided she had acted in self-defense. No doubt about it, the white man's world was walking on its head! In short, it wasn't long before everyone had something else to think about. In the markets, the gin bars, the factories, the trading houses, and the offices, in the residential districts as well as the *poto-poto* neighborhoods, conversation turned to other things.

One morning, a messenger brought Hakim another letter from Celanire. She apologized for harping on the subject. What must he think of her? But she had learned—nothing was a secret in Bingerville—that he had fallen out with Betti Bouah. Under the circumstances, wouldn't he like to reconsider her offer, to which, in fact, he had never replied? Sadly enough, Celanire was speaking the truth. Betti Bouah and Hakim could no longer bear the sight of each other. Betti Bouah realized that Hakim was a very different person from what he had imagined. When it was a question of badmouthing the French, Hakim was only too ready. But when it came to working as hard as they did, he was nowhere to be seen. He had demanded a five-day workweek, plus weekends off as was the custom in England and the colonies of the Crown. He insisted on being paid a commission on his sales. And that he was entitled to two days off for the feast of Tabaski, since he had declared himself Muslim. Naturally, Betti Bouah had not given in to any of his demands, and Hakim had sent him a stinging letter, calling him an exploiter. Betti Bouah had got a laugh out of that. Exploiter! Here was a new word! Apparently the traditional chiefs were just as much exploiters as the whites. Ever since, the two men had ignored each other and limited any contact to the business of palm oil. No more hot chocolate at four in the afternoon, no more discussions on "pacification," no more exchange of books. Hakim thought of writing a letter, this time a letter of resignation. What held him back was that once his pride had been satisfied by this act of bravado, there would be nothing or nobody to help him fill his belly. The mission would no longer want him as Mr. Philosophizer. So he would have to return to Soudan, and in order not to starve to death, he would have to live off his grandfather or one of his uncles on his mother's side.

He therefore plucked up his courage. To accept Celanire's offer was the last thing he wanted, but it was the only thing preventing him from descending into destitution.

With his mind made up, he set off for the Home one Sunday. Mass had just finished. The pupils, in freshly starched white uniforms edged in green, were filing out of the chapel, chaperoned by their monitors, now rid of their nurses' garb and dressed in identical wrappers with identical motifs, for apparently Celanire liked her surroundings to be symmetrical. Hakim took the arm she offered him. What a chatterbox! She never stopped for one minute. Without waiting to get her breath back, she told him how she had trained a choir to sing the *Beatus Vir* and the *Nulla in Mundo Pax Sincera* by Vivaldi, her favorite composer. The choir had been invited to Grand-Bassam in a month's time for the inception of the new bishop. Considering her four pupils, one of whom was a girl, had passed the native certificate for elementary studies and were preparing to become grade-five office clerks, she had every reason to be proud. Hakim remained silent. In Bingerville gossip had begun to circulate openly about the true nature of the Home. Some of the nurses whispered that once the children had been put to bed, they were paired off with those nice, gentle white officers and soldiers who gave them all sorts of presents and caresses. No comparison with those rough, lascivious Africans. Never an unkind word, a clout, or a thrashing! The first French words they learned therefore, were "cheri" or "mon amour."

Celanire and Hakim entered a drawing room furnished in exquisite taste. There she whirled around to show off her costume. For she was dressed in a fashion he had never seen before.

A full gown of rich, dark red silk was gathered at the waist over a white lace petticoat with three flounces. Her neck was encased in a collaret of frilled lawn similar to the ruffs portrayed in old engravings. Her hair was frizzed out, rolled into coquette bobs over her ears. She swamped him with explanations in her self-satisfaction. This Guadeloupean costume was called a matador gown. She had given it a personal touch by adding the collaret and leaving out the madras head tie. The traditional jewelry was also missing—the gold-bead choker and the earrings. Suddenly she stopped her hollow talk, and her face took on an expression of reproach. He had put off accepting her offer, and now Betti Bouah had let him down. Didn't he realize that once the Africans had hoisted themselves up level with the whites, they would prove to be even more wicked? Envious, that's what they were, only set on taking their masters' place. Colonization would be followed by worse events, and the name *neocolonialism* would be invented to describe them. Hakim said his mea culpa. He now wanted to turn the page and start working for her as quickly as possible. What would she like him to do? At that moment he bravely turned to face her.

Celanire stared at him like a cat about to devour a mouse or a python about to swallow its prey, before uncoiling itself to digest it in voluptuous pleasure. She stretched out her arm and stroked his neck, winding a lock of his hair around one of her fingers. Hakim stammered out the terms of her letter as a reminder. She had promised him: no love, no sex. She laughed, revealing her white teeth and blue-black gums. And he had believed her? Only a fool would trust the words of a woman, especially if she were in love! She edged closer to him and whispered in his ear. She knew of his preferences, his desire for Kwame Aniedo. Nothing shocking about that. Everyone does what he likes with his body. She herself swung both ways, as the popular saying goes. But let her show him how she could get him to like other things than boys. Thereupon she grabbed his shirt and unbuttoned it. It was this offhand manner, this way of hers of treating him like a sex object, that infuriated Hakim. He shoved her away brutally and hammered her breasts. They rolled over on the floor. As agile as an eel, she climbed on top of him and pressed her mouth against his. Disgusted, he felt sucked in by this dank cavern. He reversed the situation, nailed her under him, and in his rage, grabbed her by the neck as if he wanted to strangle her. His fingers got caught in her collaret, ripped it off, and threw it away. She uttered a shriek and clasped her hands to her throat while her eyes dimmed, like a dampened firebrand. He remained speechless, stunned by what he had uncovered.

A monstrous scar.

A purplish, rubberlike tourniquet, thick as a roll of flesh, repoussé, stitched and pockmarked, wound around her neck. It was as if her neck had been slashed on both sides, then patched up and the flesh pulled together by force, oozing lumps all the way around.

While Celanire's eyes sprang back to life and glowed wickedly, Hakim ran for the door without further ado. The recreation yard was deserted, since the pupils were back in the refectory and the garden.

For the remainder of the day Hakim stayed holed up in his room. So the superstition was true. Celanire was a "horse," and her mark was hidden on her neck. It was this extraordinary scar he had seen with his own two eyes. Consequently, he was to be the next victim: his death was foretold. Would he too be stung by a mysterious spider? Devoured by man-eating lions? How would it happen? How? He sweated and shook with fright all over.

When night fell, he could not stand its darkness. He imagined the circle of trees around the house to be the lair of mysterious creatures. He could hear them hiss, murmur, and shriek. He ran to Njiri's, where they served palm wine and *akpetseshie* smuggled in from the Gold Coast. But nothing could deaden memory and conscience like the white man's liquor: gin, brandy, and absinthe.

The following morning he was stumbling out of bed in a daze when the widow Desrussie knocked on his door again. A third letter from Celanire. The woman certainly had no sense of shame; once more she apologized. Could he really be angry with her? Wasn't he flattered that a woman desired him so violently? But that wasn't the point of her letter. He had discovered her painful secret. Her slashed throat. She begged him to come so that she could explain. Hakim thought he smelled a rat. Celanire was cajoling him the better to smother him. He tore the letter up into a thousand pieces and did not trouble to reply.

From that day on he lived on borrowed time. The yelp of a dog, the howl of a monkey, or the scurry of a rat would make him jump. At night, the rustle of an insect or a bat beating its wings as it tangled in the straw of the roof made him go crazy. On the surface it was the same routine. Every morning he watched the same sun rise above the greenery of Bingerville. Three days out of five he climbed into the same outboard, made the rounds of the same suppliers of palm oil and kernels, and loaded his booty onto the same dugouts. The remainder of the week was spent in one of the warehouses where the oil was extracted and poured into casks to be shipped to Grand-Bassam. When he returned home of an evening, he had to help Kwame Aniedo as well as overcome his fatigue and his nagging sexual desire. Yet these routine gestures were transformed by the fear that had wormed its way inside him, that had crept into every corner of his being and tainted every second of his life. The young man who once mocked superstition now seriously considered consulting a fetish priest. After the death of their sworn enemy, the Father Templar, Diamagaram and the others had reoccupied Felix Koffi's compound as if nothing had happened. They continued to work against the French but could not prevent the king from giving the Home more land. Celanire had turned it into an experimental garden where she intended planting coffee and cacao, those new plants of which the French had great expectations.

Hakim was convinced that nothing nor nobody could save him from Celanire.

And that's why he took to drink.

And that's why he became a regular at Njiri's bar.

Only there did he feel safe. After having downed half a bottle of gin or absinthe, he began to reason with himself. How could he, a liberated young man, ex-philosophizer who had read the philosophers of the Age of Enlightenment, take at face value a load of superstitions good for ignoramuses? Okay, Celanire was a nutcase! Okay, she had the hots for him. But that was all. As for her scar, she was probably operated on for a goiter or some sort of hypertrophy of the thyroid.

After a few months his liking for alcohol had utterly consumed him. His regular evening visits to Njiri's bar no longer satisfied him. He discovered a dive at Grand-Bassam, just steps from the sea, named the Fisherman's Rendezvous. From early morning, mingling with the boozers of all sorts and chronic alcoholics, you could meet landlocked hunters of tuna, grouper, and whales who no longer set off to sea. Hakim liked the spot not because of its setting, which was somewhat sordid; not because of its alcohol, which was somewhat ordinary; but because of the conversation. The regulars never tired, in fact, of poking fun at the way the French spoke, dressed, and behaved. They would enumerate the girls who had lost their virginity to the district commissioners, the number of little boys abused by the priests. They ridiculed the orders of the governor, Thomas de Brabant, and the feats of the soldiers on campaign. And, what's more, they could name the name of every senior civil servant, every high-ranking officer, who, before embarking at Grand-Bassam for his annual leave, stopped over at the Home, and could count up the number of nights he had spent there. According to them, two officers from Upper Senegal–Niger had almost renounced their career and become orderlies to the nurses at the Home. The Home was well and truly a bordello, and Celanire its madam. Once the treasure trove had been discovered, it would be like a volcano erupting. Just wait and see!

People noticed, however, that Hakim had changed. Those who worked under his orders were the first to smell his breath. The French merchants were horrified by his slurred voice and the mistakes in his syntax, which had once been so refined. His sudden change of look for the worse was a shock. He had never been a dandy, preferring a Muslim caftan and slippers to French-style jackets and boots. But he had always been washed, clean-shaven, and his hair oiled. At present his mop of hair was as thick and tangled as a fetish doll's, and he bundled himself up in dubious-looking wrappers like an Ebrié laborer.

Kwame Aniedo was worried. The date of his examination was fast approaching. Alas, evening after evening, Hakim was too drunk to think about dictations, multiplication tables, and math calculations. All he could do was sigh and gaze longingly at his student with languishing eyes. He would stammer incoherently. On other occasions he cried like a child. Kwame Aniedo arrived at the conclusion therefore that someone wanted to harm Hakim. Out of respect for Hakim, who had made a "man of letters" out of him by teaching him his alphabet, he got into the habit of joining him at Njiri's. Once alcohol had done its damage and Hakim was too far gone, he would prop him up to prevent him from collapsing into a heap and bring him home. There he would splash his face with water, then help him lie down on his straw mattress.

On that particular evening, many of the regulars could testify that Kwame Aniedo and Hakim had left the bar arm in arm well before ten. Hakim was sober and walking straight. A full moon was sailing in the sky. The buffalo frogs were croaking. Kwame Aniedo was counting on Hakim to teach him more about civics, which was his weak point. Instead of this, the schoolmaster started confiding in him. Once again Kwame Aniedo had to put up with hearing the old story of the great white colonial papa, the Tukolor princess *maman,* and the snubs Hakim had suffered as an illegitimate child. And yet, protested Hakim, the mixed bloods are the future of the world, which is in a state of miscegenation. Yes, multiculturalism would conquer all. Exasperated, Kwame Aniedo was about to withdraw to his room when Hakim started on a new chapter—the one about how he had been propositioned by Celanire. Kwame Aniedo couldn't believe his ears. He had every reason to hate the oblate who had been the cause of the quarrel with his father. But no man normally equipped could reject such a creature. He plied Hakim with questions. What had he seen exactly?

"Go on, describe her dovelike breasts, the palace of her navel, the garden of her pubis, and the fountain of her delights. Did you drink your fill?"

———

Crimes between Africans arouse little interest. Genocide, pogroms, tribal warfare, ethnic cleansing—those people kill themselves and nobody says a word.

But this murder was an exception, for Hakim was of mixed blood, the illegitimate son of a distinguished colonial adminis-trator who had served with distinction in Upper Senegal. The press had little trouble tracing the father: Robert Delafalaise, author of a remarkable anthropological study, the first of its kind in any case, *Les Bambara de Ségou et du Kaarta*. The incident was hotly debated. For those who opposed France's colonial endeav-ors— and there were quite a few, to tell the truth—it was proof, one more, of the crimes committed by the "gods of the bush," as the governors-general, governors, and district commissioners were called. When they were on a tour of inspection, they showed no respect for the local chiefs and demanded a droit du seigneur over the local beauties. If they got them pregnant, they would heartlessly pack their offspring off to a Home for Half-Castes. Hakim was a victim, nothing but a victim. For the defenders of colonization, however, this crime illustrated the dangers of crossbreeding, the savagery of those half-castes capa-ble of exterminating both the African and the European race, if you didn't watch out.

What exactly had happened that evening?

Only the *mabouyat* lizards clinging to the beams, the bats hanging upside down in the straw on the roof, and the toad squatting as usual on the threshold would, if they could talk, have been able to describe the approaching cortege of death. Kwame Aniedo had nothing to say, and for good reason. The dead are never asked to speak. Betti Bouah testified that after having reread a few pages of Jean-Jacques Rousseau's *Confessions*, he had gone to bed early. Around midnight he had been woken by the noise of a violent quarrel. He was on the point of putting an end to the din when his third wife, who had just been importuned by a nightmare and was sharing his bed that very night, prevented him from doing so. There would be enough time in the morning to tell Hakim what he thought of him. He had therefore gone back to bed. Not for long. Half an hour later, the shriek of an animal having its throat slashed put the house in pandemonium. Terrified, the infants who were sleeping in their mother's beds began to scream in unison. He had mustered four servants and, armed with a flintlock gun, had gone downstairs. The door to Hakim's room was wide open. On the ground Kwame Aniedo was lying in a pool of blood, a Sheffield switchblade stuck in his belly. Stunned, Hakim was sitting on the bed, soaked in blood. Betti Bouah and the servants had grabbed him without meeting any resistance and called the militia.

After having rotted for two months in the jail at Grand-Bassam, Hakim was transferred to the prison in Dakar, where in a state of stupefaction he was unable to reason his defense. He merely repeated he was a harbinger of death. Mr. Rozier, the astute young attorney who had been requisitioned for the case, guessed his sexual orientation. Unable to get any information out of Hakim, he came to his own conclusion. Overexcited at the idea of Celanire's nudity, Kwame Aniedo had probably got closer to Hakim and demanded a better description. Worked up by his proximity, his smell, and an excess of alcohol, Hakim had lost his head and hurled himself onto Kwame Aniedo. Horrified, the latter had drawn his Sheffield switchblade to ward off his advances. During the struggle Hakim had grabbed the knife and defended himself.

But given the date these events occurred—we are somewhere around 1903— Mr. Rozier did not dare pronounce the word *homosexuality,* as we would have done today. At that time homosexuality was considered a repulsive vice. He was afraid of alienating once and for all the jury composed of narrow-minded Frenchmen, minor civil servants, and tradesmen. He launched into a petty argument. Hakim was left-handed and would have been unable to deal such a blow. Everyone in Bingerville could vouch for the affection he had for Kwame Aniedo, who even called him "Papa." On the fateful night fifty pairs of eyes had seen them leave Njiri's bar the best of friends. The prosecution claimed a drunken brawl had broken out between the two. The prosecutor presumed. He was incapable of producing evidence, of showing why Hakim had suddenly turned on Kwame Aniedo and stabbed him over twenty times. That was the weak point in the case: the motive for the crime! It was more likely that one of those criminal types who thrived at Bingerville had followed the two men home, broken in, tried to rob them, and, surprised by Kwame Aniedo, had butchered him. This clumsy fabrication convinced nobody, and rightly so. Nevertheless, in spite of the inexperience of his defense attorney, Hakim would have been sentenced to only a few years in a colonial jail—the man he had killed, though an Akan crown prince, counted for little in the eyes of the colonial authorities—if Thomas de Brabant, governor of the Ivory Coast, had not intervened in person. He sent a confidential memo to his superior, the governor-general of French West Africa, informing him of the real personality of Jean Seydou, alias Hakim. In his classes at Bingerville he had denigrated France's civilizing mission. He was a ringleader, a hothead, a formidable agitator, a son worthy of El-Hadj Omar Saïdou Tall, his ancestor on his mother's side. Those very words scared the life out of everyone. Our unfortunate hero got the maximum sentence and was banished to the penal colony in French Guiana.

7
———

Hakim could smell the sweet baked-bread scent of the ocean.

Straining his ears, he could even hear its commotion and, depending on the day, assess its humor—ever so gentle or ever so angry. But his eyes could not see it. The prison where he was kept was housed in the ruins of a fortified residence whose back faced the island of Gorée. Long ago slaves from all over Africa were stored there awaiting shipment to the little island offshore. The prison was a round chamber where three hundred men and women once stood chained by the neck to the wooden supports bolted to the ground. At present, the only inmates were a handful of poor wretches who had not paid their taxes or refused to carry out their *corvée*. At noon, three Sisters of Charity, who treated their dysentery and their fevers, brought them a dish of fish with rice. In the evening the old Serer warden waddled in on his crooked legs and served them soup. Hakim was given preferential treatment—salad, fruit, papayas, and mangoes. He was the only prisoner they had ever seen sentenced to hard labor in a penal colony, and they were impressed. He was waiting for his transfer to Serouane, a small town on the coast of Algeria, where he would embark on a ship that would take him halfway around the world to French Guiana. For months he had remained in a cell, twelve feet by twelve, up against the side of the main building. He relieved himself in a hole dug into the ground. His youth and curly hair broke the heart of the Sisters of Charity. They knew he was a Muslim, therefore damned in advance.

Even so they could not help reciting dozens of rosaries, just in case—God is great—they could save his soul.

The only window in the cell looked out onto a wall. All day long, the sun used it like a palette to mix its colors. It began with a milky white, followed by a light yellow. Then a deeper yellow, which grew paler and paler, finally turning white again, unbearably white. His eyes were dazzled by the glare, hurt, and made him blink. The heat shimmered. And then the white began to fade. It took on every degree of blue, changed to violet, and turned an ever darker shade of gray. Finally turning to black. Jet black.

As long as there was daylight, Hakim stood in front of this window. He never tired of gazing at this wall, for him a symbol of his life. At age twenty-four his hopes had been dashed. A penal colony. What could it look like? Like a fortress. Surrounded by stone walls. Rather than think about it, however, he filled his head with all sorts of imaginings. Better not look into the past. Bamako. Bokar. Bingerville. Celanire. The Home. Kwame Aniedo. All that was over with. Gone were the rage and revolt that had racked him while he awaited his sentence. He had grown indifferent, like a lamb passively awaiting the slaughter at the feast of Tabaski. Mr. Rozier, who visited him regularly once a week, promised him a presidential pardon. He also told him that Guiana was a French territory in South America, situated between the Amazon and the Orinoco. This set Hakim dreaming. He imagined a dense, sempiternally green forest. Slow-moving, muddy rivers whose banks are eaten away by mangrove swamps. Dugout canoes loaded with naked, oily-haired Amerindians plying upstream. The men standing at the prow, armed with arrows whose heads are daubed with curare, a deadly poison. The women breast-feeding their babies, clinging to their sides like tadpoles. On their faces an expression of placid bliss. Setting foot on shore, they merged into the forest, heading for their huts in single file under the protection of the trees. At night, swaying in their hammocks, the men made love, preferably among themselves, sometimes with the women. Why had humanity shunned these mornings of the world? Why had predator nations wanted to discover other lands? And conquer and colonize them—in other words, destroy them?

As soon as night fell, Hakim's thoughts took on a darker shade. In the icy darkness, however tightly he curled himself up, however much he called out to it in tears, sleep wanted nothing to do with him. He shivered with cold. His desperately sad life stretched out forever in front of him. A half-caste mockingly nicknamed Toubabou, "white boy," growing up an outcast among other outcasts. Where was Bokar buried? He had never seen his grave. Mr. Philosophizer at Adjame-Santey, ridiculed by the Africans, held in contempt by the French. Then assistant to the merchant he had stupidly thought a friend. In reality Betti Bouah had always despised him because he wasn't an Akan, he was merely a bastard without a race. Odd as it may seem, the only person who had taken any interest in him, had desired him, perhaps loved him, was Celanire. Pity he could not return the compliment. Unfortunately, you cannot force your nature. However much a prisoner he was, rotting in his dungeon, the very thought of what she expected of him made him feel sick.

One day two white men in pith helmets and khaki uniform, their faces cooked red like those exposed to the colonies, pushed open his cell door. They looked at him as if he were a heap of vermin, muffling their noses with a handkerchief against the stink that no longer bothered him. One of them unrolled a document and in a strong Corsican accent read him a series of orders. He retained just one thing. In one week he would embark on the *Neptune* for Serouane, where he would join the other convicts, all Arabs assembled together from every corner of North Africa. From Serouane the voyage to the transportation camp at Saint-Laurent-du-Maroni in Guiana would take three months. When he had finished reading, the Corsican's voice mellowed. He added that if Hakim renounced his political ideas and proved to be a model prisoner, he might be freed before the end of his sentence. In such an event he would be granted a piece of land. He could even take a wife and settle in Guiana. Other convicts before him had married and had sons.

Meanwhile at Bingerville events were working up to a crescendo.

Blacks and whites alike were still reeling from the shock of Kwame Aniedo's murder and Hakim's banishment. Most people were convinced the latter was innocent. The truth lay elsewhere. But where? That is the question! They would have liked to accuse Celanire. But for once she seemed as innocent as the Lamb of God. She had no known liaison either with Hakim or Kwame Aniedo and had no personal interest in their killing themselves. Some of the French, however, suspected Hakim of being a homosexual, since he had never been seen with a woman. But even the most malicious hid their thoughts like dirty washing at the bottom of a closet.

To everyone's surprise, whereas Koffi Ndizi was thought to be an unnatural father, the death of his first son dealt him a fatal blow. One week after Kwame Aniedo had been laid to rest, a cold nailed the old man to his bed and snuffed him out like a candle before Queen Tadjo in her eagerness had time to prepare a concoction of *zinblannan* herb tea. His family preferred to forget he had converted to Christianity and gave him the funeral of an Akan king. Twenty slaves were sacrificed to serve him in the afterlife. Dozens of professional mourners filled the air with their wailing. During a week of feasting and drinking, gallons and gallons of palm wine flowed. Besides the slaves, the fetish priests slaughtered over a hundred oxen and as many sheep on the sacrificial stones, not forgetting the countless chickens plucked until every finger was worn out. The tradition of interrogating Koffi Ndizi's corpse resulted in some strange happenings. Normally, when the question is asked who killed the dead man and a series of names are put forward, the porters carrying the corpse take three steps forward for a yes and three steps back for a no. But this time the interrogation caused such a free-for-all that two young people were crushed to death and half a dozen others were hurt. A few days after the funeral the wives and concubines whom Koffi Ndizi had repudiated returned to reoccupy their former quarters. Alas, not for long. The king had made a donation.

The affair had been conducted expertly by the illiterate king, oddly well informed of the mysteries of French law. One day he had gone to Grand-Bassam with two witnesses and in the presence of a notary had donated all his movable and immovable goods to the director of the Home, Mademoiselle Celanire Pinceau. Informed by Betti Bouah, the council of elders in its rage endeavored to prevent this act of madness. Alas, the deeds of donation were already stamped and signed. This was the beginning of a legal imbroglio that went through a dozen attorneys and reached an outcome only in 1963, three years after the independence of the Ivory Coast. The case came to be known as *The Heirs of Felix Koffi Ndizi, King of Abila,* versus *Celanire Pinceau.* In the meantime, Bingerville experienced the sorry sight of the queen mother, Queen Tadjo, and the ex-royal wives and concubines being thrown out *manu militari* by a rabble of tarbooshed soldiers. One melancholy morning a gang of Ebriés razed the compound to the ground as part of their *corvée*. In its place a magnificent sports stadium was built for the students at the Home. The inhabitants of Bingerville had hardly got over this affront to their late king when Tanella returned, free as a bird, after having waited for two years in Dakar for a court decision. She climbed out of a fishing canoe on the lagoon and, followed by a porter, his legs bowed from the weight of her heavy green trunk, walked through Bingerville in the direction of the Home. Those who saw her pass by were flabbergasted. When she had fled Koffi Ndizi's compound after her deadly deed, she had been no more than a shy young girl with chubby cheeks. Now she had been transformed into a woman! At the prison in Dakar she had passed the native certificate of elementary studies. She had also learned to dress in the European fashion, and on that particular day she was flaunting a blue-patterned orange dress and a straw hat with a matching blue ribbon. But people had little time for their usual idle chatter as to who was the loveliest, Tanella or Celanire. It wasn't long before they had far more serious matters to discuss. First of all one of the nurses recounted how Tanella and the oblate had become as intimate as husband and wife. Instead of entertaining the white guests of an evening at the dances organized at the Home, they made whoopee among themselves. They rubbed up against each other, dancing the habanera or the beguine, a dance from Guadeloupe. They drank champagne from the same glass until they were completely intoxicated. Once the visitors had left, they locked themselves in the same room. If Tanella was shy, Celanire was excessively bold. Even in public it was a never-ending serenade of "my pet" and "my little darling" and unequivocal caresses. Furthermore, Tanella had become Celanire's right-hand woman.

She supervised the workers in the palm groves, and the cooks in the refectory, and checked the accounts to such an extent that Madame Desrussie, whose place she had usurped, never stopped lamenting and took to absinthe. In the evening you could see her totter across the garden.

Another nurse was adamant that Celanire had the power to shed her body like a snake shedding its skin in the undergrowth. One night when the wind and the rain were making the shutters bang, the young girl had entered Celanire's room unexpectedly and had seen a little heap of soft, shapeless flesh and skin in front of the wide-open window. Hiding behind a closet, she had watched as the young woman returned in the early hours of the morning. Her mouth smeared with blood, she had slipped back into her mortal coil and calmly returned to bed. No doubt about it, Celanire was under the spell of powerful *aawabo*.

Can one really believe such nonsense and malicious gossip?

One thing for certain was not a pack of lies; the Home entered six candidates, including four girls, for the native certificate of elementary studies in June. All passed, even the girls, and were immediately hired by the mission schools and the administration. As a recompense for her extraordinary results Thomas de Brabant was to award Celanire the medal for academic excellency, a large bronze medal attached to a purple ribbon. From two o'clock in the afternoon all that Bingerville could muster in the way of civil servants, merchants, missionaries, members of the royal family, cooks, nannies, tarbooshed guards, and militia had gathered on the lawns of the Home out of curiosity and were drinking barley water. People arrived on foot and in fishing canoes from Grand-Bassam and Assinie. In everyone's view, the transformation of the Home in such a short time was pure witchcraft. How could the palms, the orchard, and the bamboo groves have grown so fast? How could the fruit trees be loaded with so much fruit in such a short time? Lemons as big as grapefruit! Mangoes that looked as though they had been grafted! Avocados as heavy as pears! All eyes were turned on Celanire and Tanella. At a quick glance they could have passed for twins. They were the same height, same weight, same velvety black-black skin. They were dressed identically except for the bouffant scarf of raw silk tied around Celanire's neck. They wore the same Soir de Paris perfume, and their makeup and hairstyles were identical. Despite this resemblance, it was obvious that, between the two, Celanire was the leader and the brains while Tanella, in spite of her unusual, murderous act, simply followed her instructions. It was also obvious that Celanire was the less infatuated of the two. Tanella looked up to Celanire as if she were the holy of holies or the Eucharist, and Celanire was overjoyed to be the object of such boundless admiration.

The ceremony opened with the Home's choir singing Vivaldi's *Gloria* a cappella. Then the governor gave his speech and pinned the medal on the oblate's breast, followed by the official embrace in the name of France. The pupils bellowed out "La Marseillaise." There was a ripple of applause, and the celebrations began. The nurses, dressed in yellow-patterned blue wrappers, handed around petits fours, salted almonds, and Job cigarettes.

It was only once the sun began to bleed over the lagoon that the guests, stuffed to bursting, made up their minds to set off home. The inhabitants of Bingerville had scarcely finished grinding, chewing, and masticating the pittance of the memory of that lovely afternoon when two Ebriés, out fishing one night, hauled up the body of Madame Desrussie. They first thought a cayman, a sacred animal, had got tangled in their nets and were already thanking Heibonsha, the water god, for their miraculous catch, promising prosperity for many years to come, when they recognized the unfortunate widow. Her face had been beaten to a pulp. In fact they could only identify her officially from her dentition, a masterpiece fashioned by the colony's only dentist, a soldier stationed at Assinie. This event caused quite a stir.

The widow was born Azilin Dossou. The Dossous, however, a well-known family in Adjame-Santey, had converted to Catholicism very early on, given two catechists to the mission, and changed the pagan name of their daughter to Rose. Rose, the jewel of the mission, had been one of the first to learn how to sew, read, and write. She had also been one of the first to enter the bed of a Frenchman. He had never taken the trouble to "regularize" her situation, even though everyone called her Madame Desrussie. Yet there was scarcely time to wonder whether it had been a suicide or an accidental drowning before another event followed almost immediately afterward that fired people's imagination. They learned that Thomas de Brabant was to slip a wedding ring on Celanire Pinceau's finger. Notified by his services, the governor-general of French West Africa cabled the Ministry for the Colonies in Paris. At that time, marital union between colonial civil servants and "native" women was frankly never heard of. What complicated matters was that Celanire was not a "native." She was a French citizen from Guadeloupe who spoke French French and rendered remarkable services to her *metropole* in its civilizing mission. Moreover, she took good care of the unfortunate widowed governor's child. After much debating, the ministry cabled its approval to the governor-general. In Bingerville itself, public opinion was divided: some of the French demanded the "nigger-loving" governor be replaced. Because of the controversy, Thomas's wedding took place in the strictest privacy. Two witnesses: Tanella and

Cyrille Sérignac de Pompigny, his right-hand man, an energetic recruiting agent for the new wharfs in Grand-Bassam. A carefully handpicked congregation: four or five district commissioners from the vicinity, all respectably married with their wives. These ladies of noble birth, more often or not with a title, eyed Celanire scornfully, this negress who was marrying their husbands' hierarchical superior and consequently was going to have precedence over them. It was not only her color that infuriated them, but her impudent freshness. Whereas they wilted and yellowed from the heat, the humidity, the fevers and biliousness, she positively glowed. On her wedding day Celanire ignored the tradition of a white bridal gown and dressed all in pink, a pink as pale as cherry blossom during springtime in Osaka. She replaced the traditional bridal veil with a hat veil. Around her neck she wore a wide moiré silk ribbon fastened by a cameo. She looked at Thomas and Tanella in turn as if to say they must love each other as she loved them. In the great drawing room of the governor's palace the servants uncorked bottles of champagne that kindled few bubbles, and Cyrille Sérignac de Pompigny proposed a toast to the happiness of the newlyweds.

The real festivities, however, took place at the Home. After a festive dinner—including Celanire's homemade coconut sorbet—the pupils went up to their dormitories. The nurses then slipped out of their uniforms and got themselves up as they saw fit. Well, almost. No European-style dresses, since Celanire had very set ideas on the matter. In her opinion, an African woman who dresses in the European fashion is like a dish without condiments. Then a gang of Ebriés on their *corvée* hung resin flares from the trees, and the night turned as bright as daylight. Muslim houseboys busied themselves roasting meat and grilling kebabs and legs of lamb. Cooks prepared fresh and saltwater fish, pepper and groundnut stew, and pounded mountains of yams and plantains. For once Christians and pagans alike had a whale of a time until four in the morning.

Ludivine did not attend her papa's second wedding. Just before lights-out, Thomas and Celanire walked into the dormitory, holding hands. Celanire had pushed back her veil, and her eyes gleamed like carbuncles. They sat down beside her bed and informed her of her good fortune. She was going to leave the Home and come and live with them. She was no longer an orphan in this world: she had a new *maman*.

"I did it for you as well," Thomas kept repeating. "I did it for you."

<hr />

8

People in Bingerville still remember Celanire after so many years as a kaleidoscope of negative facets, whereas as a rule time tends to soften any bitterness. For them there was no doubt she was the "horse" of an evil spirit who had brought nothing but death, mourning, and desolation. Paradoxically, they also judge her as someone who should have been bound by the rules of society. Men think of her as a dangerous feminist. Yet what exactly do they mean by this word, which has so many significations? They cannot forgive her stand against excision. They swear she made the women rebellious, demanding, and disrespectful of the male species. They are particularly outspoken about the center she created for sheltering women who wanted nothing more to do with suitors or husbands. But despite its grand-sounding name, the Refuge of the Good Shepherd, a rickety wattle hut under a straw roof, the center never filled its function. One year it sheltered a group of wives arbitrarily repudiated by their husbands. Another year, a group of battered women. Around 1905 the mission turned it into a native dispensary. Some men go even further and claim that Celanire was a corrupting influence. They expatiate on what went on at the Home but have nothing to prove it. The African woman, they say, must be the eternal keeper of traditions. If she prostitutes herself, society is shaken to its foundations. But was it really a question of prostitution? It seems that the nurses received gifts in exchange for the favors they freely consented to their partners. Some of the French clients were extremely generous. Captain Emile Dubertin, for instance, left his entire estate to Akissi Eboni, who bore him a son. She made the journey to Nantes to receive her inheritance and was very well treated by the Dubertin family, who kept the child. Generally speaking, the generosity of the colonial civil servants allowed the ex-nurses to live the rest of their lives free from financial worries. Relatively well off, therefore, knowing how to read and write, they married into good families and helped form a genuine aristocracy in the country. As for the orphans, they made up the first contingent of teachers in the Ivory Coast. Some of them dabbled in politics and sat on the benches of the National Assembly in Paris.

Above all, nobody would admit that Celanire gave the town a certain character that it has lost only recently in the name of development. Besides the Home for Half-Castes, she transformed the sumptuous Governor's Palace, which was a constant reminder of Charlotte's death. A mournful and morose building, it had become a warehouse for storing pell-mell the packages of medicines, books for the mission school, and spare parts shipped from France for the factories. Thomas only occupied a small part of it: four rooms on the second floor—a study, a real shambles, a bedroom, unfurnished except for a deathly pale bed under its mosquito net, and a washroom where, among the pitchers and basins, all sorts of creepy-crawlies reveled in the humidity. The houseboys regularly killed snakes there of the most dangerous sort, those they called "masters of the bush." The only attractive feature was a small living room, pleasantly furnished, where he would read at night.

With Celanire, all that changed.

Like Betti Bouah, she sent for Apollonians from the Gold Coast. Under her direction they worked for months, standing in the pale light of dawn and lying down in the black of midnight. She had no intention of imitating the style of the Home, and consequently, Bingerville could boast of two architectural treasures, each a source of pride in its own way. She had balconies suspended on the north facade of the palace, where the arabesques of their wrought-iron balustrades relieved the hardness of the stone. She also installed French windows to let in the light and the air, and extended the south facade with a terrace overlooking a garden that she stocked with monkeys and all types of birds— commonly found birds such as hyacinth macaws, brightly colored parakeets, large-billed toucans, budgerigars, and other chatter-boxes, as well as rarer species like those American yellow-tailed parrots called Amazonas. Clusters of *kikiris* hung on the branches of the *azobé* and ebony trees, while red ibis transplanted from the mudflats of the Aby lagoon waded through the grass on their long, melancholic legs. The roof of the palace was another open-air terrace where three hundred people could listen to music in the dry season. Once it had been restored, the palace was boldly painted ocher and pistachio green.

The interior was as sumptuous as the exterior. Two Fridays a month Celanire invited her husband's compatriots to dinner and led her guests on a guided tour of the apartments. Even today, despite all the waste and excessive logging, the Ivory Coast is not lacking in wood. So with the help of the books of her "beloved little papa," as she never failed to call him, Celanire initiated the Apollonians in the techniques of the furniture makers from Guadeloupe. They reproduced *buffets à deux corps, arbalète* commodes, spider consoles, recamier-style sofas, four-poster beds, and rocking chairs. Standing in front of the planter armchairs, she would explain that the arms pivoted into extensions so that the person seated could rest his legs in a horizontal position while sipping a rum punch, the traditional drink in Caribbean climes.

Finally Celanire turned Bingerville into an artistic capital. The highlight of the palace was its museum. It first took up a living room, then two, then the entire ground floor, and became the first "ethnographic museum" in Black Africa, far superior to the IFAN museum in Dakar. It is still a major attraction today. Its aim was to prove not only to the orphans at the Home but also to all those doubting Thomases that Africa has a culture of its own. The collection included Dan, Wobè, Gouro, Yaouré, and Baoulé masks, but especially masks from the Guéré people, masters of the art. The finest pieces in the museum were a series of nine Guéré masks: one singer's mask, two warriors' masks, two dancers' masks, a mask for wisdom, a mask for running, a fool's mask, and a griot's mask. Celanire threw herself passionately into her treasure hunt. She had no qualms soliciting the chiefs and elders or mingling with secret societies and initiation ceremonies. This deeply shocked the Africans, who complained she was looting their sacred heritage. It would bring her misfortune. Women are not allowed to look at masks, let alone lay hands on them. Consequently, she would never give birth, neither to a son nor a daughter.

In actual fact the Africans could never forgive Celanire for marrying because she no longer had time to look after the Home and left Tanella in charge. For them, Tanella deserved to be stoned with a hail of rocks after murdering Mawourou and to rot without a grave on the land she had insulted. Her acquittal was scandalous. It was true Tanella did not have Celanire's iron hand, capable of bringing to heel a troop of rebels. Under her management the Home foundered. Guinea grass overran the lawn. The papilios died in the aviaries. The nurses no longer wore white uniforms. The students' success rate dropped to nil. Discipline became lax, as did hygiene. Epidemics returned at an alarming rate. One serious incident alerted the French authorities. An officer on leave from Upper Volta, Jean de Brezillac, stabbed a colleague, Melchior Marie-Marion. According to him, Melchior had stolen his "fiancée," Akwasi, a nurse at the Home for Half-Castes, to whom he had given a gold ring. The latter denied everything. An inquiry was opened. But the inspector, housed at the Governor's Palace, fell under the spell of Celanire. Consequently, his report boiled down to a panegyric of the "lovely Creole," Madame de Brabant, and matters remained that way right up to Celanire and Thomas's departure for Guadeloupe a few months later. This departure stunned blacks and whites alike. It was true Celanire never stopped talking about her childhood island to anyone she met. She liked to repeat that she kept the memory of it in her heart like a candle burning in front of the high altar, for a country, just like a mother, cannot be forgotten. She confided in close friends that she had a sacred duty to carry out: find her parents, especially her real mother. Yes, her birth had been darkened and marred by tragic events. That beloved little papa she spoke of so often was not her real father, even if their feelings for each other had been unparalleled.

Despite all that, watching her bustling with activity in Bingerville, you wouldn't be alone in thinking that Africa had replaced her island home in her heart and she would have trouble leaving. And yet she left.

One morning in February, a host of porters swarmed into the palace gardens. The strongest loaded onto their backs Celanire's fourteen trunks. The others grabbed Thomas's trophies—elephant tusks, a stuffed lion he claimed to have shot during a hunt, and miles of boa constrictor skin. The nurses had come down from the Home and were comforting Tanella, who seemed on the point of giving up the ghost. Celanire bade her an emotional farewell before setting off for the Ebrié lagoon. However, once she was seated in the fishing canoe under a canopy of woven palm fronds, she seemed to forget those she was leaving behind. She perked up as if the life she had just led no longer mattered. Ludivine, watching her, was shocked by so much insensitivity. Her own heart was grief-stricken. To what unknown destiny were they taking her? She already regretted the end of an era. She knew that the older she got, the more nostalgic she would feel for her childhood and Bingerville, and in spite of herself she would portray the Home as a lost paradise. She would forget its charged atmosphere, loaded with mystery. She would forget the way the nurses took good care of their boarders during the day and then the way everything changed from six in the evening onward. The way the children were hurried up from the refectory to the dormitory. As soon as the last Hail Mary was recited, the nurses locked the doors and vanished. The glow of a large lamp was scarcely reassuring, for once it had drunk its oil it generally went out before midnight, which plunged the room into darkness and a host of eerie shadows. The tots who couldn't get to sleep thought they heard the hullabaloo of music, noisy conversation, and shouts of laughter.

In early August a new governor arrived in Bingerville, as well as an officer who took over the management of the Home. Without further ado, he removed Tanella and dismissed the nurses. He kept only the cooks, matronly Ebriés and sturdy mothers who would not appeal to anyone. He restored order to the curriculum. For the boys, arithmetic and grammar; for the girls, cutting and sewing. We have to admit, we shall never know what really went on at the Home for Half-Castes. This splendid edifice, which appears in the book on colonial architecture by Frédéric Grogruhé, keeps its secret closely guarded. Closed down for many years when it almost collapsed into ruin, it was later entirely restored and became the Orphanage of the Ivory Coast.

As for Tanella, her life dragged on in sadness and came to an even sadder end. As she was one of the few "women of letters" of her time—let us not forget, this was the term for those who could read and write in the white man's language—she was hired as a schoolmistress for the mission. This unusual status aroused the lust of Chief Bogui Yesso from the region of Abreby, who hastened to make her one of his wives. But he married her merely for the sake of adding a woman of letters to his harem. During the first year he paraded her around like an expensive piece of jewelry. Then he abandoned her in one of the huts of the women's compound and neglected her to such an extent that she turned to Catholicism and became deeply religious. Catholicism in fact had spread like wildfire along the Alladian shores. It was conversion upon conversion, christening upon christening. The catechists were too many to be counted. Churches sprang up like mushrooms. At first modest buildings made of bamboo, they were now built of prefabricated materials shipped from

France. Tanella, christened Marie-Pierre, died giving birth to her third daughter, for she could only produce babies of the vagina variety. In fact, she had stopped living many years before that—once Celanire had left her.

The day before Tanella's death—when she was already in her death throes— a dog such as had never been seen before in Abreby, a black hound with gleaming jaws, as tall as a heifer, as muscular as a bull, appeared in the compound. It lay down in front of the dying woman's hut and uttered the most frightful yelps, groans, and whines. Africans have no particular liking for dogs, that's a fact, and this one received a hail of mortars and a volley of machetes. Yet nothing would make it budge. If it retreated a few feet, it was only to return to the attack a little later and reconquer lost ground. During the wake ceremony, the commotion it made almost outdid the wails of the professional mourners. It kept watch during the church ceremony. It followed the cortege to the cemetery and stretched out on the black-and-white-tiled grave that Bogui Yesso, still enamored with prestige, had built for his family. It only vanished at nightfall as suddenly as it had arrived, and nobody ever saw it again.

The Alladian fetish priests concluded it must have been the messenger of a spirit—a spirit far away who was lamenting the death of Tanella.

The inhabitants of Bingerville have nothing good to say about Thomas de Brabant either. He is not credited with any accomplishment. What surprised everyone was that once he was married, he lost interest in everything, he who was so authoritarian, meddled in everything, laid down the law, pontificated and exasperated Africans and Europeans alike. He lost interest in the roads, the bridges, the wharfs, and the railroad. He let his wife wear the pants, as the rather vulgar saying goes. He only stopped by his office long enough to absentmindedly sign the papers his secretary presented to him. At the same time his appearance changed. The former dandy now dressed any old how. His skin grew flabby; he lost the thick black hair he had liked to oil and became potbellied. In short, from a dashing man of authority he turned into a fat stick-in-the-mud.

They discovered the key to this transformation when they found out he was imitating another Thomas, Thomas de Quincey, whose book *Confessions of an English Opium-Eater* Celanire had given him for his thirtieth birthday. Like him, he was drinking laudanum. Under the pretext of treating a toothache, he had vialsful shipped from Grand-Bassam.

Morning, noon, and night he gorged himself on this lovely, amaranthine tincture.

Cayenne
1906

Hakim thought Guiana looked like the Ivory Coast. Same sweltering forests. Green and more green everywhere you looked.
Rivers, now in slow motion, now suddenly raging torrents.
Only the ocean was different, swamplike, without a line of
breakers or rollers. Cayenne especially looked like Bingerville.
The same smells of almond, mango, and palm trees. Here too
seven months out of twelve the sky was like a wet rag oozing
dirty water that overflowed the storm drains and soaked the
streets. The houses of the administrators were identical. There
were the same public buildings under their rusty roofs, the Governor's Palace housed in an authentic Jesuit monastery, the bank
and the transatlantic shipping company. In short, the same
colonial ugliness encrusted amid the splendor of the forest like
lice in a magnificent head of hair. The only difference: the buzzards, which ambled across the Place des Palmistes in Cayenne
and perched on every available branch, were bigger and smellier
than the African vultures. At first he couldn't help comparing
Cayenne to Saint-Laurent-du-Maroni, where he had stayed
weeks, perhaps months, perhaps years (it was all so muddled in
his head) at the transportation camp. In contrast, Saint-
Laurent-du-Maroni was a little jewel. The convicts had built

such lovely little houses for the penitentiary administrators, they had christened it "Little Paris"! Men are such wonderful creatures! Even reduced to the scum of the earth, they continue to be artistic geniuses. They built magnificent edifices and designed and painted friezes, frescoes, and paneling. From the transportation camp Hakim should have been sent to the Ile Royale, one of the Iles du Salut. But the cells there were already overflowing. So they sent him to Cayenne, where he became, like so many others, a houseboy, a domestic. Houseboy to Monsieur Thénia, governor of the Banque de Guyane, who lived on the promontory at Saint-François. He did not know exactly when he began forgetting the charm of Saint-Laurent-du-Maroni and started liking the wilder, rougher city of Cayenne. He knew the city inside out, from its mangrove swamps and grassy squares to its streets cluttered with handcarts and its magnificent clapboard facades. He wallowed in its few corners of sunlight, soaked up its trails of shadows, and got drunk on its stench. In short, he became attached to its atmosphere of gloom. The town only came to life at carnival time, but the gaiety didn't suit it. Its smiles looked more like grimaces. Its bursts of laughter rang out like moans.

A few months after arriving in town, he was referred to a certain Papa Doc for a nagging dysentery. Papa Doc was doing time for rape of a minor, and his ten-year sentence had been commuted to life. He had built a shack made out of planks and corrugated iron within the prohibited zone along the seashore, but the authorities had turned a blind eye, since his reputation was known from Saint-Jean-du-Maroni to Mana, and from Iracoubo to Organabo and Sinnamary. He was the living proof that saints ended up in the penal colony. On Devil's Island he had treated the lepers. At Saint-Joseph he had cared for the insane.

At Charvein he had saved the wardens and prisoners from epidemics of scurvy, yellow fever, and yellow jack. At the New Camp he had put the bedridden and the crippled back on their feet again and comforted the dying on their final journey. He cured every form of gut ache, even ankylostomiasis, which tears the intestines to shreds. And all that with remedies of his own invention. When he was on the Ile Royale they let him roam freely around the penitentiary, examining the plants with a makeshift magnifying glass, plucking and stuffing them into the bag he kept tied around his neck. He captured anacondas with his hands and made ointments out of their grease. Sometimes he could be seen braving the wrath of the ocean, defying the sharks, always lurking, attracted to the smell of meat from the slaughterhouse, and catching manta rays he would eviscerate on the spot. Then he would dry them, grind them, and pound them to make unguents, lotions, and poultices. At Cayenne he had not wanted to live like the former convicts who banded together out of common misery, pilfered by day, and slept in the marketplaces by night, where they quarreled, hurled insults at each other, and squabbled. He had continued to invent remedies and treat the "Creoles," as the descendants of slaves were called, now free, yet worse off than they were during slavery, as was everyone else. Even the Indians and the Maroons, the Boshs, the Bonis, the Djukas, and the Saramakas came down from their villages to consult him. All of them put their trust in the power of his hands. He meted out his treatment free of charge or almost, in exchange for the joy of a little wild honey, a slice of grouper, an agouti, turtle eggs, or a gourd of cassava *kwak*. So from five in the morning the sick, dressed in identical rags, with skins of every hue, lined up in front of his door.

Where did he come from? From Guadeloupe. He must have

once been light-skinned, high yellow or frankly mulatto. Now his skin wavered between brick red and muddy brown, with grayish fissures at the folds in his neck. He no longer had a hair on his head. Nor on his eyebrows. A kick from a screw had broken his nose and knocked out all his front teeth. Smallpox had pocked his face with purplish stains and indelible scars. Chiggers had eaten away his toes, making him limp. Nevertheless, there remained his deep brown eyes, mirroring his compassion. Nobody had heard the sound of his voice, as if the suffering and ignominy he saw around him every day had once and for all stifled his throat. He communicated with his patients through a language of signs and gestures, the same way he communicated with a hard-faced, wild-looking Galibi Indian woman who had stayed with him ever since he had cured her of a case of yaws. She cooked his meals with an expert hand and of an evening gave him pleasure, for there was still the hint of a generous and capable body under her rags.

As for Hakim, he tended the gardens at Monsieur Thénia's, which was no small matter. He was up before dawn, and it was only at day's end, around six in the evening, that he had time to sit down with Papa Doc, side by side, always in the same spot, on the pebbles on the shore, facing the ocean. Looking blindly out to sea, they drew on their pipes stuffed with excellent tobacco smuggled in from Oyapock. What lay on the other side of the dark line of the horizon? They could no longer picture it, no longer imagine the time when they had been free to come and go and roam wherever they pleased. When the breeze began to bite and make them shiver, they would make their way back toward the promontory of Saint-François, walking one in front of the other, breathing in the smell of brine. The hut had a single room and therefore only one hammock. So Hakim had hung his outside on the branches of a silk cotton tree. The Galibi Indian woman would be waiting for them on the doorstep, savoring her pipe as well. She had already lit the grease in the oil lamp and on the kitchen range was heating up the wretched meal she had prepared. All three would chew in unison, without a word between them, lost in their thoughts. Then the woman would clear the table, wash up, and put everything away before slipping into her hammock. The men went and sat outside in the darkness. They would down one, two, three, four glasses of rum and separate, teetering on drunkenness. Papa Doc would go and join the Galibi woman, and Hakim, somewhat disgusted, could hear them moan with pleasure.

"Even so! At their age and in their state!"

He himself believed his body had long vanished along with any desire. On nights when he was lucky, hardly had he closed his eyes than he would fall into an opaque, dreamless sleep. On other nights he would toss and turn like a man possessed until the early hours of the morning.

One evening, the moon was in its first quarter and an ylang-ylang tree was endeavoring to perfume the smells from the swamp and the mangrove. Papa Doc was sitting with Hakim among the roots of the silk cotton tree when a sound rose from his mouth. An eerie sound. Like an out-of-tune piano. A rusty clarinet. A muffled trombone. A punctured saxophone. Accompanied by a high-pitched shrill, the clack of a *rara* during Holy Week, and here and there, the tinkling of a bell. During all those years he had not spoken a word; it was only natural he had lost the knack!!

"I was twenty-three or twenty-four, a student at Pau, when Aurélie, a girl who was in love with me, gave me a book that was to transform my idea of medicine and change my life forever. It was a novel written by an Englishwoman, and *Frankenstein* was its name. It was the story of a scientist who got it into his head to create a human being and ended up fabricating a monster. He took an instant dislike to it, and this triggered a series of unfortunate events. This sad story taught me that medicine is more than just curing typhoid, amoebic dysentery, or lymphomas, and we have to look further and decipher the secrets of human nature.

"I'm here for a crime I did not commit. I've told the lawyers, judges, jury, and every Tom, Dick, and Harry, over and over again, I am innocent. As innocent as the newborn fresh from his mother's womb. But I'm not disgusted, I'm not embittered. Because there are at least two other crimes on my conscience that nobody suspects, except for the Almighty up in heaven. They're the ones that landed me up in this hell. One day my sins caught up with me and consumed me with a raging fire. It's the Good Lord's justice. That's why I bow down before Him, ask Him forgiveness, and accept His will.

"Like I've just told you, I'm no bush doctor, no leaf doctor. I did my medical studies at the university of Pau in France, the first Guadeloupean, a descendant of slaves, to set foot in a faculty of medicine for whites. You understand what I'm saying? I should be rolling in money with a doting wife and kids. And look where I am. I haven't got a penny to my name. I'm dressed in red stripes with a black number on my chest. My father was a Royer Belle-Eau, a family of white planters who refused to pass their name on to me. But since he worshipped my mother, a seamstress, he sent me to school and paid for my education. But still I hated his guts. I dreamed of eating them in a salad, of making black pudding out of his blood. My mother wept every time I talked insanely about him. Because, after all, he was only concerned for my welfare. At Pau, Aurélie loved me although I was half black. I could have married her. Had quadroons with her. Whitened the race. But I didn't want to. On the contrary, I wanted to blacken it. The race, I mean. Go back to Africa. Become a cannibal again. Climb back up my tree. That's why I married Ofusan, a Wayana.

"The Wayanas were runaway slaves who had fled the plantation and settled on the slopes of the Soufrière volcano. When the whites finally got round to abolishing slavery, the Wayanas stayed put. The only difference, twice a week they came down to the villages to sell their garden produce. Hidden under their *bakoua* hats, you couldn't tell the men from the women. Same blackness. Same shaved heads, same scarifications—everyone was scared of them. They didn't speak Creole, but an African language, *Kilonko*. It was rumored brother slept with sister, and even with the mother. A real pig swill. When they had finished selling their stuff, they piled their baskets onto their heads and went back up the mountain. One day, they came to fetch me. A Wayana girl had slipped on a rotten mango amid the market filth. Her head had hit a rock so violently she had fallen into a coma.

"I had returned home to Grande-Anse two years earlier and opened my practice on the square in front of the church. There was no lack of patients. The sick came from as far away as Grande-Terre to consult me. They couldn't get over seeing a mulatto, an islander like them, doing what I was doing. They begged me to go into politics, to run for a seat in the Conseil Général. I had other ambitions. I researched, I experimented. I had invented a cure for dengue fever. I had invented a way of replacing broken hips in older people with an artificial one. But Frankenstein remained my dream, and I too burned with desire to assemble the elements of life to produce my creature. In secret, I conducted experiments on rats, mice, and voles. That morning, I grabbed my bag and ran to the market. The Wayana girl was lying on the ground, her head dripping with blood. I had a great deal of trouble reviving her. She finally opened her eyes. I must confess I soon realized I didn't love Ofusan. For me, she was a way of getting my revenge. On my father. On my mother, who had lived her whole life in servitude and adoration of the whites. On all those light-skinned girls she presented me with to whiten her blood. On the mulatto clique in Grande-Anse, who aped the very same families who had lashed their parents. On our wretched society, whose only concern was the color of money. Whereas poor Ofusan worshipped me. She was a saint. But men like me have no time for saints. They're only interested in *bòbòs,* loose women who stink of sweat under their patchouli. For me, Ofusan learned to speak Creole and French, two languages the Wayanas despised. For me, she had herself baptized. She attended catechism classes. She took her first communion, and then on April 27 we were married before God and before mankind. Ever since our wedding night, making love to her had been a problem. Her purity repelled me. My member, always sprightly, had never, oh never, played tricks on me—you know full well up till this very day it has never let me down—it became as squishy as blotting paper soaked in water. In order to get the tiniest erection I had to imagine she was one of my whores lying in bed beside me.

"I should now give you a description of Grande-Anse. It lies on the windward side of the island, in the middle of the sugar-cane basin. On one side, the green of the cane fields; on the other, the blue of the ocean. It used to be a fairly big agglomeration: a mess of cowpatlike huts piled into neighborhoods—

Front-de-Mer, Bélisaire, Carénage, and Bas-de-la-Source. What
they called the town, Grande-Anse itself, was the residential district. It was composed of the cathedral Saint-Pierre-et-Saint-
Paul, the balconied, mansarded houses belonging to a handful of
dignitaries, the boys' school for Christian instruction run by the
monks, the girls' day school run by the sisters of Saint-Joseph-
de-Cluny, the Saint-Jean-Bosco orphanage, city hall, the dispensary, and the police offices recently opened in a former rum
purging station. All around it were the whorehouses. Whorehouses galore! There must have been at least a dozen. The black
and mulatto women whom emancipation had liberated from the
cane fields and the great houses, and who had nothing to fill
their bellies with, flocked to them. As for the white Creole
planters, they did same and paid a fortune for what they had
always taken free of charge. Behind every girl there was a black
or mulatto pimp. On the side I was the physician to the most
popular whorehouse in Grande-Anse, called the Ginger Moon.
There's a long story to it! My mistress at the time was a certain
Carmen, a *bòbò* from Santo Domingo, matured by experience
the way I like them, whom I had cured of a case of furunculosis.
One day she came to ask for help. She was fed up selling her
body to one and all. She wanted a rest and to get others to work
for her. So she had the idea of opening a whorehouse and asked
me to lend her some money. I accepted on one condition. I
would be in charge of hygiene. The place would be spotless. Dis-
infectant and bleach. Every three months I would give the girls a
checkup so they wouldn't contaminate the customers with the
chancre, clap, syphilis, and what have you. She said, You've got a
deal, and we were on a roll. And what a roll! Sometimes the
white Creoles would be lining up in the corridor. There were
mulattoes too, whom I used to see take communion on Sundays

beside their wives. As for the blacks, it wasn't girls they fought over. Believe me, they had other things to think about at the time. One night, I had an urge to see Carmen. I shall never forget that night. It was in September. It was pouring down in bucketfuls, and the claps of thunder would have awakened the dead. Since d'Artagnan, my Arab stallion, was scared of lightning, I walked to the Ginger Moon, wading in water up to my stomach. Soaked to the skin, I was about to go up to see Carmen when a young girl came out of one of the rooms. I had never seen her before. She must have been fourteen or fifteen, in any case no older. No taller than a tuft of guinea grass. Certainly no bigger. Her skin was shiny black. Her hair, a stream of oil flowing down her back. Even so, despite her hair, she didn't look like a coolie. Rather a hodgepodge of Chinese and black mixed in with Carib blood. The way she swept past me without even a glance, I can't even begin to tell you the effect it had on me. I arrived quite out of breath and asked Carmen:

"Tiny. Slender. A spark on a bonfire. Who is she?"

"She burst out laughing. 'The way you speak! It's Pisket. She hasn't been here a week. And already the men are mad about her. Do you want to try her?'

"And how! I had no sooner tried the girl, I was mad about her as well. I had to have her morning, noon, and night. She was my morning cassava bread, my noontime red snapper, and my evening bush tea. Soon, I could no longer bear another man touching her. I would have liked to lock her away and keep her all for myself. But I imagined the scandal it would have caused in Grande-Anse and all over Guadeloupe. A man like me whom everyone respected. Me, Dr. Jean Pinceau—"

Hakim gave a start, since the name rang a bell in the thick fog of his stupor.

"What did you say your name was?" he asked.

"Pinceau. Funny name, isn't it? It's the name of my mother's family, a family of talented free blacks since the early eighteenth century. The Pinceau men were locksmiths. The women, seamstresses and milliners. . . . So I didn't dare do anything more about it and merely settled Pisket in a room next to Carmen's in the attic. She had her own washroom with her pitchers and basins. I paid a servant to cook, wash, and iron her clothes. Believe me, Pisket was a real character. I never knew where she was born, who her parents were. . . . At first I didn't even know her real name. Pisket was a nickname she had earned because she was so slender. She was all skin and bones. Carmen knew no more about her than on the day she picked her up while she was making love on a plot of waste ground in Grande-Anse. The fact was, she seldom uttered a word, barely a sound came out of her mouth. You never knew whether she was happy or upset, whether she liked doing it, whether she wanted more. A real autist. It was probably that which got me so excited. I never knew whether she was fond of me or what her feelings were. I had to have Carmen watch her. For as soon as I had my back turned, she took in men. Not for money. Not for pleasure. Just like that. Like a machine. It made me so angry! Can you imagine, me jealous of a *bòbò!* But she always managed to outsmart Carmen and put a man in her bed. There was this Kung Fui, a Chinese half-caste like herself, a weird guy, who was always in her room and even slept in her bed. When I got angry, she vowed he was her brother! There was also a third rogue, more Chinese than black or Indian, always in their company, but who never stayed at the Ginger Moon. What's more, Pisket smoked opium. However often I smashed her instruments and broke her pipe, she would always begin again. She was allergic to hygiene too. She was like a cat: hated water. When she got too funky, I would stuff her in a tub of hot water. I would scrub her shoulders and her you-know-what with a bunch of leaves. But there was nothing I could do about it. I wallowed in her filth.

"Alas, my happiness didn't last. After a few months I realized she was not menstruating. She was so ignorant, she didn't know what it meant. I had to explain it to her. Can you believe she jumped for joy, someone who didn't care a damn about anything. A baby! A baby! For the first time, she was happy. But I was in a predicament, to tell you the truth. A baby with a *bòbò!* And first of all, was it my child? Despite my words of warning, Pisket had slept with a great many other men. I don't trust those teas and decoctions women take for an abortion, so I proposed operating on her. Oh, nothing complicated. No need to be frightened. She didn't say anything, and I took that to mean yes. Three or four days later, she disappeared.

"I can remember it as if it were yesterday.

"It was December 22, to be exact. Lights and Christmas carols in every home. The children from the Saint-Jean-Bosco orphanage had decorated a giant crèche, which they had placed in front of the high altar in the cathedral, and folk from Grande-Anse came to admire baby Jesus, Mary, Joseph, the ox, and the donkey. I had gone up to her room and found it empty. She had taken all her stuff. Nobody had seen her leave. Nobody knew where she had gone.

"I wanted to die, but had little luck. I began by accusing Carmen of not keeping an eye on her. That was unfair; she had no reason to distrust Pisket, since she never set foot outdoors. One of the girls told us that the day before she had surprised her with Kung Fui near the cathedral deep in conversation with Madeska, a notorious mischief maker who was friends with a certain Madone, Pisket's only friend. This struck her as being odd. What could she be doing with such an individual? Except for Madone, all the girls used to run and hide when he turned up. They were scared of him. What's more, he was fat and filthy as a hog in his African *boubou*. Obviously Carmen didn't have the courage to kick him out. But that didn't tell me where Pisket had gone. Where should I look for her? On Grande-Terre in the vicinity of La Pointe? Over by Basse-Terre? Among the cane fields? On the mountain slopes? In the waterfalls or along the rivers?

"In desperation I haunted the places of ill-repute. I mounted d'Artagnan and scoured the countryside. I interrogated the rum guzzlers and players of dice, checkers, and dominoes. I visited one by one the whorehouses on the windward side of the island and dragged the whores from their beds. I lost my appetite for everything. I was a real bag of bones. Don't laugh, I suffered like I had never suffered before. People were convinced I was working too hard and begged me to take a rest. Don't ask me how long this hellish state lasted. I was like a drug addict in withdrawal. Then finally I snapped out of it. I conducted more and more daring experiments, endeavoring to transplant rabbit hearts into mongoose and vice versa. In particular I began a crusade against opium. I have to tell you that at the time there were as many opium poppy fields in Guadeloupe as there were cane fields. The plant had been introduced by those Asian workers come to replace the blacks in the plantations. They dried the seeds themselves from the poppy flowers.

"Old Chang, for instance, owned an opium den right in the middle of the Bélisaire district, which, by the way, was thick with Chinese. When the police had had enough, they raided the den, rounded up all the customers, and threw them in jail. After two days they had no choice but to set them free, since there was no law against smoking opium. You could count us on the fingers of one hand, those of us who protested that opium was far more dangerous than rum. I began writing columns in *Le Courrier de la Côte au Vent*. I worked together with a childhood friend of mine, Dieudonné Pylône, the police commissioner. I opened a small center for treating drug addicts that I called the Refuge of the Good Shepherd. In short, because of all the fuss I made, they awarded me the medal for social merit. More and more, people took me for a role model. They were so adamant I should go into politics, I ended up creating a party that I prosaically called the People's Party. Unfortunately, I never won an election. The absurdity of my situation, I am convinced, must have stuck out like the Soufrière volcano: me a bourgeois belonging to an old family of freed coloreds, I dared to speak in the name of the slaves.

"One morning I was in my surgery, about to operate on a small boy for tonsillitis, when Carmen sent urgent word that Pisket had reappeared. I left the child laid out on the operating table and ran outside like a madman. Yes, Pisket had come back. But not the Pisket I knew! A zombie. She now smoked as many as fifty opium pipes a day and had reached the stage of bondage. She could no longer stand on her own two feet, walk, or eat, and it was Kung Fui who did everything for her. He of course had reappeared, together with his Chinese friend. Eyes wide open, at night she had hallucinations and sometimes screamed like a hog having its throat slit. At that stage, all my learning was to no effect. She gradually drifted into a state of terminal cachexia, and one morning, while I was leaning over her, the life went out of her.

"You can't imagine what happened next. No doubt because of the opium she had consumed, her body turned rotten in next to no time. She passed away at five in the morning when dawn mass was being said. At eight, she reeked to high heaven. At noon, the stench made it impossible to remain in the house. A thick juice, as black as tar, oozed from her private parts, which liquefied, and stained the bedsheets. I had to run to the undertakers. The undertaker quickly cast a lead coffin, which he placed inside a second ironwood casket. But the smell! You can't imagine! During the wake we had to beat off the swarms of blowflies, bigger than beetles, that settled on everything and everyone. The removal of the body was a great relief. The priest, of course, refused to give her the extreme unction. But I had a tomb built in which we buried her on Sunday, August 30, the day of Saint Fiacre. The bad talkers of Grande-Anse were not surprised to see me in deep mourning because of my work with the drug addicts. They thought I was trying to show the young people an example of what not to do. Little did they guess that the sun had set forever on my life and that I was laying my only love to rest. I envied Kung Fui, who had nothing to hide and was crying his heart out as he followed the hearse, propped up by Yang Ting—that was his name, I remember now. A nasty piece of work he was, you only had to look at him, but you couldn't help feeling sorry for him. I didn't give him long to live either. He was already an old bag of bones, as yellow as saffron. Emaciated. Eyes dilated—red and swollen. A certain Tonine was also walking behind the coffin. They said she was Pisket's sister. I had never seen her before. I remember she looked a lot like Pisket except for that shy, gentle expression, which Pisket never had. A few weeks later, grave robbers came and opened Pisket's coffin and scattered her remains. All her fleshy parts had been eaten by worms. Only the skeleton was left, but broken into a thousand pieces. It was all the more surprising, since grave robbers as a rule go straight for the tombs of the white Creoles and make a beeline for the jewelry, gold necklaces, cameos, gold chokers and beads of the women, and the pocket watches, the rings, and the bracelets of the men. What did they hope to find on a wretched prostitute? And yet the biggest surprise was yet to come. One morning I got a letter from a notary in Grande-Anse informing me that Kim Lee Fui—that was Pisket's real name—had left me and Kung Fui an inheritance. She had left a considerable sum of money in the Crédit Colonial and a laundry in her name, Le Blanc Galop. We then discovered she hadn't gone very far. To Bélisaire. She hadn't gone into hiding. She had opened this laundry on the ground floor of her house, where she employed not only her so-called brother and the inseparable Yang Ting, but also two Chinese and the girl called Tonine, who was the close friend of this Yang Ting. Instead of looking under my very nose, I had gone looking for her as far away as Basse-Terre. Pisket had made pots of money! I didn't understand how she had amassed such a fortune, nor why she left me half. Obviously, I refused every penny of it and gave my share to Kung Fui, who pocketed it and vanished from Guadeloupe with Yang Ting. And no one was any the wiser.

"Dieudonné Pylône was right to be intrigued. He put Mangouste, one of his assistants, on the case; like his nickname, Mangouste was as cunning as a mongoose. He went and prowled around Bélisaire, but turned up nothing. The neighbors had never seen Pisket's face, since she never went out, never even attended mass. One morning they had seen Le Blanc Galop all shut up. They couldn't care less what happened to Pisket, Kung Fui, Yang Ting, Tonine, and the two employees. Dieudonné was about to close the case when the manager of the Crédit Colonial sent him a confidential memo stating that Pisket's money had been deposited by a rich white Creole, a certain Agénor de Fouques-Timbert. What was the relationship between the *bòbò* and the planter? Dieudonné and Mangouste thought Agénor should be interrogated. But they were apprehensive. At that time the eyes of the whites drilled into ours. They finally picked up enough courage and set off for the plantation. The story of the Agénor de Fouques-Timbert family is part of the history of Guadeloupe. It was an open secret that the Fouques-Timberts had black blood in their veins. For that reason, some of the white Creoles refused to have anything to do with them. Nevertheless, they were perhaps the richest planters on the island. Not only did they escape bankruptcy following the abolition of slavery, but Agénor was clever enough to modernize and expand his sugar factory. He was the first to have replaced the so-called Père Labat system with modern sugar-making technology. Megalomaniac, he planned to invest in a large factory on the windward side of the island, which would rival that of Darboussier. To increase his fortune and his whiteness, he had no scruple marrying Elodie, the only daughter of Emmanuel des Près d'Orville, who was hunchbacked and so ugly that nobody wanted her despite all her papa's money and estates on northern Grande-Terre. Even so, she gave him seven fine children, all boys. Nothing was lacking, except a position in politics. It nagged him like the urge to piss. One morning he began stomping for votes. With no trouble at all he was elected to the Conseil Général. At the time, you see, it was a lucrative affair. The Conseil Général was in complete control of taxation. It was there to protect the rich. Agénor's secretary received Dieudonné and Mangouste on the doorstep and told them anything that came into his head. That Agénor was in the habit of making gifts to institutions and the underprivileged at Christmas. That he had Pisket on his list of charities. They didn't believe a word of it, but they didn't dare pursue the matter. And yet they sensed they were on to something."

Hakim cleared his throat.

"And Pisket's baby, your child, what became of it?"

"There's nothing to prove it was my child! But I'm not a complete scoundrel. When they reappeared, I asked Kung Fui what had happened to Pisket's pregnancy, since she was no longer in a position to answer for herself. He replied that she had had a miscarriage, which didn't surprise me. Opium had become her only food, and her body was unable to nourish a fetus."

"And what about Ofusan?" Hakim insisted.

"You oblige me to return to the scene of my crime. For pity's sake, you're making me live it all over again. Where we come from, our wives are used to being neglected and spending their nights all alone in bed while their husbands are out having a good time with their mistresses. If they have the nerve to complain, they are beaten. Ofusan was not used to that. She did not come from a society like ours, where the male is God incarnated. What's more, she didn't have a friend in the world. Nobody could say anything bad about her, that's a fact. She was beyond reproach. At confession every Friday. On her knees at the altar every Sunday. Plus vespers, rosaries, and the month of the Virgin Mary. Despite all that, she was only barely tolerated at Grande-Anse. They never forgot her family were Wayanas, maroons, black as sin, who on weekdays sat in the market.

"One morning in early September, the seventh, the feast day of Sainte Reine—I can remember it as if it were yesterday— shortly after Pisket's death my friend Dieudonné Pylône rushed into my surgery in a frenzy. He was carrying a kind of package in his arms. He unwrapped the bloodstained cloth and revealed a baby. A baby girl, a few hours old or a day at the most. A plump little body, her tiny almond slit between her thighs, her umbilical cord neatly cut under a scab of blood. But horrors, I'm not kidding, her head was hanging on by a thread. A blunt instrument—a machete, a cutlass, a butcher's knife, or garden secateurs—had virtually sectioned it from her body. The baby had completely drained itself of blood through this hideous wound. Clinically she was dead. Her heart had stopped beating. Her encephalon showed no signs of life. Anyone else would have called a priest. But I saw the opportunity I had been waiting for. Defy nature and coax back life like a docile bitch into the body she had deserted. While I was frantically preparing my instruments, Dieudonné told me the story. He had been chasing a common thief in the infamous neighborhood of Bas-de-la-Source when he stumbled upon this mutilated baby at the Calvaire crossroads, lying amid rusty nails, pieces of iron, shards of mirror, and red rags. Visibly there had been a sacrifice. He had gathered up the little victim and dashed to find me.

"To give you a better idea, remember what happened forty years after the abolition of slavery. Society was still reeling, and you were witness to all sorts of horrors. Virtually nobody had profited from emancipation. It had ruined most of the white Creoles. As for the former slaves, none of the promises made them had been kept. No schooling, no work, just poverty. The indentured Indian workers who had replaced them were a dead loss. As for the Chinese, they were worse. They systematically bled the island dry with their robberies, their rapes, and their banditry. They had raided a munitions depot at Fort Saint-Charles and, armed and masked, would hold up and rob carriages, attack the great houses and homes of the rich. There was a thriving traffic in newborns. The black and mulatto women were fed up with letting their men have a belly for free. Those babies that were not left in orphanages were sold. Or else they were kidnapped, and for a small fortune the evildoers would perform human sacrifices for those who wanted to succeed in business or politics. Sheep, fowl, and black bulls from Puerto Rico were no longer enough. It had to be babies. Babies, and nothing but babies, and more babies. For instance, everyone knew where Madeska, the mischief maker who made the fortune of the most powerful politicians, got his money from. Oh, it was a dreadful time. You were ashamed to be a Guadeloupean.

"My eyes had never seen anything so hideous as this baby with her throat slashed. I set to work. The operation lasted seven hours. I had to reconnect the severed arteries, veins, nerves, and tendons. For that I used the sharpest needle and the softest catgut. Then I sutured the flesh. I grafted a strip of skin taken from her thigh onto the jagged suture that twisted around her neck. I was sweating profusely. My heart was thumping, but my hands were steady. I needed blood to irrigate my work. I transfused the blood from two chickens that I sent Ofusan to fetch as fast as she could. The whole time I felt that here I was at last emulating my hero Victor Frankenstein, and it spurred me on. I too was equal to the Creator, and when the child began to sneeze and cry I was overcome with pride. What I didn't predict was that Ofusan, to whom I confided the baby for motherly care, became obsessed with her. In her solitude she looked upon the child as a gift from the Good Lord to console her for her barren womb. She begged me to adopt her. How could I refuse her? So we adopted her. Registered her officially as our daughter on September 24, the feast day of Saint Thècle, under the name of Celanire Jeanne Pinceau."

"You said Celanire Pinceau?"

"That's right, Celanire Pinceau. Celanire was my mother's name, whose memory Ofusan wanted to honor. Not that Mother treated her very well. Behind her back she called her 'tar girl.' May God bless her soul!

"In the meantime my friend Dieudonné instructed Mangouste to go and interrogate Madeska, who knew a thing or two about children in the region with their throats slashed. Mangouste stumbled into a house of despair. Madeska had just fled, abandoning women and children. Every day now for years he had gone for a dip in the sea at the same spot. He would lay his clothes under the same almond tree. Since he couldn't swim, he never went very far. That very morning, much to their surprise, the fishermen had seen him hoist his fat body and potbelly into a fishing boat and row frantically in the direction of Montserrat. What was he running away from? That was anyone's guess.

"All these signs hinted to us, Dieudonné and me, that Celanire had not been sent by the Good Lord, but by Beelzebub himself. As for me, I was wondering how we were going to get rid of her, especially as I had brought her back to this world. Unless murder was committed, there didn't seem to be an answer. And there was my wife going into raptures over her, embroidering baby clothes, decorating her bedroom, gurgling silly names, and looking so much younger. I didn't dare tell her what I suspected.

"I have to say that Celanire was a beautiful baby. The older she got, the more beautiful she became. She was so lovely that once they tried to steal her. One day the nursemaid was walking her along the seafront when a young girl came up and begged her to let her cuddle the divine little angel in her arms, which she naively accepted. The young girl then ran off and almost got away. People said that Celanire looked like me, only darker, since it is always said children take after their adopted parents. Like

Frankenstein, I soon came to loathe the creature I had created. Don't ask me why. I took a dislike to everything about her. Above all, I couldn't bear to look at her obscene scar, purplish as an infibulated labium, which was a constant reminder of what I had done! I asked Ofusan to hide it, and she got into the habit of tying silk or velvet ribbons around the child's neck. The terrible thing was that despite this aversion, which I had trouble hiding, Celanire took a special liking to me. Her chuckles and gurgles were directed at me, something that Ofusan suffered agony over. Because, oddly enough, the child never showed her any affection. This gave Ofusan the opportunity to invent another excuse to torture herself. If nobody loved her, it was because the ancestors, her *maman* and her papa, had put a curse on her. She had to make peace with them again and ask their forgiveness. She subsequently concluded she had to return to her mountain home. The way of life there was less corrupt. She could bring her daughter up in a healthier environment. I have to confess that I exploded on hearing this litany of insanities. One morning, when I couldn't take it any longer, I told her in no uncertain terms that if she wanted to go back to her boondocks, I wouldn't lose sleep over it. And above all to take her Celanire with her! I could do without her even more. Stung to the quick, she decided to leave the next morning. Okay, I said, just like that. Good-bye, farewell, and good riddance!

"The following day I lost her.

"The next morning she went to the market to inform her own people she was returning home when a dog, a huge Cuban hound, like those used to hunt down the maroons in olden times, black, as big as a calf and strong as an ox, leaped on her, clawed her face, and sunk its teeth into her neck. She died on the spot while the hound, its chops dripping with blood, vanished before anyone could make a move. It's this second crime I am paying for today. The cur is me. I killed Ofusan as clearly as if I had been the one commanding it to sink its jaws into her throat. And the saint got her revenge, because I found myself lumbered with this child I couldn't stand and who was to be my downfall. If I had had any sense, I would have left her at the Saint-Jean-Bosco orphanage. Or else with a scalpel I would have undone my surgical masterpiece and sent her back to the hell she deserved. I couldn't, because of Ofusan. *In memoriam.*

"My friend Dieudonné Pylône began to get suspicious. That dog, that Cuban hound, had nothing to do with the scrawny, mangy pack of stray dogs that roamed the market. None of the sellers or customers had ever seen it scavenging the garbage. Where did it come from? Was it really an animal? Wasn't it rather an evil spirit? I was unable to help him solve the mystery.

"Ten years went by. My friends urged me to remarry. In their opinion, I couldn't raise a young girl all on my own. Many a young wench made eyes at me, for without boasting, I was still a handsome man. A full head of curly hair, a good set of teeth. But I wasn't interested. At the age of thirty-three I had finished with sex. Women of the night or well-bred young girls, it was all the same to me: nothing interested me any longer. I kept clear of making medical experiments. I immersed myself in politics. With no success, as I've already told you. That scumbag Agénor de Fouques-Timbert beat me twice. Even so I made a name for myself electioneering against assimilation, which all the other parties at the time were hankering after.

"Looking for someone to take care of Celanire, both as a nursemaid and a bodyguard, for that crazy woman was still prowling around her, I hired a certain Melody. Knowing myself as I did, I hadn't hired her because of her references; she didn't have any. It was because she was so ugly and cross-eyed that even the devil couldn't have made me make love to her. That woman, in whom I confided everything, became so devoted to me that I ended up treating her like a close member of the family until that day when she dealt me the coup de grâce.

"In 1894 Celanire was ten years old. Still just as pretty and, as they kept telling me, just like me but blacker! She was a child with a most pleasant nature. Happy, cheerful, and amusing, inventing all sorts of stories. Not scatterbrained, however, extremely intelligent. Top of her class. At home she would pester me with questions I couldn't answer: 'Why don't girls get more schooling and why are they considered inferior to boys? Why do men cheat on their women? Why do they beat them? Why are there so many illegitimate and unwanted children with no *maman* or papa?' Contrary to the custom at the time, I told her outright she was an adopted child whom I had operated on to save her from dying. Sometimes I caught her looking at her monstrous scar in front of the mirror. Her eyes would brim with tears, as if she were wondering who her real parents might be. She had got it into her head that they must have given her away because they were too poor to raise her, and this afflicted her deeply. She swore that when she was older she would do everything to find them and build them a palace for their old age. In fact, she was beyond reproach. For most families, she would have been their pride and joy. But my feelings toward her hadn't changed. It was something beyond my control; I couldn't stand her. She had the loathsome habit of constantly calling me 'darling little Papa,' pestering me with her little treats, entering my surgery without knocking with cups of hot chocolate and slices of marble cake, kissing me on the neck, and rubbing herself up against me like a cat. Every evening, when she was tucked up in bed, I had to read her a story and end it with a kiss, and this was a pretext for all kinds of unbearable cuddling and fondling on her part. Precocious as she was, she had her first period early that year. And she would chatter about it right in the middle of a meal in front of the guests, as if it were our little secret. 'Darling little Papa, I've got the curse . . . I can't go swimming today! . . . Darling little Papa, I've got stomachache, you know why? . . . Darling little Papa . . .'

"I was livid. From one day to the next, a boil as big as the knob on a cane swelled up on her groin. I had no other choice but to examine her, and she openly offered herself to me. You think I'm lying? I swear I'm not. Too many loose women have swooned in front of me for me not to know their little game, and this child was doing it to perfection. It happened one morning in her room. I was wondering whether to lance her boil when she began to roll her eyes, wriggle, uncover her budding guava breasts, and guide my hand into the most inappropriate places. In response to my protests, she moaned: 'Darling little Papa, take me. I love you so much!'

"Disgusted, I dealt her two slaps; I had never laid hands on her till that day, and rushed down to my surgery. My patients commented on how I looked. I felt sicker than they did. What was I going to do with Celanire? How could I get rid of her? At lunchtime, she didn't come down. Melody, whom I always believed to be on my side, announced she had a fever. At dinner, same thing. At night, I couldn't get to sleep. I tossed and turned. I could hear her moving about over my head and talking to Melody. Suddenly I was frightened, like a homeless person who knows the hurricane is heading straight for him. I was right, because two days later the police came to handcuff me in my surgery in front of my flabbergasted patients. Dieudonné Pylône preferred to resign rather than be mixed up with this masquerade.

"Me, Dr. Jean Pinceau, I was accused of sexually abusing Celanire, my adopted daughter. Melody, my faithful Melody, was a witness for the prosecution. Alarmed by the child's behavior of crying for no reason and losing her appetite, she described how she had plied Celanire with questions. After weeks of her insisting, the child ended up telling her the truth. Encouraged by Melody, Celanire finally went and revealed everything to the police. When I heard Melody churn out all that nonsense, I got the impression I was dreaming. Worst of all, the jury believed every word of it!

"My trial lasted over a year. I became a cause célèbre, the subject of conversation of every bourgeois and country yokel, every white, black, and mulatto. If you read the papers from Guadeloupe, Martinique, and Guiana for the year 1894, I made front-page news. Few of the columnists called me a common pedophile. Instead, they reported my career record: brilliant student in France, successful medical experiments, an antidrug crusade, and unmatched devotion to my patients. Ah! Dieudonné was a loyal friend during these tough times!

"Because of me, he left the police force, became the head of my defense committee, and had petition upon petition circulated. But it wasn't easy for him. Because of the color of my skin! As a mulatto, I'm too light-skinned. The masses would have mobilized for a black. Nobody felt like defending a guy whose class is traditionally an ally of the white Creoles. Dieudonné adamantly repeated that I was not being sentenced for rape, which was a ridiculous accusation for anyone in his right senses. Who was this Melody whose testimony was so damning? A real mystery. Before she worked for me, no decent family had hired her. Nobody on Grande-Terre or Basse-Terre had ever set eyes on her. What I was paying for, Dieudonné asserted, was my nationalistic stand. During the last electoral campaign I had openly canvassed for the end of French tutelage. Poor guy, he did what he could. He had no idea that at meetings the presence and encouragements of a cheering crowd has the effect of a rum punch, and you say anything that comes into your head. At heart, I've always been a bourgeois, a small-time bourgeois.

"My family didn't want her, as you can imagine; they were scared of her. So the court entrusted Celanire to the sisters of Saint-Joseph-de-Cluny, who sent her to the Sisters of Charity in Paris for her education.

"After I was sentenced, I was transferred to Grande-Terre. From Grande-Anse a prison cart took me to Petit-Bourg, where, shackled hand and foot, I embarked on the sailboat linking the town with La Pointe. Along the Lardenoy wharf Dieudonné had managed to muster a few demonstrators shouting 'Free Pinceau!' But most people had come out of curiosity to gaze at the likes of a future convict. There were a good many high-society ladies under their lace parasols who looked me up and down. The jail at La Pointe was the most revolting place you could imagine. Obviously it was nothing compared to what we saw in the penal colony, but believe me, it wasn't a pretty sight. It was the first circle of hell. This is the last. The prisoners were piled in eight or ten to a cell, where in the dark the mosquitoes had the feast of their lives. Once a day the guards gave them a ration of green bananas. Once a month they were lined up in the yard, given a piece of rough soap, and hosed down. The rest of the time they fought as best they could not only with the mosquitoes, but also with the rats attracted by all this filth. No need to tell you that with so much diarrhea, the holes for doing your business were filled to overflowing. I can't begin to describe the stench! Oddly

enough, in the high-security area we were slightly better off—
only four individuals to a cell. I found myself with a Chinese
guy who had hacked a woman to pieces, a black who had raped
his sixty-year-old mother before slitting her open, and an Indian
who had sent his father's head flying with one swipe of a cutlass.
In the evening all these poor devils wept like little children. All
shouted they were innocent and gave their own version of their
story. They then sodomized each other by way of consolation.
Nobody could escape it. I even ended up rather liking it.

"On Christmas Day, 1895, I sailed on the *Biskra* for Guiana
in a raging sea. All around me my traveling companions were
vomiting left, right, and center. Although I had never been
known for aggressive or disruptive behavior, they locked me up in
a blazing hot cell, one they reserved for violent prisoners, right
above the boilers. Throughout the entire voyage I was unable to
stand upright, which explains why to this very day I walk
hunched over, bent in two. On arrival they began by thrashing
me, considering it arrogant on my part to ask to be transferred to
the camp at Saint-Louis to treat the lepers. They didn't understand I felt like a leper myself. Birds of a feather flock together."

"So you haven't heard from Celanire since she was a child?
You've no idea what became of her once she left Guadeloupe?"

"No. The last time I saw her was at the courthouse in
Grande-Anse with Melody, when her mouth uttered those outrageous things which everyone took to be gospel truth. Even I was
troubled by what she said. I began to wonder whether my sex,
which has always had a mind of its own, had not won the better
of me. Perhaps unknowingly I had gone up to her room and
committed the horrors she accused me of. After all, how could
an innocent mind invent such terrible things? Where would she
have got such ideas? What Satan had put them in her head?

Then I regained my senses. I was innocent. Celanire must be twenty-four or twenty-five by now. I imagine she is capable of driving the most serious, the most virtuous, guy out of his mind. I am positive she continues her mischief making, and I tell myself I am somewhat to blame. If I could have loved her, if, when Ofusan died, I had been there for her, treated her like my daughter, it might have curbed her wicked instincts. At the end of the day, perhaps all she needed was a little love from me."

"Unfortunately," murmured Hakim, "you couldn't be closer to the truth. I have met her, your Celanire. Far, far from here. In Bingerville, in deepest Africa. It's her, it's the same person you're describing, there's no mistake about it. Her beauty you've described so vividly, her black-black skin, her long, oiled hair, the terrible scar around her neck, especially that scar. You can't forget that scar once you've seen it. It haunts you. It must be terrible for her not to be able to get rid of it. It's funny, Celanire talked about you all the time in the most affectionate terms. 'Darling little Papa' here and 'darling little Papa' there. She claimed you were dead, and she had never managed to get over it. She also described her island of Guadeloupe, which, in her eyes, was the most perfect place on earth. She swore she would return there one day to clear up some unfinished business. I dread to think what exactly, since she wreaks evil wherever she goes. I know for sure, without being able to prove it, that she is the cause of my suffering. It's her and nobody else who has brought down misfortune on my head. Tonight, my friend, I'll tell you my story, and you can judge for yourself."

For in fact the sun had risen, brightening the sky, a patch of crumpled cloth above the eternally muddy sea. Papa Doc had needed the entire night to unravel his sad story. Since the Galibi woman had already left to sell her wares at the market he set about heating up some watery coffee, which he poured out equally into tin mugs. The two men dunked their pieces of cassava, drank, and ate, both locked in identical thoughts. How amazing life is! There they were, side by side, sharing the same fate, victims of the same Celanire! Each of them had been born and had lived on opposite sides of the world, one in the Americas, the other in deepest Africa. Each of them had been separated by so many lands, oceans, and mountains! Did it mean they were going to die together? What nature of spirit was driving their common enemy? Why was she bent on doing evil from sunrise to sunset, from north to south? What caused her rage? What did she want to destroy in the world? Reluctantly, Hakim set off for Monsieur Thénia's house. Out of the two, he was perhaps the more shaken. In dismay he realized he wouldn't be able to tell his story before nightfall, and he felt something he had not felt for a very long time. Certainly not since he had been in Cayenne, where he lived as if in a daze. In fact he got the impression he had been born in this patch of forest and that the memory of what he had left behind had been erased from his mind. Had he ever been anything else but one of life's rejects, thrown into the last circle of hell? That morning, his memory returned, and with it, the memory of the terrible injustice he had been a victim of. Abandoned by his father. Spurned by his family. Rejected by society. But suddenly another thought crossed his mind, interrupting his litany of woes. What if, like Papa Doc, he was paying for a crime unbeknown to him? Hakim had seldom thought of himself as a pervert. Fondling Bokar had not left him with a feeling of guilt. On the contrary, it had given two lonely, tortured teenagers a taste of happiness. Simply the death of his beloved had convinced him that because of something abnormal about him he was never meant to be happy. For the first time, he realized he was a degenerate who deserved the most terrible punishment.

In the past the promontory at Saint-François was known for its unhealthy vapors, rising up from the white and black mangrove trees soaking in the brackish, snake-infested waters, and capable of causing deadly diseases. Then some convicts had cleaned up the area and built dwellings for the notability. Monsieur Thénia's house was the most remarkable of them all. As a safeguard against the risk of fire, the governor of the bank had shipped a metal framework from Bordeaux. The building's slender columns and its numerous apertures gave it an impression of airiness. But people did not just admire the zinc friezes, the scrolled consoles made of iron, or the elaborate balustrades. They went into raptures over the gardens. Hakim, who had under his orders a horde of gardeners, the 'banished,' as the convicts were called, simply common-law criminals but paradoxically the most dangerous type, had them hoe, weed, rake, and graft until they were ready to give up the ghost. He had invented an irrigation system of pulleys and paddle wheels. In his new frame of mind he realized that morning that unconsciously he had taken as inspiration the gardens at the Home for Half-Castes in Bingerville. The bamboo grove, the hibiscus hedges, the clumps of crotons, the beds of periwinkles, the English lawn, and the aviary where all sorts of nocturnal and diurnal butterflies, as striking as those in the Ivory Coast, beat their powdery wings—nothing was missing.

He now understood that his entire past was embedded deep inside him. Nothing had been exorcized. Bingerville and the never-ending rainy season. Koffi Ndizi. Thomas de Brabant. Betti Bouah. Every one of these ghosts was alive and well and living inside him. Papa Doc's story had opened the door of their jail, and now, liberated, they were prowling around him.

Among his team of gardeners were three Arab convicts, Mimoun, Rachid, and Ahmed, who were serving a sentence for peccadillos committed in their *bled*. They spoke to no one, didn't mix with either black or white, and all the convicts knew they only had intercourse among themselves. When he approached them, Hakim was aware of something being triggered inside him. He realized his old passions were not dead. He looked the three men straight in the face. Blackened by the sun, as angular as a vine stem, tattooed from top to bottom, Mimoun was certainly the handsomest. Trembling with a secret emotion, Hakim assigned him his day's work. Mimoun listened to him without saying a word, walked away, then, turning to his companions, said a few words in their gravelly, hermetic language and all three of them burst out laughing.

Hakim hung his head. Mimoun had seen through him. No, he hadn't changed. He would never be cured of what he carried inside him. He would never be anything else but what he was.

He had such a reputation as an expert gardener that in the afternoons Monsieur Thénia lent him to the colonial administration to weed the public squares and plant jasmine and mignonette. On his way to the town center each day he would meet processions of escaped convicts, their numbered prison uniforms in tatters, returning to the fold at gunpoint. The dream of escape was the convict's obsession. The idée fixe was freedom. Although the men knew only too well that the end of the line would be Charvein or the Ile Saint-Joseph for life, they never gave up trying. There was the story of a convict who had escaped twenty-four times, had been recaptured twenty-four times, and on his last trip to his cell slit his belly open with a cutlass. Since Hakim no longer had any dreams, he had never tried to escape. When he was at Saint-Laurent-du-Maroni he had been told about the gold that lay hidden upriver. Boats loaded with gold diggers on their way upstream would pass the convict vessels. It was said that the gold formed in the heart of the Tumuc Humac Mountains, then the rainwater washed it down along the riverbeds, where it glittered supreme, the object of the gold diggers' lust. So sometimes he pictured himself as a marauder, scraping the sand and the gravel, pocketing his gold nugget. Yet what would be the point? Even if he managed to sell it, what would he do with the money?

When the eye of the sun began to droop low in the sky, Hakim hurried to go and join Papa Doc. All he wanted was to start telling his tale; he wanted it to be his turn to tell his story, which he now saw in a different light. He was cursed before he was born because of those wicked instincts planted inside him. When he arrived at the shack, the Galibi woman, her hands reddened with blood, was busy scaling a skewer of grouper fish. Crouching a few steps away, a Saramaka, as tall as a *mapoo,* a bow and arrows slung on his side, holding a cutlass, was waiting for Papa Doc. The latter no sooner appeared than the Saramaka leapt to his feet. The two men embraced like old acquaintances. Then the Saramaka began to explain in his grating, incomprehensible (at least to Hakim) tongue that he had traveled all this way because a terrible epidemic was ravaging his village. Countless villagers were being carried off. Men, women, and children were burning with fever and bleeding to death through every orifice. Papa Doc nodded. It sounded very much like hemorrhaging dengue fever, which he had successfully treated in the past at Grande-Anse. While he was quickly collecting together his vials and unguents, Hakim was seized by an irresistible compulsion. To hell with Monsieur Thénia's garden: he would follow the two men, even though he knew full well that any unjustified absence was immediately reported to the penitentiary adminis- tration. The price he would have to pay for absconding might very well be landing up again on the Ile Royale.

They left Cayenne in total darkness under a delicate, luster- less moon that was emerging from its sleep. To reach the river, they first had to cross the banks of the Cayenne, then wade for miles with mosquitoes on their heels across a swamp, through soft mud strewn with tree trunks whose rotten stench grabbed them by the throat. It was almost daylight when they arrived at the spot where the Saramaka's pirogue was bobbing patiently, half hidden by the thick vegetation on the bank, to which it was leashed by two stakes. A whitish vapor wafted over the surface of the water, apparently dormant under its duvet. Soon the current picked up speed, and the boat sped along like an arrow. The Saramaka and Papa Doc, perfectly at home on this shaky, precar- ious craft, silently manipulated their paddles, and Hakim envied them their quiet assurance. Once the river slowed down, nar- rowed, and they glided between two sheer cliffs. Flocks of birds flew from one wall to the other. Then the waters widened again. At noon the sun pitched itself vertically, and all at once the smoldering sky burst into flames. In agony, Hakim slaked his thirst as best he could by drinking the river's muddy water in the cup of his hand. At one point, the Saramaka pointed out amid the mangrove trees a solitary hut standing on the bank, fringed with white sand and teeming with equally white birds.

"Mami Wata," he cawed.

Hakim knew the legend. It existed in the Ivory Coast as well. A siren with long, shiny hair spends her days swimming in the river depths. At night she emerges and retreats to her house on the bank. There she sings song after song, so melodious they sound like a heavenly concert. But woe betide the traveler who hears her and approaches her house, for she throws herself onto him and drags him down to her watery palace, the better to devour him.

Toward the end of the afternoon they swung away from the center of the stream and finally landed. As they stepped out of the canoe, their feet sank into a sticky humus that stuck to their soles. They had to walk for a good hour before the ground became firm again. Daylight was fast fading. A bitter smell of bruised vegetation reached their nostrils as the Saramaka hacked their way through the poisonous flowers, the lianas and wild plants. At a bend in the path the village loomed up in a clearing. Hakim was not surprised to find the same charming appearance as the villages in the African bush! The ground was covered with fine sand. Large huts perched on stilts were arranged in a semicircle. All around the forest had been cleared and neatly planted with plots of tobacco and cassava. Now he was convinced it was the hand of Europe that defaced everything, blindly imposing its architecture and its discipline. There was only one dark side to the picture: surrounded by mourners, a dozen bodies lay unburied, waiting for the night to be carried to their final resting place. Without wasting any time, Papa Doc entered one of the huts. Hakim climbed into a hammock hung under a *carbet.* As night fell, the clouds of mosquitoes became bolder and joined the bats in flight. Insects and birds, emerging from every tree branch, chirped, warbled, and screamed. In the distance monkeys burst into laughter, while some animal howled in response. The music they composed was enough to frighten the most intrepid.

Hakim could not help shivering, as if he had caught a fever, and he wondered what had got into him to follow Papa Doc to such an inhospitable spot. Just then the Saramaka women, who had finished their cooking, brought him a copious dinner of haunch of venison and freshwater fish. Every one of them had an infant clinging to her side who was intrigued and frightened by this stranger. Hakim could not touch his meal. Instead, he greedily sucked rum from a bottle, something he seldom did.

He finally fell asleep.

Hardly had he done so than a young Saramaka woke him. In a daze, Hakim first thought it was Kwame Aniedo. The same jet-black skin, the same hair tied into small braids, above all the same smell, the smell he could not forget, a mix of sweat and vegetable fat. Then he realized his mistake. This one was darker, not so tall, slightly built, with filed teeth. Smiling, the young man placed a finger to his lips and motioned him to follow. He obeyed and stumbled to his feet. As fast as his senses returned, the more frightened he became. He was sure he would never forget that night. Sheer pandemonium! A sinister drumming was unable to cover up the screams of the women mourning. Pyres burned in front of the huts silhouetted against the dark backdrop of trees. Their eerie glow exaggerated the flickering shadows of the men and women who with heartrending wails were burning their dead. The young Saramaka left the village and fearlessly plunged into the forest. By magic, every noise stopped on their approach, and they walked on in muffled silence. Soon they reached the river, rippling with tiny iridescent waves in the darkness, and climbed into one of the small boats anchored among the mangrove trees. Straining with all his muscle power, the Saramaka paddled against the current, and after an hour they landed on the other bank. They cautiously set foot on dry land. Then suddenly the moon emerged from its hiding place and illuminated every nook and cranny of the landscape. Blinded by its glare, Hakim got the impression he was living a nightmare and thought he recognized the spot. The isolated creek. The wreath of mangrove trees. The wattle hut, its doors and windows mysteriously closed. It was the home of Mami Wata! The Saramaka, however, still smiling, motioned to him to wait and climbed back into the boat. He remained alone under this glare of moonlight, even more frightening than the dark, listening to the fading sound of water lapping as the boat disappeared into the night. He couldn't say how long he waited, standing motionless and paralyzed on the sand. Finally the boat returned, and he could make out two shapes. Next to the Saramaka was Papa Doc who did not seem to be afraid of being where he was. The only sign something was wrong was that Papa Doc, who had been so nimble up till now, almost stumbled as he set foot on the shore. When Hakim saw his friend, his terror vanished and his serenity returned. He knew what awaited him, and it was no coincidence they were both together in this place. The two of them were going to live their final adventure.

One morning some gold diggers paddling upriver discovered the bodies of Hakim and Papa Doc near a jetty. They were scarcely recognizable, swollen by their long immersion, drained of their blood by vampire bats, and half eaten by birds of prey and ants. They came to the conclusion that the two companions must have left Cayenne by night and tried to reach one of the villages along the river for one of those illegal card games, the only means for a convict to get cash to buy cassava flour, one or two liters of rum, cans of sardines, and, if they were lucky, some black-eyed peas. Unfortunately, on the way there, their boat must have overturned. Although convicts, both Hakim and Papa Doc were baptized Christians. The gold diggers brought them back to Cayenne, where the duty of the penitentiary administration was to find them a final resting place. They planned to throw them into the communal grave. But they misjudged popular opinion.

United in life, Hakim and Papa Doc were separated in death. Nobody was affected by Hakim's death; he was, after all, nothing but a convict like so many others, and had never made a name for himself. He seemed good only for growing flowers. Nobody understood why he was such close friends with Papa Doc and why he had followed him deep into the forest to their death. Papa Doc, however, was a living god to the hundreds of wretches he had cared for in the poor districts of Cayenne. As soon as they learned the news of his death, they marched to the penitentiary building and demanded the body. Then they carried his rough pine coffin to his shack on the Saint-François promontory. Meanwhile the Indian and Maroon villages along the rivers emptied, and long processions of canoes converged on Cayenne, swelling the crowds streaming toward the shack. Breaking with the legendary impassiveness of the Indians, the Galibi woman was weeping hot tears for her man. She was frantically talking with those of her tribe who had come to console her. There was something unnatural in his death, there was something mysterious about this business. Among the numerous Saramakas present at the wake, not one of them looked like the beanpole who had dragged Papa Doc off a few days earlier. None of them had heard of a terrible epidemic, neither on the Oyapock nor on the Approuague. The only three convicts from the French Caribbean, two from Martinique and one from Guadeloupe, obtained leave from Charvein, where the prisoners had forced the warders to fly the tricolor at half staff. They had never met Papa Doc. But his body was their property. After all, they were from the same island womb. Too bad if there was not enough rum or thick soup! They would make do with a wake, and the farewells would be heartfelt and passionate. One of them grabbed a flute, another a mandolin, yet another a guitar, and they played mazurkas and beguines from their native land. Then, with his tongue loosened by a little rum, one of them grew bold and improvised as a storyteller.

Soon the traditional words reverberated:

> *Yé krik, yé krak*
> *Yé mistikrik, yé mistikrak*
> *A pa jistis à nonm ka konté*
> *Ta là, sé la jol i té yé*
> *Kan mem, sé té an mal nèg*
> *Se té an nèg doubout.*

These loyal followers of Papa Doc refused to let his body be thrown into the communal grave as if he were a common mortal. They found enough money to buy him a burial plot and erected a tomb, which they covered with black-and-white flagstones, in the very middle of the cemetery on the promontory at Saint-François reserved for high-ranking officials. It's odd that in his book on the penal colony Albert Londres does not devote one line to Papa Doc, who was a real character in his time and left his mark on people's memory. To prove it, even to this very day, the descendants of the convicts have not forgotten him, and every All Saints Day his tomb is lit with candles in his memory. In 1960 a delegation of nationalist militants traveled from Guadeloupe and laid claim to the corpse. Taking up the arguments of Dieudonné Pylône, they asserted that Papa Doc had in fact been banished as a political opponent. According to them, he was one of the first to have demanded independence for Guadeloupe. But the colonial authorities categorically refused to accept their request, and the delegation returned home empty-handed.

Ever since, the Guadeloupeans, who come to let off steam at the carnival in Cayenne and admire the costumes of the *touloulous,* have made the graveyard a place of pilgrimage and laid fresh flowers on their compatriot's tomb.

Guadeloupe
1906-1909

1

In early June 1906, the inhabitants of Guadeloupe were as stunned, flabbergasted, and topsy-turvy as if on the morning after a hurricane they had emerged onto their verandas to discover the extent of the disaster—not a leaf to be seen, not a tree with branches, the land brown and scorched by the brine carried by the rain. Some of them couldn't believe their eyes and had to put on their spectacles twice. But the news was well and truly there, spread across page 3 of the most widely read daily, *Le Nouvelliste*.

SOCIAL CALENDAR

The new governor of the colony, Monsieur Thomas de Brabant, arrived yesterday from Marseilles on board the SS Elseneur. He was accompanied by his wife and daughter, the young Ludivine. May we remind our readers that Madame, née Celanire Pinceau, is a native of our small island, from Grande-Anse to be exact. She left in her tenth year under dramatic circumstances that few Guadeloupeans have forgotten. Interviewed on her arrival, she simply expressed her joy at setting foot once again on a land of which she had vague childhood memories.

A murmur went up across the island. Incredible, but true! Celanire, Celanire was back! What could possibly bring her back to her native land? Didn't she know what her compatriots were like? Didn't she realize they would be quick to dig up the cadaver of a rape that had made such a scandal at the time, and gorge themselves again and again on its stinking carcass? Although she had become the wife of the governor, both she and her husband would find themselves sullied. Unless she had come back to put the finishing touches to all the evil she had already committed? In any case, this return was a bad omen. Nevertheless, nobody was more troubled than the police commissioner of the Arbre-Foudroyé district in Basse-Terre. It was as if the news had dragged him out of a deep sleep.

Unable to work, Matthieu Dorliss stood up and went over to the window. He wasn't looking at the garden. He wasn't looking at the square either, with its mango trees loaded with fruit, or the church, with its miniature replica of the grotto at Lourdes, complete with miraculous waters. He was reliving the past. They used to call him Mangouste. When he was the tenacious, idealistic, lanky sixteen-year-old assistant to Dieudonné Pylône. When Dr. Jean Pinceau, the first physician of color from Guadeloupe, who was more than a brother to his boss, had been sentenced ignominiously to serve ten years as a convict. Unable to prevent the sentence, Dieudonné had resigned from his job and reconverted to trading tropical hardwood. There was absolutely no doubt that his feeling of helplessness had hastened his premature death a few years earlier. Matthieu recalled the promise he had made to him on his deathbed, a promise he had never been able to keep—to find out Celanire's identity and clear the name of a just man.

Racked with emotion, he went out.

In Basse-Terre the deepwater harbor had still not been developed due to the negligence of the Conseil Général, and the ships remained anchored offshore, surrounded by a flotilla of small craft. Matthieu strode on, oblivious to the tremulous greetings of people who recognized him and the authority he represented.

It had been ten years since he had last been involved in this murky affair. He had received an anonymous letter. As a rule the police do not pay much attention to anonymous letters. They know it is a favorite tool of cowards, malicious minds, and madmen! But in this case the writer claimed what Dieudonné Pylône had always suspected, i.e., that Pisket had sold her belly to Madeska at the request of Agénor de Fouques-Timbert. The white Creole, who wanted to get into politics, had sacrificed the infant at the beginning of September 1884. But if that were true, in a manner of speaking it merely deepened the mystery of Celanire, who was very much alive, despite her patched-up neck. What belly had she come out of? Unless . . . unless Pisket's daughter and Celanire, saved from death at the last minute by Dr. Pinceau, were one and the same person. Here the brazenness of his thoughts made Matthieu gasp.

When he arrived home in the Redoute neighborhood, a servant woman handed him an invitation: Governor Thomas de Brabant and his wife requested the pleasure of his company at a reception. Celanire was not wasting any time!

In the eyes of those who saw them for the first time, Thomas de Brabant and Celanire made a surprising couple. As a rule, husband and wife are expected to be well matched. It is even said that after living together for a certain time, they begin to look alike. But Thomas had aged prematurely; his paunch was squeezed into the brocaded poplin of his governor's uniform, his bald head hidden under his flat cap, and he was constantly dabbing his oozing red eyes. Celanire was at the peak of her charm. But let us not jump to the hasty conclusion that because they were ill-assorted they did not get along together. They expressed their adoration for each other at every moment. They fondled each other, held each other's hand, and whispered in each other's ear. To the great surprise of those who had not seen her for fifteen years, Celanire had changed very little. Grown hardly any taller, she had maintained the figure of a young girl—hardly any fatter either. Her cheeks were still velvety from childhood, and her eyes kept their juvenile sparkle. Her admirers compared them to stars, diamonds, carbuncles, and other clichés. The fact remains, however, that it was difficult to sustain the look in those gleaming eyes of hers.

That evening she had boldly revived the Directoire fashion, and her breasts hovered on the edge of her bodice like two birds eagerly awaiting flight. The inevitable ribbon wound tightly around her neck was held in place by an amethyst clasp of the same color. Following in her wake was a young girl of about ten, tall for her age, with a solemn face as white as the *broderie anglaise* of her dress, and very black hair tied with a bow on her neck. The reader will have recognized Ludivine. Celanire devoured her with kisses, squeezed her hand, called her "my darling little pet" at the slightest opportunity, and seemed in every respect to be the affectionate stepmother, which was especially embarrassing, as the girl looked perfectly exasperated by this billing and cooing.

There was a crowd of guests. All the colony's officialdom; white Creoles, yellowed and wrinkled as parchment; mulattos, waved and brilliantined, done up in their Sunday best; blacks puffing up their chests out of timidity at finding themselves in such a place; old people who had lived through the events of the past; young fellows who knew of them only through hearsay—all had been in a hurry to come and examine Celanire at close quarters. They were surprised to find her in such good spirits, so natural, and not at all ashamed of past events. The evening had a piquancy about it that was usually lacking in receptions of this kind. This could no doubt be ascribed to the extraordinary charm of the hostess, but also to some amazing innovations. First of all the buffet: neat little rum punches, codfish and *tannia* fritters, crab patés and spicy black pudding. But above all the band—the cabaret sort, not the type of official receptions. A saxophone, a guitar, and a singer churning out beguines. Even the people who deep down considered such music vulgar couldn't help humming the familiar songs, and this brightened up the atmosphere considerably.

Matthieu had come with his wife, Amarante. Three years earlier he had married this sixteen-year-old Wayana beauty in the hope of shaking up conventions. The Wayanas had been forced off the slopes of the Soufrière volcano and made to settle along the seashore. They were ordered to send their children to school to recite "Our ancestors the Gauls" like everyone else. But nothing had changed, and they continued to be despised and labeled *nèg mawon*. An exception was made for Amarante because she possessed a voice powerful enough to split a rock, an organ with a remarkable range and sweetness. In actual fact, few people had ever heard her, for in her modesty she only sang for a privileged few. Matthieu and his wife had come to the governor's reception for different reasons. Bracing himself once again, Matthieu had not forgotten he had promised to avenge poor Jean Pinceau. As for Amarante, she was bursting with curiosity. The story of Ofusan, little Celanire's adopted mother, who for the love of a mulatto from the flatlands had turned her back on her people's traditions, had become a legend among the Wayanas. The Wayanas attributed the arrival of the baby in her life to her sudden death. For them there was no doubt the infant harbored an evil spirit! Amarante therefore stared at Celanire with amazement. She was not expecting so much juvenile charm and seduction. She was almost prepared to believe it was the Good Lord Himself who had sent her to lighten our darkness. A feeling she had never felt before crept into her and set her heart pounding while, spellbound, she couldn't keep her eyes off Celanire. Matthieu was oblivious to this, relying on the reactions of his nose. Literally. Ever since he was small, he only had to open wide his nostrils and sniff hard for smells to tell him the hidden truth. At the age of four, he had discovered a thief among the guests at a wedding who had tricked his way in. Amarante poked fun at him and claimed he sniffed even in his sleep, even while making love. He was gazing around the room when among the ocean of black, white, and cream-colored faces, the features of Agénor de Fouques-Timbert, president of the Conseil Général for almost twenty years, emerged. Despite old age, which was creeping up on him—he was over sixty—despite debauchery and depravity, Agénor remained a handsome man. As wiry as a guava tree. Not an ounce of fat. Not one white hair. A corn-colored beard and mop of hair, and patches of blue sky in lieu of two eyes. He had scandalized the most broad-minded by burying the mother of his eight boys at eleven in the morning and setting up house with a Chinese whore, young enough to be his daughter, at three in the afternoon the same day. Agénor stared at Celanire with a look that aroused the curiosity of an already intrigued Matthieu. As if, among all those present, Agénor was the only one to know who she was. How could he prove that she was well and truly the survivor of his sacrifice, Matthieu frantically pondered?

There were a number of leads in this affair that had never been followed up. They had never interrogated Madeska's wives, now destitute, who would surely reveal all his secrets in exchange for something to eat, nor questioned his children. His eldest son, Zuléfi, used to follow him everywhere. Even though he was a kid, he must have seen something! Why, for instance, did he give up the family tradition of mischief making and become a traveling preacher, living off the charity of his followers? Matthieu swore he would go and get a closer look. He took hold of Amarante's arm and, surprisingly enough, still unforewarned by his nose of her infatuation for Celanire, went out onto the veranda.

The Governor's Palace was set on an elevation halfway between the ocean and La Soufrière. As dusk fell, mist rolled up from the sea while the vapors and humidity of the massive volcano behind lay heavy as a clamp. In other words, the evenings were freezing. It was an ungainly wooden edifice all on one level, similar to a plantation great house with a steep sloping roof and clapboard walls. Plans for it to be replaced by a building of reinforced concrete, more fitting for its function, were constantly toyed with by the administration. Yet still no decision had been made, and the governors complained of the discomfort for themselves and their families. They would have to wait for many long years and for the architect Ali Tur before things changed. In fact, at the time, the principal merits of the place were its gardens, a dozen acres of outstanding beauty where the rarest of tropical trees grew. Lit by flares, a podium had been erected in the very middle of the lawn. A dozen drummers dressed in white short-sleeved shirts conspicuous against the darkness of the night were seated in a semicircle behind their instruments. The guests, already disconcerted by the beguines, wondered if they were going to start beating the *gwo-ka* drums. They could not believe their ears when Celanire, who had leaped onto the podium, began praising the merits of cultural traditions, of which the *gwo-ka* drum was the *poto-mitan,* in an eloquent, articulate speech. Why be ashamed of it? Why be ashamed of Kréyol, our Patwa mother tongue? The guests liked her singsong accent, which was so Guadeloupean, but not what she was saying. Kréyol, a language, whatever next? However, if they had learned how to listen, they would have noticed that Celanire's words were empty of meaning or emotion. She paid no attention to what she was saying. She had climbed up to where she stood to be seen by everyone, to thumb her nose at her guests and mock them:

"You came to get a good look? Well, take a good look. Look at me. Take a long, hard look. I'm going to drive you to distraction. I'm going to shake Guadeloupe to the core."

When she had finished speaking, the guests exchanged scandalized looks. They would remember Governor de Brabant's first reception for a long time to come! Only Thomas clapped in hearty approval. His face, drained by laudanum, beamed in beatitude like a parent attending a school play in which his child has the star role. His Buddha-like countenance, however, hid an agile mind. He considered his wife to be a kind of artist or poet who operated in the realm of fiction. Anything could be true, as anything could be false, in what she said. Above all, he made no attempt to distinguish fact from fiction in what she did. In Bingerville she had amused herself playing topsy-turvy with people out of sheer fun. She had returned to Guadeloupe for far more serious reasons—to find her real parents, to discover those who had abandoned her. Wasn't that only natural? Thomas was prepared to swear that Celanire was the best of wives. She was cheerful, full of good humor. You were never bored in her company. She adored Ludivine. He liked to think that she was fond of him in her own way. Since laudanum had purged him of any carnal desire, the frenzy of their early years had passed, and he was content with their virtually platonic relationship.

In the meantime, Amarante stared at the dark curtain of trees beyond the illuminated podium. Darkness had locked the palace in its grip and would not let go for some time. Not until throngs of seabirds, messengers of dawn, had begun to flock across the sky. Darling little Celanire, darling little Celanire. That evening she had been revealed to her, and her beauty struck her like the flash of a frigate bird. Svelte yet strong. Good-humored but serene. Knowing what she wanted in life and determined to get it. The glow in her eyes betrayed the passion burning deep down. Was it so that they could meet that fate had brought Celanire back to Guadeloupe?

2

Three months after her arrival Celanire opened an academy of music, Au Gai Rossignol, in an old building in the Carmel district. Polite society began by disapproving. In fact, besides the violin, piano, and recorder, students were taught the seven rhythms of the *ka* drum; besides the "Hallelujah Chorus" in Handel's *Messiah* or the barcarolle from *The Tales of Hoffmann*, students were trained to sing Creole melodies such as "Doudou, Ban Mwen Lanmou." Then snobbery got the upper hand. In next to no time the bourgeoisie elbowed their way in under the low entrance to enroll their offspring. After a few weeks Celanire was on first-name terms with a good many of these bourgeois *mamans* who compensate for the absence and cheating ways of their husbands by fussing inordinately over their progeny. It

wasn't long, we have to say, before these ladies had other things
to think about besides their kids. They rediscovered their youth
and began to get a life for themselves. Off they went again to
dances, cotillions, and banquets. At carnival time they organized
a procession of floats. They formed an association under the
recent law of 1901 and named it Lucioles. Henceforth, in addition to the picnics, excursions to the sea, the river, and other
amusements, there was a whirl of cultural afternoons, evenings,
and retreats. They read short stories, they recited poetry, they
performed short plays. Members of the Lucioles association even
went so far as to create a publishing house. Unfortunately, to our
knowledge, it never published anything more than some illustrated calendars and *Fulgurances,* a collection of poems by Elissa
de Kerdoré, now out of print. Today there is every indication
that Celanire opened Au Gai Rossignol solely as a means to draw
closer to Amarante, whom she had noticed during the reception
at the Governor's Palace.

Amarante was not an easy conquest. Her Wayana education
had made her virtuous, preoccupied with the concerns of her fellow men. In the Redoute neighborhood where she had lived
since her marriage, there was no counting the number of poor
children who called her Godmother and on New Year's Day
lined up on her doorstep for their present. Noon and night her
maid would take food to the bedridden, abandoned by their
families. Amarante never forgot she descended from a dynasty of
feisty women. Her ancestor, Sankofa, leading a battalion of
Maroons hiding out on the slopes of Les Mamelles, had pelted
the French soldiers climbing up for the attack with a rain of
flaming branches. She also wore herself out every day walking to
a one-class school for Indian children at Monplaisir. Celanire
sent her one of those flowery letters she was so good at and

offered her an exorbitant wage so that she could devote herself to her favorite pastimes of music and singing. Up till then Amarante had tenderly cherished her papa, her *maman,* her brothers and sisters, and respected the husband they had chosen for her.

Suddenly, she discovered passion, turmoil, desire, and the burning need for another person. In her distress, she read the letter out to Matthieu. She was counting on his nose to sense something suspicious in this offer, to prevent her from accepting it and thus save her from herself. Unfortunately, Matthieu saw here an opportunity to get closer to the mysterious Celanire and begged Amarante not to refuse. Some people make their own bed of misfortune.

So Amarante left her little Indians and the school at Monplaisir. From that day on her life was transformed. Accustomed to a husband preoccupied with himself, she now spent her days with an attentive, considerate, and thoughtful person. Celanire's company was a delight not only because of her good-heartedness and intelligence but also because of her good humor and vivacity. At the Gai Rossignol the hours flew by like minutes. No sooner had classes begun than the bell for recreation would ring. Celanire communicated to Amarante her love for classical music, especially Vivaldi, and in their mezzo-soprano voices they sang together the *Lauda Jerusalem.* When they didn't have classes, they strolled together in the governor's gardens and lunched tête-à-tête on the veranda before retiring for a siesta and savoring even greater moments of delight. The only blot on this idyll, Amarante noticed, was that Celanire did not miss Ofusan, her adopted mother. Not only was there no treasured memory of Ofusan kissing her or leaning over her cradle, but Celanire seemed to harbor a grudge against her. Amarante decided she would right matters. But every time she broached the name of the deceased, Celanire would hurriedly change the subject. If she insisted, she sensed her companion's irritation. What could have opposed mother and child during their short life together? It was unfair; only "darling little Papa" got Celanire's attention. She embellished him with all sorts of virtues, and it was hard to believe that this highly educated, highly trained doctor, noble crusader against drugs, and nationalist politician, had taken advantage of her like the first uncouth *nèg kann* to come along.

That particular year, the month of September was midwife to a number of hurricanes. Thank goodness, they spared Guadeloupe and spread their desolation elsewhere. One of them, however, wreaked havoc on Montserrat. Sometimes heaven is unrelenting: a few months earlier the tiny island had been two-thirds destroyed by the eruption of its volcano, Chances Peak. The population, terrified by this second blow fate had dealt them and thinking themselves cursed, took to the sea in makeshift boats. Those who did not sink to the bottom of the ocean were washed up along the windward shore of Guadeloupe. The distress of these poor wretches was such that the governor, Thomas de Brabant, ordered the military to erect tents along the seafront and urged every Guadeloupean who could to help these brothers in their misfortune. Regretfully, however, although the seafront became a popular stroll for the bourgeois, who noised their sorrow in front of the tents, gifts in kind like cash were rare—so rare that Celanire decided on her own initiative to organize a collection and sail to Montserrat with the booty: barrels of fresh water, sacks of rice and French flour, and cases of saltfish and smoked herring. At that time it was quite an expedition getting to an English island. So Thomas chartered an old schooner called (don't laugh) the *Intrépide* for his wife, Amarante, and the domestics accompanying them. For three days the

Intrépide, with timbers cracking, pitched and heaved and rolled with the swell of the waves. With the exception of Celanire, standing bolt upright in the prow, breathing in the air, all the other passengers were as sick as dogs. Finally, one morning, the island loomed up over the horizon, and presented a harrowing sight. The flames from the volcano had first of all scorched the earth, then the pouring rain had loosened the crater, burying hundreds of individuals. For days the moans of the dying had cast a pall over the island. Human arms and legs, corpses of rotting animals, patches of tin roofs, and uprooted trees emerged from tar-colored ponds and craters of mud. Packs of mangy dogs, herds of hogs, and worse still an army of rats driven frantic by the flood following the hurricane, roamed all over the place. In Plymouth, the capital, every shack had been blown away, and only the ruins of Fort Barrington remained.

About a hundred ragged victims of the disaster, all that remained of a population of over a thousand, were assembled on the shore and hurled themselves onto the victuals. It required the firm hand of Celanire to restore law and order. Then the newcomers settled into the few remaining houses in the village of Sotheby. Celanire was welcomed by a certain Melody, whose roof had miraculously survived these natural calamities. Melody greeted her enthusiastically like a beloved long-lost friend and served up a callaloo soup thick with spinach and ham bones. Amarante, exhausted by the journey, withdrew to the bedroom, got into bed, and fell fast asleep as soon as her head hit the pillow.

When she awoke, she was still alone in bed. The moon was smiling through the louvered shutters as if to say she had nothing to do with the evil forces of the elements. Gilded clouds gamboled around her. The cool night air was fragrant with the scent of gardenia. Where could Celanire be? Amarante got up and took a few steps in the dark. The hovel was divided in two by a printed calico curtain. In what served as a dining room, around the glow of a hurricane lamp, Celanire was still conversing with Melody. Amarante had been too tired to take a good look at Melody on arrival and was only now getting her first glimpse. As black as the bottom of a calabash blackened from the cooking fire. Cross-eyed. A mole embossed on her cheek as big as a birthmark. Teeth as pointed as a warthog's. She was gazing at Celanire in adoration, clutching her hands, and smiling at her in raptures with those formidable teeth. As for Celanire, she never stopped talking, as usual. Finally the two women stood up. Melody grabbed the lamp, and preceding Celanire, stepped out into the night.

Amarante went back to bed, unable to fall asleep. Where were Celanire and Melody going at this hour of the night? From where did they know each other? The darkness and strangeness of the place made her feel even more frightened. She recalled what the Wayanas used to whisper. Celanire was the child of evil spirits and spread misfortune to those around her. She was worse than a *soukouyan,* an old hag in league with the devil who preys on victims until the light of day and gorges herself on fresh blood. The hours passed. Gradually insects and buffalo frogs grew silent. The sky turned white. The roosters began to crow. The dogs began to bark. The commotion of the day, so different from that of the night, started up again. Despite the warm air, Amarante shivered under her sheets. Finally, around six in the morning, the door creaked open, and Celanire came and slipped into bed. As soon as she felt her beloved up against her, all her imaginings seemed unworthy of a person endowed with common sense. Celanire had an answer for everything. Melody? She had been her nursemaid when she was a child, and you couldn't wish for anyone more affectionate and warmhearted, despite her looks. She hadn't seen her since she was ten, although she knew she lived on Montserrat. What a joy to embrace her at last! They had gone out intending to conceal the victuals from thieving hands. What a mortifying sight had met their eyes! There were signs of a cholera outbreak. Some of the storm survivors had taken refuge in trees, others in the mangrove. The latter had survived by drinking brackish water and swallowing oysters buried deep beneath the roots of the mangrove trees. The adults had made it through, but they had had to bury the children, and the mothers' despair was unbearable. There were miracles, though. They had discovered a ten-month-old baby playing quite contentedly in a puddle. He had no doubt been dragged for miles by the mud from the volcano. Nobody knew where his parents were, and for him, the tragedy had turned into a game. Ah, sometimes the Good Lord doesn't know what He's doing. How were they going to treat the diarrhea, the cholera, and malaria?

On waking Melody had prepared a breakfast that contrasted shamefully with the surrounding misery: soft-boiled eggs, creamy vanilla chocolate, fruit, and toasted *dannikits*. Celanire's appetite always seemed phenomenal to Amarante. That particular morning, she excelled herself and devoured enough to feed an entire family. The looks Melody gave Amarante as she fussed around Celanire made her feel so uncomfortable, she choked. Finally Celanire began organizing the rescue operation. For almost a week they had to climb up and down dizzying cliff faces under a scorching sun, cross arid savannas, and stumble along the edge of gaping precipices. Everywhere lay rotting corpses in various states of decomposition for which they had to dig graves.

The day of departure arrived, and the *Intrépide* returned the way it had come. They passed boats of fishermen casting their nets, oblivious to the perils of the ocean. The old schooner increased its speed over the quietened waters, and at the end of the second day the shacks of Guadeloupe came into sight, some of them clinging to the green blanket of the volcano like children clutching their mother's apron strings. As they neared the wharf, they saw a crowd had gathered: Thomas de Brabant, the governor, the mayor of Basse-Terre with his tricolor sash, His Grace, Bishop Chabot of Guadeloupe, in his purple robe, a group of schoolchildren dressed in white, including Ludivine, supervisors done up to the nines, and the members of the Lucioles association in their silks and jewelry. They couldn't help but notice the flowing mane of curls of Elissa de Kerdoré. Everyone applauded when Celanire set foot on dry land as fresh in her blue polka-dot dress and matching kerchief around her neck as if she had just come back from a picnic. There were speeches and more speeches. A little girl presented Celanire with a bouquet of canna lilies, roses, and anthuriums. Then Thomas pinned to his wife's breast the medal of the Ordre National du Mérite Social. While he hugged her to him, applause broke out once again.

For Ludivine, all this seemed nothing more than a masquerade. She did not know why her stepmother had risked her life going to sea. But she had no doubt whatsoever that Celanire couldn't care less about the trials and tribulations of the population on Montserrat. Going from the expression on her face, the gleam in her eyes, and the trembling on her lips, she guessed that Celanire was getting enormous fun out of all these ceremonies in her honor. Ludivine knew her father was blind regarding anything to do with his wife. Were the rest as blind? Every single one of them? What was the point of having eyes if they couldn't see? Ludivine was convinced Celanire was responsible for her mother's death, but she did not believe in African super-stitions. She had her own logical explanation. Not content with being Thomas's mistress, Celanire dreamed of marrying him. So she had bribed the houseboys to mix into Charlotte's favorite drinks, from her morning fruit juice to her evening cup of chocolate, those herbs that slowly but surely secrete a mind-debilitating substance. And one day the poor woman, com-pletely off her head, left her home far, far behind, lost in a flesh-eating forest like Tom Thumb without a pebble or a bread crumb to find her way home. Ludivine almost burst into tears in front of everybody, just thinking of her poor *maman.* The older she got, the more her love for her mother and the desire to avenge her grew. But she was crushed by a feeling of helpless-ness. She swallowed back her tears as best she could. The cere-mony was over, and turning their backs to the sea, the pupils set off back to town.

Stupid Amarante standing there, gazing at Celanire in adora-tion! When Celanire had finished with her, there would be noth-ing left for her to do but sink into a watery shroud like the widow Desrussie.

3

The heat of the day was over. It was still barely daylight. Clouds of fireflies already streaked through the air. You sensed that night was in a hurry to stuff into its bag of mourning the green of the cane fields, the deep blue of the sea, and the gray of the sky. The crater of the volcano had already disappeared in the dark, and its slopes were cloaked in mist.

Agénor de Fouques-Timbert hated the place he was going

to—the Bois-Debout Great House at La Regrettée, abandoned for over thirty years. Unfortunately it was always there that Mavundo, his trusted mischief maker from Santo Domingo, arranged to meet him. He whipped Colibri, who restlessly snorted the air. The horse lumbered down the slope of the Morne du Calvaire, quickened its pace across a series of savannas, and stopped abruptly as soon as they came in sight of the Great House. An alley of royal palms, a hollow facade like a trompe-l'oeil, and the remains of the washhouse walls—that was all that was left of one of the most magnificent mansions in the region. After having carried away the furniture, the rugs, and the family portraits, thieves had gone to work on the bricks and roof tiles, leaving not one stone standing. On the other hand, they hadn't touched the slave shacks, and their dingy quarters stood intact at the foot of the Great House buildings like a mangy herd. Their doors gaped open onto mounds of beaten earth once used as beds or tables, as well as the wretched shelves still fixed to the wall. Once separated, the two graveyards now merged into each other: the masters', with its arrogant marble tombs and wreaths and crosses of pearl, the slaves', where under the nettles and sensitive plants, the only signs of a tomb were the white bones of conch shells. The two chapels had also fallen into ruin, overrun by the creeping leaf of life. Agénor was suffocating in the stifling atmosphere. Even after so many years the place still recalled the groans and lamentations of those long buried, the tears they had shed, and their unanswered pleas and prayers. The smell of this suffering humanity seemed to cling to the branches of the trees.

Colibri had come to a standstill, frightened by all these ghosts looming around him, and only when Agénor whipped him on did the horse reluctantly amble off again.

Mavundo was waiting for him in the old slave chapel. He

was a puny, reptilian, red-skinned individual who outwardly appeared perfectly ordinary but inwardly concealed an immense cunning. He commanded a multitude of dwarves hidden in the wind and scattered to the four corners of the globe. Thanks to them, he could see and hear everything. He had studied with the great Rwaha of Ethiopia and lived seven years under his wing in Addis Ababa. Agénor understood from the expression on his face that he was about to announce something terrible. He was right. Mavundo had just learned from one of his dwarves that Madeska had died on Montserrat, where he had been living as a recluse outside Plymouth. His death could be attributed neither to the volcanic eruption nor to the hurricane. The dwarf had found his body, his belly slit open with his guts oozing out, in the very middle of the mangrove swamp. The racoons had made such a good job of mauling his face and neck that his new wife, a young girl from Montserrat, had trouble identifying him. At the end of the day, therefore, the spirits had finally caught up with him. After all these seemingly peaceful years, they were now embarked on the road to war.

In fact Agénor had been expecting this news for the past twenty-five years and accepted it with resignation, almost with relief. When he had decided to go into politics some years earlier, his father-in-law, who had always considered him a despicable fortune hunter, had shrugged his shoulders in disbelief. He wasn't the only one. The whole of Basse-Terre scoffed at the idea. Too many people saw him as a poor-white country bookie, barely capable of growing sugarcane. So he swore to himself he would surprise them. He got the idea of asking Madeska for a human sacrifice as the best way to win the support of the invisible spirits. The mischief maker's family had been close to his from time immemorial despite the difference in color. Madeska couldn't possibly turn him down. As a wise precaution, they had come to an agreement. He was never to meet the belly donor, a certain Pisket. Madeska, who was on intimate terms with her best friend, a certain Madone, took the matter in hand. The deal between the mischief maker and the *bòbò* had cost him a fortune. What's more, in order to carry out the rites that had to be performed every week of the pregnancy up to the final sacrifice, Madeska wanted the girl to be entirely under his control. They had had to find lodgings close by and open a laundry in her name so as not to arouse suspicion. Madeska had just informed him that the birth had gone according to plan and the sacrifice would take place that very night, when suddenly, badabim, badaboom, in rolls misfortune blacker than the ass of a Congo! As a rule Madeska left the sacrificed newborn deep in the woods, haunted only by raging wild animals. This time, goodness knows what got into his head to set the newborn down right in the middle of the Calvaire crossroads. Not surprising that wretched police commissioner Dieudonné Pylône stumbled onto it and that meddling Dr. Pinceau got the idea of patching things up! What happened when a sacrifice was misappropriated? Agénor had prudently waited a few days before going down to ask Madeska for details. Alas, when he had finally made up his mind, the bird had flown! The mischief maker had split. Sobbing their hearts out, his wives added that they hadn't a cent to their name and had fifteen children to feed. Worried out of his mind, Agénor had gone to consult a well-known Nago soothsayer who read the grains of sand on the shore. He hadn't minced his words. Darling little Celanire had become a darling little devil. Dr. Pinceau had done exactly what he should not have done. He had brought her back to life! Moreover, he would pay dearly for his foolishness and would be one of her prime victims. In fact, snatched from death, the baby would become even more formidable. You see, what is difficult for a spirit, good or bad, is to be reincarnated. Thanks to her docile little body, the evil spirits, starting with Ogokpi, the superdemon, would be able to parade freely among humans. Right up to her death, they would use her to commit any crime that caught their fancy and any mischief that came into their heads. Furthermore, convinced they had been swindled, they would savagely take their revenge on all those who had participated in the aborted sacrifice. Madeska thought he could save his skin by crossing the ocean. A waste of time—the spirits would catch up with him whenever they wanted, wherever he was. Likewise, they would hunt down every single one of those who had been involved in the affair, one by one.

Confronted with these dire predictions, Agénor had spent half his fortune protecting himself. His head bursting, he sometimes wondered whether it wouldn't be better to give up. Lie down and sleep. Lie down and die. Be reunited with the mother of his children. Once again the fools had got it all wrong. That cross-eyed hunchback, who had become a laughingstock, was the only woman he had loved with all his heart. Before sinking into the void, she had given him a smile that meant "Don't take too long! Remember, I'll be waiting for you."

He knew that one day his learned assembly of mischief makers, sorcerers, magicians, soothsayers, *houngans, mambos,* obeah men, *kimbwazé,* marabouts, and *dibias* would be of no use and he would die in torment. When he had set eyes on Celanire again at the Governor's Palace and met her gaze, he knew his time was finally up. How odd! After all these years, he had recognized her. Twenty-five years earlier he had been unable to contain himself. He who never set foot inside a church, he had gone over to the cathedral of Saint-Pierre-et-Saint-Paul at the hour of mass to get a closer look at darling little Celanire, the miraculous baby who was the talk of Grande-Anse. Standing on the steps, Ofusan was cradling her in her arms, showing her off like the Holy Sacrament, and everyone kowtowed in front of her. The infant, only a few weeks old, was dressed ostentatiously in silks, satins, and lace, the way mothers proudly deck out their offspring. A large lace bow frothed around her neck. When he leaned over her, with the pretense of a smile, the baby looked up. Then she eyed him scornfully with her unrelenting gaze, as if to say, "So there you are. Yes, I'm still alive, no thanks to you. I'm in no hurry to settle our business, I'm going to take my time."

He had gone inside the church without really knowing what he was doing and fallen on his knees in front of the statue of Saint Anthony of Padua, a saint he loathed, with his tonsure, his missal, and his silly expression. For the first time in his life he was shaking with fright, as helpless as a child!

Poor Mavundo! Since learning of Madeska's death, he had gone to a lot of trouble. He had worn out his dwarves. Now he was giving Agénor *wangas,* potions, powders, unguents, and lotions of his own making. He lit candles in a circle around him. He made scarifications in the fleshy parts of his arms and thighs and inserted amulets. He whirled around and drew circles in the undergrowth. Agénor looked at him in pity. He knew full well all this agitation was a waste of time. His days were numbered. When the mischief maker had finished aping around, Agénor paid him generously and climbed back onto his horse. Delighted at leaving, the animal, now with wings on its hooves, flew through Grande-Anse and galloped without stopping until they reached the Fouques-Timbert plantation. On leaving La Regrettée, Agénor did not notice the flock of egrets scatter in a commotion behind Colibri's rump. He did not realize that what had scared them was another bird, attired in black plumage like a frigate bird or a buzzard. During the conversation between Mavundo and Agénor it had kept its distance, perched motionless on the branch of a guava tree, observing the scene with its cruel, round eyes. Once the conversation was over, it had taken flight, following Agénor and Colibri from afar, its wings spread wide like the arms of Christ on the cross.

When Agénor arrived home, the bird wheeled around for some time above the estate, as if it were deciding on where to settle. Then it made up its mind, swooped down on a magnificent mahogany tree, and nestled among its shiny leaves.

4

Every Sunday at three in the afternoon, the fatal hour of the death of Our Lord Jesus Christ, the same scene never failed to occur. Zuléfi, Madeska's eldest son, his tall body draped in a white robe, took up his position on the seafront. Behind him, the crumpled fabric of the waves and the silhouette of the ships leaving for Veracruz. Above his head, the yellow eye of the sun that seemed to mock his antics. A few feet away, Hosanna, his wife, and their six children, dressed in the same white, rang their bells and harangued the tired, poor, and huddled masses, who were convinced there was a curse on the black race, to draw closer to the Master's Envoy. Oh, yes! The black race had suffered in the holds of the slave ships. It had suffered in the sugarcane plantations. Its blood had reddened the earth. Its sweat had drenched it. First and second slave emancipations alike had changed nothing. They were still eating out of the same bowl of misery. And they would continue to do so. And for what reason? Because they were paying for unspeakable crimes, vile and horrible acts, acquired while they were in Africa and perpetuated in Guadeloupe—human sacrifices, fornication with animals, and depravity of all sorts. But those who reasoned along these lines, preached Zuléfi, were not entirely within reason. The Good Lord knows no curse. God forgives. He forgives everyone, even those who are black of skin, vile, and crouching in the gutter. If they learned to ask for forgiveness, the black race would be rewarded with a wondrous thing. In the afterlife they would be equal among nations.

Difficult as it may seem to believe, this sermon had a considerable following. As early as Saturday morning folk from La Pointe crowded onto the bridge leading out of town, and the procession set off in the direction of Basse-Terre. Crowds poured in from the Leeward Coast, from Deshaies, Vieux-Habitants, even Sainte-Rose, plus a few fanatics from the Grand Cul-de-Sac. By noon the seafront in Basse-Terre was swarming with people: women and more women, but also men, even teenagers. While they waited, they sang psalms, some sitting on the ground or small benches, others standing, drawing themselves up to their full height. The more the priests thundered from their pulpits against Zuléfi, the more the politicians scoffed at his "naive rhetoric," the more the crowds kept coming. After the sermon in Creole, which usually lasted two good hours, Hosanna and the children passed around the small wicker baskets for people to give what they could—from brand-new bills to penny coins. Then came the solemn moment of communion. Zuléfi asked the Good Lord to fill the bread twists with His presence before handing them out. Every time there was an incredible commotion. There was never enough to go around. People elbowed their way through the crowd, clawing and fighting like the possessed, and one wondered why the Good Lord did not simply repeat the miracle of Canaan and the multiplication of the loaves.

That Sunday, the three o'clock sun was especially harsh. The worshippers sheltered as best they could under parasols, *bakoua* hats, pieces of toweling, and jute sacks. Now that the hurricane season was over, the experts predicted a volcanic eruption, given the baking heat. Folk who slept on the volcano's slopes had been woken by rumbling noises. Up by the Yellow Baths, it stank of sulfur. Ashes had blackened the bed of the river Galion. Zuléfi himself dripped great drops of sweat. Though he looked as if he were lost in prayer, he was watching every movement among the crowd and could have described every one of his congregation. When he saw Matthieu arrive, he was not surprised. He had been expecting this visit for the past twenty-five years. He knew that one day some smart police officer would think of interrogating him, now that his father was gone. Yet so convinced he was of divine indulgence, he was not scared of mortals. Matthieu's impeccable behavior never betrayed the real reason why he was present. Like everyone else, he knelt down in the scorching sand. Like everyone else, he sang the psalms. During the sermon he devoutly placed his head between his two hands. He struck his breast twice as hard demanding the Lord's forgiveness. However, he did not budge for communion and merely watched as his fellow disciples filled themselves with the presence of God. As the crowd dispersed, he stood up, dutifully made the sign of the cross, then walked over to Zuléfi with a look that meant, Now it's our turn.

Zuléfi had often imagined this moment when he would be able to get this weight off his chest and confess.

———

"Who put you onto me? You must have been surprised that I, the child of a mischief maker, raised amid vice and magic, suddenly took refuge in the Good Lord. You want to know why?

"Because one day the scales fell from my eyes like Saul on the road to Damascus. The stench of my sins and those of my father grabbed my nostrils. I can't tell you which smelled the worst. All I know are those that wake me up in the middle of the night. I, Zuléfi, committed the mother of atrocities—I performed human sacrifices. It's no use telling me I was still a little boy. I was twelve. I understood perfectly well what I was doing. And to be honest with you, I had already dabbled in the waters of women. My father's ancestor landed here in 1640. He came from the kingdom of Abomey. He was a Yavogou from a noble family and one of the court's highest dignitaries. The Yavogous are not merely princes. They can see and talk with the spirits, like I'm talking to you at this very minute. The invisible world holds no secrets from them. That's why they alone perform the supreme sacrifice—the human sacrifice. When it comes to the annual celebrations and royal funerals, they are the ones who decide how many widows, slaves, virgins, and albinos must be sacrificed. On the death of a member of the royal family, they decide who must follow them to the grave. Once the sacrifices are over, as guardians of the spirit world, they knead the earth around the shrines with fresh blood. You can imagine that, coming from a tradition like that, my father wasn't going to break his back under the sun cutting sugarcane. He used his powers to turn the heads of the Fouques-Timbert family. Fair's fair. He helped them become the most powerful family of planters. In exchange, he and his family were virtually free.

"Like his father and father's father before him, Madeska had inherited the *lithalam,* the name for the sacrificial knife made from a bull's horn, so sharp that as soon as its tip touches the flesh, it slits the skin in two. Blood was its staple diet. From the age of seven I attended every one of my father's sacrifices. Fowl, sheep, goats, bulls, humans—I didn't miss a single one. But my favorites were the newly born. Every time I was fascinated by the incredible sight. My father would pray out loud, kneel down, then do what he had to do. With one stroke of the *lithalam*—it should never need two—he sliced the neck of the infant, no bigger than a quail's. The blood gushed out in great spurts; at first bright red, then slowing to a black trickle. Finally, the baby uttered a muffled gurgle. Its eyes clouded over with a gray film and slowly faded into oblivion. For a long, long time afterward its body shook with violent convulsions. It was as if there were frogs hidden under its skin who were all trying to escape the agonized little body at the same time.

"When it was over, my father would grab the soul as it wandered around in a daze and shove it into a jar, which he stored in a shed behind our house, in case a reincarnation proved necessary. At the age of ten, I became my father's official assistant. My job was deadly serious. The ceremony always began in the secret of midnight. My father would hand me the *lithalam* in its leather sheath. Reciting the prayers, I would draw it out and hand it to my father. Once the sacrifice had been performed, I would ceremoniously wash the blade dripping with blood, coat it with sacred unguents, and return it to its sheath. Then just before dawn I would carry the bleeding victim, still warm, wrapped in seven pieces of cloth and squeezed into a goatskin, to its final resting place. This would traditionally be the clearing at Malendure, way up in the depths of the forest near the Dead Tree Falls. There I laid it on a pile of earth with its head facing the rising sun. At its feet I set down the sacrificial food of smoked herring and ground corn cooked with no salt; I made a circle of ceremonial objects such as candles, nails, and a crucifix and recited the farewell prayer. Then I left without ever looking back. If I did, my two eyes would have been gouged out by the spirits come to feast on the victim's body.

"That night a baby girl had gone under the *lithalam*. Everything had gone as planned. Just before sunrise I was about to set off for the clearing at Malendure with my bag when Virgilius came to fetch me. Virgilius was my best friend, the son of another mischief maker, somewhat less expert than my father. He had been looking for me since the day before. His cousin had been taken to hospital with a pleurisy. We could borrow his boat and take off for the island of Antigua. We'd been longing to go to Antigua for ages! I wanted nothing better, but what was I to do with my wretched load? It would take me almost a whole day to walk to Malendure and back. Then Virgilius had an idea. His father didn't go to all that trouble, not him. He dropped his sacrifices off at the Calvaire crossroads, where he left his magic baths. I hesitated; then the longing to set off to sea got the better of me. I let him be my guide. When we arrived at the Calvaire crossroads, the sky was barely turning white. We hurriedly laid the baby on a mound of grass, set down the sacrificial food, scattered the nails, pieces of iron, and red rags, and rushed off as quickly as we could. We launched the boat into the water. The sun caught up with us around eight in the morning. I shall never forget the color of the sea at that hour. Green like the back of an iguana. We threw out our nets and drew them back in loaded with all sorts of fish—wrasse, largemouth bass, and porgies. We hauled in crayfish. When we returned to Grande-Anse the following night, the place was abuzz with talk about darling little

Celanire, the baby girl found at the Calvaire crossroads by Officer Dieudonné Pylône. Miracle of miracles, Dr. Jean Pinceau, they said, had spent the entire day sewing her together again. A crowd had gathered in front of his door. My heart missed a beat. Terrified, I ran home. *Maman* and her cowives were in tears. Refusing to eat or drink, my father had locked himself in his prayer hut. He let me in. 'You didn't take her to Malendure, did you?' he quietly asked. 'You set her down at the Calvaire crossroads, didn't you?' All I could do was nod. 'Well,' he sighed, 'I'm a doomed man. Ogokpi, the great demon, has broken his pact with me. He's convinced I tried to trick him and rob him of what I promised him. My only chance of escape is to cross the ocean.' I fell to my knees. My head felt as if it were about to burst. 'Can I go with you?' I begged him. He shook his head. The next morning he set off in the direction of Montserrat without troubling to say farewell to anyone. Not even to my mother, whom he loved more than any of his wives. I cried my heart out.

"At noon I went and stood in front of Dr. Pinceau's door in the hope of catching a glimpse of this darling little Celanire. I stood there with the vague hope that, after all, it might be some other infant. I spent the entire day standing in the sun. But all in vain. Out of fear of infection for the baby, the doctor's surgery was closed and nobody went in or out. In fact it was only several weeks later, on the day of her christening, that I saw darling little Celanire with my own two eyes. No doubt about it. In her yards of lace, English embroidery, velvet and silk ribbons, blouse, smock, and bonnet, it was the very same infant I had left naked, covered in blood, throat slashed, on a bed of guinea grass. Due to my thoughtlessness I had brought misfortune on all those I loved most in this world.

"I've heard that the woman they call Celanire has returned

to Guadeloupe. She's now a very important person. The governor's wife. I know she has come back to take her revenge. But I'm not scared of her. She can only hurt my body. The Good Lord has shown me the way. There are no crimes that can't be pardoned. Both Father and myself have gravely offended Him, that's true. Yet I need only repent to appease His anger.

"With such faith I have been atoning for my sins for years. I have nothing more to confess."

Zuléfi stopped there, for the words were spinning in his head. This was no place for such a confession. Tomorrow, in the darkness of the police station, he would get this weight off his conscience. Without another word he took the summons, murmuring many thanks, as if Matthieu had just done him an act of kindness. He would obey the law and tell the truth that he had kept secret for far too long.

With his mind at ease, Zuléfi set off for home with his wife and their children in tow. The children, sulky and tired out by the never-ending ritual, were dragging their feet, whereas their mother was overjoyed: it had been a good collection. The congregation's contributions had filled all the little wicker baskets to the brim. They would be able to resole the younger children's shoes and buy some white thread to sew the robes of the older ones. There would still be money left over to buy some pork she would salt herself. It was then she heard a great commotion and shouts:

"Baréye! Baréye!"

Snorting and foaming at the mouth, shaking its mane, a black horse was galloping down the rue du Sable. It had thrown its rider, who was hobbling after it, brandishing his whip, and was now stampeding down the middle of the road unbridled and out of control. In a frenzy it headed straight for Zuléfi, who was standing on the sidewalk, and rearing up, dealt him two mighty kicks full in the chest. Zuléfi collapsed in a pool of blood. The horse trampled him in its rage, reducing his chest to pulp, then continued its flight.

Oblivious to the tragic incident that was playing out at the other end of town, Matthieu walked away from the seafront. His nose itched more and more every day. Soon, he thought, he would discover who Celanire was.

He knew that on that Sunday the members of the Lucioles association were meeting just steps away from the seafront on the Champ d'Arbaud. For some time now Matthieu no longer recognized the woman he had married. She had become Celanire's alter ego. Powdered and perfumed, she followed Celanire like her shadow and never missed a single dance, masked ball, reception, cotillion, banquet, or book club. Matthieu practically never saw her. They no longer took their meals together. She came home when he was leaving for work and began her day when he had finished his. They hadn't made love for ages. When they did happen to find themselves side by side in a bed, she would push him away, feigning menstruation, headache, or fatigue—unusual affectations for such a docile wife.

The Lucioles association was housed in a magnificent edifice with a courtyard behind and a garden out front that a penniless white Creole rented to Celanire. Besides the copper-potted palms and the gilt mirrors, the hall was crowded with men and women, mulattos and blacks, all perfumed, pomaded, and powdered alike. The afternoon session was already well under way. Elissa de Kerdoré had finished her poetry recital, and they were now launching into opera. Matthieu recognized his wife's voice

singing Johannes Brahms's Rhapsody for Viola, opus 53. There
was something shocking about this sudden obsession for singing
in public. And for singing this type of music. It might have been
acceptable if she treated everyone to the Kilonko epics of the
Wayanas! In a bad mood, Matthieu looked around for a seat.
After a while Amarante bowed to the applause. Celanire, who
had been standing at the foot of the stage, gazing reverently at
the artist, dashed up the steps with her usual enthusiasm and
handed her a bouquet of flowers. Another burst of applause. The
two women embraced each other, then kissed.

There was something so shameless in the way they hugged,
in the way their breasts rubbed against each other and their lips
greedily sucked on their kisses, that Matthieu stood up in horror.
Didn't anybody else see what he saw? His nostrils itched like
mad, and in a flash the truth exploded in a fit of sneezing.
Celanire and Amarante were on the closest of terms. As close as
husband and wife.

We should point out that at the start of the century female
homosexuality in Guadeloupe was not something completely
unknown. The lovely Elissa de Kerdoré championed the cause.
Twice divorced, she had devised a theory that, for want of a pub-
lisher, she expounded on every possible occasion. In her opinion,
heterosexuality was an obligation imposed by society. In fact,
marriage was unnatural. The proof: it failed under every clime
and in every country! If women followed their natural inclina-
tions and kept to themselves, they would experience greater happiness, intimacy, and tenderness. There was more pleasure and
voluptuousness to be had from the caresses of a woman than
being screwed by a man. Moreover, she didn't mince her words
when censuring motherhood, that straitjacket in which women
were imprisoned. Elissa's discourse struck a sympathetic chord,

especially among the women of the upper classes who deliberately sought out their *doudous* from the dregs of society and paraded them openly in public. Branches of the Zanmi association had been created at La Pointe, Basse-Terre, and Le Moule. Its members lived openly as couples, some of the partners dressed in men's trousers and pepper-and-salt-striped twill frock coats, even wearing top hats. For the church, it was an abomination. The priests recalled the sacred duty of procreation and the virtues of motherhood. Alas, they were wasting their time!

Celanire and Amarante descended the steps arm in arm. Matthieu leaped to his feet. As he bounded toward them, Celanire pushed Amarante to one side and, shielding her with her body, confronted him with such an insolent expression that he stopped dead in his tracks. What could he possibly do in front of so many people? Hit them? Insult them? He turned and ran outside.

That particular Sunday evening the Champ d'Arbaud was crowded with people, for the weather was so glorious that the inhabitants of Basse-Terre, who much prefer to sit inside behind closed shutters, had consented to enjoy the fresh air. Children were bowling their hoops. The older ones were playing hopscotch. Lovers strolled down the paths, gazing into each other's eyes. Mothers were sitting on the park benches, whispering secrets and exchanging the latest gossip. In the shade of the mango trees, unsavory characters were hatching more mischief. Matthieu climbed into a carriage for rent stationed at a corner of the square and returned home to the Redoute neighborhood. He went to bed but was unable to fall asleep. The hours passed.

The guilty party arrived home in no hurry at the stroke of midnight. Matthieu, tucked up in bed under his mosquito net, heard the horse pulling a tilbury whinny, piss heavily, then leave in a clatter of hooves. Then he heard Amarante messing around in the washroom, indulging in her ablutions. Finally she came into the bedroom, protecting the flame of her candle with her hand. It had been a long time since Matthieu had really looked at his young wife. He had not noticed how much she had changed. He had married a young beauty, that was for sure, but shy, gauche, and demure so as not to attract the attention of strangers. Now she held her head high and was as succulent as a Kongo cane. She no longer shaved her head as smooth as a coconut in the Wayana tradition. She had let her hair grow, and straightened and curled it with a hot iron like the women of the upper class. For a moment he was jealous of this transformation in which he had no part.

Amarante slipped into bed, bade him good night as if nothing could be more normal, blew out her candle, and calmly turned on her side. It was then he grabbed her and immediately asked what was going on between her and Celanire. She shook him off and confronted him. Elissa de Kerdoré was absolutely right. Women are meant to live among themselves. Thanks to Celanire, she had discovered infinite bliss. And she didn't mean simply a sexual or physical attraction, but an incredible communion of minds. Celanire and she had the same tastes, the same desires, the same dreams. They caught themselves sharing the same thoughts and doing the same things at the same time. As a result they had decided their liaison would no longer be kept secret. On the contrary, they would openly flaunt it. At this point, Matthieu couldn't help snickering. She didn't really think that Celanire was going to leave the governor, his prestige, and his money to live with Sappho on love alone? Amarante inclined her head and calmly repeated what she had just said. While she shamelessly described her vice, Matthieu gradually filled with anger. He might have forgiven her if it had been a man, a strapping stud, well equipped where it was needed! But horrors! Cheated on by a woman! Cuckolded by a female! His anger bubbled up, suffocated him, boiled over like a pan of milk forgotten on the stove, and he set upon Amarante. He kicked and pummeled her like a common drunkard, he who had never raised a hand to her. She received his blows and his punishment, eyes closed, like a martyr. He ended up throwing her to the floor and then fell upon her. She managed to shake him off and ran for the door. He thought about running after her, but a violent remorse lacerated his heart. He began to sob uncontrollably like a child while a torrent of abuse flowed from his mouth. He heard himself scream at her and throw her out. "Out, shameless hussy! I no longer want to set eyes on you! Never set foot inside my house again!" After this fit of anger, he collapsed onto the bed and burst into tears.

The sequence of events that follows is not entirely reliable. It is a collection of eyewitness accounts gathered here and there that we have pieced together. The next-door neighbors, surprised by the noise, since the Dorlisses were not in the habit of making a commotion, didn't budge during the quarrel. Only the neighbor opposite picked up courage and peeped through the louvers and outer doors, despite the late hour. She saw Amarante leave the house with a look of defiance, holding a suitcase, and set off in the direction of the seafront. Two homeless people at a street corner comparing their lot saw her pass by and wondered where she could be going at this late hour with such a heavy load. Apparently she sat down on a rock at some distance from the road. After the splendor of the sunset, the night was a magnificent deluge of India ink. A sliver of a moon tucked into a corner of the sky had a hard time illuminating even its own nook. Reassured by the darkness, the cohort of invisible spirits was creating a terrible din. They capered along the shore and swung in the branches of the almond trees. Sometimes they even dived into the ocean from the clifftops, and you could hear a great splash, but not a ripple could be seen on the surface. Other times the spirits mischievously crept up close to Amarante, hissed into her ears, or clasped her neck with their icy cold hands. Just before dawn Amarante walked back to the road. A vegetable grower, lugging his dasheen and gherkins to the Carmel market, hoisted her up exhausted into his cart. He stacked her case among the crates of vegetables and pityingly noticed her swollen face. Another one who had been manhandled by the heavy hand of her husband! Nevertheless he respected her silence and did not pry. He set her down in the Colchide neighborhood where, like every battered wife, she would probably take refuge with her *maman*. But at seven in the morning, Dorisca, the fishwife, had bumped into Amarante at the coach station, where she took the first carriage to set off for the center of Basse-Terre. There witnesses saw her walk in the direction of the Gai Rossignol conservatory, whose doors were still closed. She remained for a long time, leaning motionless against the iron gate. At 8:30 A.M., Celanire arrived to give the first flute lessons. Nothing had transpired from the conversation the two women had. A student who had been there since nine claims that Amarante emerged from the office around 9:30 A.M., in tears and shaking. One hour later Celanire went to practice her singing exercises with Elissa de Kerdoré, who had just arrived and was smoking cigarette after cigarette under the mango trees in the yard. Several children can confirm that at ten Amarante lay prostrate in the garden, her heavy suitcase standing beside her. Others say she wandered like a lost soul through the neighboring streets. At the stroke of eleven they lost sight of her as she was swallowed up by the flow of women returning from market, the crowds of children running to school, the stream of workers and civil servants and politicians dashing for the Conseil Général.

What is absolutely sure and certain is that around six in the evening two boys who were flinging pebbles at the mouth of the river des Pères saw a woman walk into the water fully clothed. She strode out toward the open sea, purposefully threw herself into the water, and disappeared among the waves. The boys looked at each other and hesitated. They were afraid of Mami Wata, the water spirit, who had the power to lock up the fish in order to starve humans, drive foolhardy swimmers to their death by unleashing a raging storm, or attack them by changing herself into a shark. But their finer feelings got the better of them. Bravely they tore off their clothes and rescued the drowning woman.

5

When, after several long months in the hospital, Amarante had fully recovered, she did not go back to live with Matthieu. Celanire had given her the taste of another life. She felt a kind of shame when she thought of all those years depending on a man and all that care and attention lavished on him that she seldom received in return. She remembered how she would hurriedly get up at midnight to reheat his dinner and, on Sundays, warm his bathwater and cut his fingernails and toenails as if he were some Oriental potentate. In short, she had been his servant. She didn't go home to her mother either. All those precepts they had rammed down her throat when she was young—Love thy neighbor, Return good for evil—bored her. What was the point of them? Did she deserve to be hurt and neglected like this? As a result of all those scandals, there was no question of her going back into the teaching profession. So she bravely rented an upstairs-downstairs house on the rue du Soldeur and hung a sign over the door that read, "Singing and Music Lessons." But owing to the proximity of the Gai Rossignol and Celanire's reputation, she was unable to attract sufficient numbers of pupils and soon lacked the basic necessities of life. She experienced hunger. Consequently, bitterness and resentment mixed with her love for Celanire. While Celanire wallowed in opulence, she had become the victim. Memories of their moments of passion together woke her up during her nights of solitude. If she lived to be a hundred, she would never get over the shock of hearing Celanire laugh that morning she had come seeking refuge, naively reminding her of her promise to live openly as a couple.

Her grief knew no bounds when some good souls informed her that Celanire had quickly got over her loss and was carrying on openly with Elissa de Kerdoré. It didn't surprise her: she had always thought those two were made for each other—equally attractive, provocative, and diabolical, with that touch of nonchalance of the leisured class. At their initiative, the innocent little island of Fajoux, which is anchored in the crystal-clear waters off the Grand Cul-de-Sac, was transformed into Lesbos. A cohort of Zanmis set up tents and wattle huts, each with her one and only. They swam in their altogether, shamelessly baring the cups of their breasts, the curves of their buttocks, and their fountains of life. They barbecued red snapper and crayfish that they caught themselves. They brazenly caressed each other as they rolled in the burning blanket of sand. Owing to her official duties, such as inaugurating maternity homes, nurseries, and orphanages, Celanire had to stay in Basse-Terre and only joined

Elissa on the island at weekends, when she would stimulate intellectual activities, such as never-ending verbal jousting and theatrical entertainments. She inaugurated a poetry competition in Kréyol, a language she had always encouraged. When Elissa, who hated Kréyol and considered it vulgar, criticized her for not speaking it herself, she retorted that the mouth does not always need to express what the heart cherishes. Sometimes Thomas de Brabant came with her, spending the night in the open so as not to get in the way of her lovemaking with Elissa. The fishermen, shocked by the copulation going on almost under their noses, quickly hauled in their nets, and it wasn't long before there was a shortage of fish in Grande-Terre.

The priests frowned upon all this. But they didn't dare protest. The governor's wife had connections in high places. Bishop Chabot's purple robe covered up for her. They had recently made a deal. The overpopulated orphanages that the church had trouble running had just been handed over to the colonial authorities. Celanire scrubbed and modernized them and hired a dozen girls, whom she sent to be trained in Lyons, where she had kept in touch with the missionaries. As for the orphans, some of them already sang in a choir and had performed at Saint-Pierre in Martinique.

Gripped by jealousy, Amarante began to harbor ideas for revenge. Old rumors came streaming back to her. It had been gossiped around that the young Celanire had been the cause of Ofusan's death as well as the ruin of Dr. Pinceau. And goodness knows what else. Amarante, who had always been a sensible, down-to-earth person, grew frightened of all these shadowy figments she felt accumulating inside her.

One morning, to escape her inner self, she turned her back on Basse-Terre and set off for La Soufrière.

Three thousand feet up, the forest of Guadeloupe becomes stunted. Gone are the *châtaigniers,* the mastwoods, the mountain immortelles, and the red cedars. The earth is covered with a mass of purple-flowered, scentless bromeliads and white orchids streaked with cardinal-colored venules. Amarante, born and raised on the coast, just steps from the remorseless splendor of the ocean, discovered a landscape whose beauty is on a human scale. Here the sun can veil its face so as not to dazzle the newcomer, the sky clothe itself in gray, and the air grow soft with streaks of blue as cool as a mountain stream. Despite the advent of a new society following the abolition of slavery, a group of Wayanas clung stubbornly to the slopes of the volcano. Others had returned when they realized that nothing had changed down below. Down on the plain or high in the mountains, life always had the same bitter taste. The same bowl of misery was served wherever you were. To avoid being harassed by the gendarmes, the recalcitrant Wayanas had simply climbed higher and hid their wattle huts behind the camasey trees, whose leaves are embossed in greenish black. They slashed and burned plots of land. Then they cultivated whatever they needed to subsist—*soukous* yams that grow well high up, sweet potatoes, a little tobacco, and hemp, which the women wove like flax. If the leaf-cutter ants became too bothersome, they would abandon the plot and begin again farther up.

When Amarante loomed into sight at the end of the day, the yellow-and-white Creole dogs did not bark. On the contrary, they came and rubbed themselves up against her. After all she was still a Wayana for these years. Under the soap and rouge of the town, her skin had kept the smell of her people. According to Wayana hospitality, the guest is a gift from heaven. So no questions were asked. They gave her food and drink. When the night turned black, they hung a hammock for her on the veranda of the communal house. Amarante was delighted with this newly discovered monastic life, which her mother and father had experienced during their childhood and yearned for all their lives. She understood that happiness does not reside in a restless mind, as Celanire had taught her to believe. It resides in dispossession: wrapping oneself in a cloth dyed and woven by hand, washing oneself with the others in the icy waters of the gully, lighting a fire between four stones, cooking with the women, listening to stories under the lenient gaze of the moon. Only the insipid taste of the food bothered her, since for the Wayanas salt belonged to the gods and was not to be eaten by humans.

After a few weeks she became involved in communal activities. Although she hated scratching her hands planting, hoeing, and digging up sweet potatoes or yams, she took a liking to hunting. The Wayanas did not use firearms, coward's weapons that kill from a distance. They hampered and fettered the animal with a lasso and fought with it close up, using a knife. When they finally got the better of their prey, they thanked the gods with a prayer and quartered the animal alive, then lay the chunks on a crisscross of young branches to cure them. Amarante also learned how to recognize each plant by its shape and its smell and began to read nature like an open book. All these activities purged her of her ill humor. She noticed that gradually she forgot the way she had been abandoned and betrayed, the love between Celanire and Elissa de Kerdoré, and all that nonsense that had caused her so much pain. She craved for a different way of thinking; she hungered for a new life.

One evening, in accordance with the Wayana tradition, a young man named Wole came and hung his hammock next to hers.

"No, I didn't come here for that," she sharply rebuked him. "I don't want anybody. Men have shown me their limits and women their cruelty."

Wole shrugged his shoulders.

"Don't generalize! You speak of a man who made you suffer, for he was set in his heart on satisfying his ambition. As for the woman you were infatuated with, everyone knows she was a demon. Didn't she kill our noble sister Ofusan?"

Amarante, who had often heard such nonsense, burst out laughing.

"I'd like you to explain how a baby can kill a grown-up."

Wole's expression turned serious.

"You Wayanas from the town, your minds have been completely distorted. You always need to have an explanation. You need logic and reason! Do you want me to tell you what happened?"

In spite of her expression of disbelief Amarante was dying to hear the story of Ofusan. Wole collected his thoughts.

"Noble sister Ofusan came into this world in the black of midnight. She was such a lovely little girl that all those who were present at her birth were overjoyed. Yet Gongolosoma, our protector and god who followed us from Africa, looked worried and predicted she would cause serious trouble for those she loved. This turned out to be true soon enough. All through her childhood and adolescence she was rebellious, pestering, and disrespectful of the elders. So nobody was surprised when at the age of sixteen she left the mountain to go down and marry a mulatto in the plain, a ladies' man and womanizer with the airs of a patriot. When she left she broke two hearts—her mother's and that of Agboyefo, to whom she had been predestined by the elders ever since she was a baby. Mothers' hearts are always prepared to forgive. But not the betrothed's. Outraged, Agboyefo went and asked Chéri Monplaisir, the *dibia,* who resided down at Saint-Sauveur, to help him take his revenge. 'What do you want me to do?' asked Chéri Monplaisir. 'I want her to suffer like I'm suffering today. Invent for her the most terrible of punishments. Make an example out of her. It's not just me and her mother she has insulted. She has offended the sacred traditions of the Wayanas. She has preferred the white man's gods to ours.' Chéri Monplaisir began by requesting a white heifer without a single blemish on its body and three hens of identical color as a sacrifice. When Agboyefo returned three days later, the *dibia* was overjoyed. 'Things are looking good. I've made a deal with the superdemon Ogokpi. He'll take care of Ofusan.' Ogokpi is the master of the seven circles of hell. One day, he swallowed his daughters by mistake and gorged himself on their blood. Ever since, he has been asking for sacrifices of children and babies. The younger they are, the happier he is. He adores newborn babies. As promised, he took care of Ofusan. During the seven years of their marriage her mulatto husband cheated on her with all the *bòbòs* in Grande-Anse and thereabouts. As a rule women console themselves for their husbands' philandering with a litter of kids. But her home was filled with nothing but hot air. In her solitude, then, she almost went mad. So she fell headfirst for the bait Ogokpi sent her: a little girl as radiant as the new moon. Anybody in her right senses would have been suspicious: a newborn discovered with her throat slashed at a crossroads! But no, not her! She blindly adopted the child and made her the queen of her house.

"Celanire has always testified that ever since she was a baby, it was her foster papa she loved, whereas she couldn't stand the *maman.* Ofusan had the most magnificent baby clothes made for her. Nothing was too good for her. But every time Ofusan fin-

ished rubbing her with lotion and dressing her up, Celanire
would deliberately vomit all over her baby smock. Staring her
straight in the eyes, she would fart and defecate such a foul-
smelling custard of caca that the whole house stank. Ofusan
could not help but notice this aggressive attitude and complained to her husband. But all he had in response was a series of
mollifying clichés, such as, 'Everyone knows little girls always
prefer their papa.' Gradually Ofusan got tired of being neglected. She was still young and lovely; she could make a new life
for herself. When Celanire heard her talk of leaving her husband
and going back up the mountain, she first of all fell ill to stop
her from going. One fever after another. Diarrhea after diarrhea.
This only made Ofusan even more determined; she concluded
that the air in Grande-Anse did not suit her little girl. Moreover,
she worried a lot. Once some crazy woman had tried to steal the
child. Ever since, she always kept close behind her whenever they
strolled along the seafront, or else stood standing for hours in
front of the house. So Celanire took drastic measures. She summoned her protector to rid her of her stepmother. Ogokpi, the
superdemon, ran to her rescue, and changed into a dog. He
adores this type of masquerade. It was when he turned himself
into a dog and sank his teeth into his great rival Beelzebub,
drawing blood, that he took over the reins of hell. It was in the
very middle of the market he hurled himself onto Ofusan. We
know the rest of the story."

While Wole had been speaking, the moon had made its
appearance and was rubbing its round cheek against the
branches of the candlewood trees. Amarante knew full well this
was just a tale for young girls so that they didn't run off with a
husband of their own choosing. Yet it moved her to tears. She
ran her hand over Wole, who placed it firmly in the right place.

Wole had attended the local elementary school in Basse-Terre and had been expelled for insubordination. He was now getting his revenge. Every morning he gathered the children around him and incited them to hate white folks who had led the ancestors into captivity and shipped them to Guadeloupe to slave in the cane fields. Although she appreciated the strength and force of this unexpected companion, who was a balm to her humiliated heart and body, Amarante thought these lessons narrowed the mind. Humans need more than just memories of yesterday and yesteryears. They need hope, poetry, and music! Her mother had naturally taught her old Wayana songs, but Amarante didn't stop there. She remembered how Celanire had initiated her in other music. It wasn't long before the natural cathedral of the woods echoed with children's voices exuberantly singing the *Regina Coeli* and the *Exultate, Jubilate*. Even though Wole did not really like Mozart, the motets were so beautiful, he did not dare protest.

Soon, however, Amarante desired something more. She was no longer content with sounds collected by others. She asked those going down to the town to buy her exercise books, pencils, rulers, and erasers, and she began to compose. Up before dawn, lying on her stomach on the carpet of green, it was as if her past suffering and the discontent of her heart and body flowed out of her and changed into this precious, magical stream of sounds. She spent days on end like that forgetting to eat or drink. She no longer needed anything or anyone.

She was free. She had been healed.

Meanwhile, deprived of a wife who had always been beyond reproach, Matthieu suffered martyrdom. A slow degeneration set in. First of all he was seen downing glass after glass in the rum shops, where men of his standing wouldn't be seen dead. Then he stumbled along the seafront at ungodly hours. His clothes became filthy. He discarded his frock coat and jacket for a shirt and twill trousers. He began to stink of sweat. His hair remained uncombed. His superiors sharply rebuked him for not taking it like a man. How could he lose face over a woman! They would have turned a blind eye if he hadn't cornered anyone and everyone to churn out his spiel. He swore he could sense Celanire's true identity. His mistake during all these years was having believed there were two children, whereas it was one and the same baby. Celanire was Pisket's child. Don't ask for any proof! He didn't have any! And he never would. In this sort of investigation, instinct was convincing enough. He had arrived at his conclusion by supposition, deduction, and sneezing, and nothing would make him think otherwise. His stunned listeners endeavored in vain to get him to see reason. Imagine if such stories reached the ears of the governor, Thomas de Brabant! And if he heard that his beloved wife was the daughter of an unknown father and a *bòbò!* Nothing good could come out of angering someone with connections high up. But Matthieu continued to do exactly as he pleased. He wrote letter after letter to the Ministry of the Colonies, the Ministry of the Interior, and the Ministry for Public Safety. He swamped the papers in France, Guadeloupe, and Martinique with open letters that never got published. Drastic measures had to be taken. He was retrograded to watchdog, stationed outside the schools. Unfortunately, he insisted on recounting his tribulations to the dumbfounded teachers and pupils. Then he mobilized his socialist colleagues at La Pointe. Always prepared to back the wrong horse, they went to a lot of trouble inquiring why this superior mind was being picked on.

They then had the idea of transferring him to Grande-Anse. There he could discreetly continue his investigation.

Matthieu arrived then in Grande-Anse at the height of the dry season. The heat was suffocating. The sea and the sky boiled in sulfur. The flowers of the hart's tongue clinging to the slopes of the hills were scorched by the sun. He no longer recognized the place he had grown up in. Everything had been freshly daubed and painted. Under the influence of an invasion of rosy-cheeked Mormons from Salt Lake City, the bordellos had been transformed into respectable houses. The turpitudes of the Ginger Moon had slipped its memory, and it now housed a harmless mom-and-pop store on the ground floor. The Saint-Jean-Bosco orphanage had been turned into a college for whites, mulattos, and blacks. The seafront had been planted with royal palms and made into a promenade where families could take the air. Yet despite all these modern touches Matthieu could see that the people remained the same. Acquainted with the purpose of his visit to Grande-Anse, everyone wanted to help him. With the passing of time the memory of Ofusan was revered like that of a saint. Almost twenty years later they still lamented the fate of good Dr. Pinceau. If they could, they would do everything possible to help him reveal the identity of "darling little Celanire," who without a doubt had caused the couple's misfortune. But they didn't have the slightest clue. No sooner had he moved in than Matthieu set to work. There was no doubt in his mind. Since he believed Celanire to be Pisket's child, the first thing to do was to go back over her tracks. Here was a girl who was probably born in Grande-Anse, had grown up there, died, and was buried there, and yet nobody knew a thing about her. How come there was not a single friend to flower her grave? Not a single enemy to badmouth her? He focused his investigation on the

Ginger Moon. Alas, however much he prowled around the upstairs-downstairs house, which could have come straight out of the French Quarter in New Orleans, he came up with nothing. The former owner, Carmen, had turned to religion before being called to God. As for the former residents, who had now settled down and had their own pew at church, it would be unwise to recall the time when they were *bòbòs*. Matthieu did not give up hope, convinced that finally he would get lucky. He took his meals in a cheap eating house inappropriately named the Delights of Gargantua.

One evening when he was about to rinse out the bad taste of codfish and rice with some white rum, the owner informed him that her mother would like a word with him. Under her cottony white hair combed into four buns, she must have been in her sixties. Everyone dutifully called her Mama Sidoine after the name of her late husband, a respected fisherman.

"In actual fact, my real name is Madone," she said in a mysterious tone of voice.

As this did not seem to mean anything to Matthieu, she had to refresh his memory.

"Pisket's good friend, the only one she ever had. She came back to die in my arms, that's proof enough! Two people loved her on this earth. Me and her twin, Kung Fui."

Matthieu lowered his voice and went straight to the point.

"Do you know the name of the child's father?"

"Do I know it? Of course I do!"

She lowered her voice as well.

"It's Dr. Jean Pinceau!"

Matthieu leaped to his feet, drew himself up to his full height, and shouted furiously, "*À pa vwé! Manti aw! Manti aw!* It's not true! You're lying!"

She eyed him scornfully.

"What's got into you to shout like that! You really think some men are different from the rest? The best of them are not worth the rope to hang them with. All of them are scumbags. In fact few people know that Dr. Jean Pinceau was stinking rotten to the core. Everyone in Grande-Anse respected and worshipped him like the Holy Sacrament, whereas he liked the ladies of the night and was a regular visitor to the bordellos! At the Ginger Moon his favorite was Pisket, the dirtiest slut of them all."

Matthieu was no longer listening to her, and was pacing up and down like a madman. The idol of his youth had bit the dust. So the paragon of virtue wallowed in vice. The slayer of opium eaters worshipped a drug addict. He recalled the fervor in his handsome face. He could still hear the brazen speeches of his electoral campaign: "Guadeloupe is not France, and France is not Guadeloupe. It is an entirely different country whose inter-ests are in contradiction with those of colonialism." Such bold words at the time! He tried to tell himself that this old woman was lying. But no, his nose sensed the truth. Ignoring him, she prattled on, coming out with everything she had kept bottled up inside her for too long, her hands deformed by arthritis resting on her knees.

"The poor girl was naive enough to believe that with all his money the doctor would at least promise to help take care of her baby. Despite their wicked ways, that's what the white Creoles did when they had children with black girls. But all he could say was, 'An pa sètin sé ti moun an mwen! Fo ou fin èvèye. I'm not sure it's my child. Get rid of it.' This upset Pisket, despite her shame-less ways. She cried a lot, I know. But she didn't let on to the doctor. When he offered to give her an injection for an abortion, she pretended to accept. And then she let Kung Fui make a deal with Madeska. When they left the Ginger Moon, they didn't tell anyone where they were going, except me. You should have seen Dr. Pinceau that day. He was like a lost soul, a zombie. You'd have thought he'd go mad or die. He didn't want any of the other girls as a consolation. You couldn't help pitying him.

"I seldom visited Pisket at Bélisaire. People in our line of business don't like going out in broad daylight. When the children meet us, they shout 'Shoo!' as if we were dogs or else 'Zouelle, an *bòbò!*' and respectable persons make the sign of the cross. And then visiting them wasn't very pleasant. The Blanc Galop was a real hornet's nest. Kung Fui had brought his inseparable Yang Ting with him, who was living with their sister, Tonine. But Pisket and Kung Fui couldn't stand Tonine. They hurled insults and abuse at her. Sometimes even Pisket tried to hit her. Yang Ting would intervene, and there'd be a hell of a commotion. And then Madeska and Pisket didn't get along. She complained that the mischief maker's food was tasteless, since salt was taboo. Once a month he wanted to cut her, take her blood and bits of flesh. But what I really want to tell you is that you're barking up the wrong tree in your investigation. Celanire, the governor's wife, is not Pisket's child. She couldn't be! Seven months pregnant, and the child slipped out."

"I don't believe it!"

"But it's true! The child slipped out! Pisket had a miscarriage. But Kung Fui was an artful one! I don't know how he did it. All I know is that he and Pisket came to an arrangement."

"An arrangement?" Matthieu yelled. "What do you mean?"

"Well, they found a belly for sale. Don't ask me where or how, I haven't got the slightest idea. I had my own troubles at the time: I ate some conger eel, which gave me blood poisoning. I spent three and a half months in the Saint-Félix hospital at death's door. When I came out, Grande-Anse was in a hullabaloo. Madeska had vanished; the only talk was of 'darling little Celanire,' 'darling little Celanire,' the baby Dr. Pinceau had miraculously saved. They said she was so lovely, so beautiful, a woman had tried to steal her. One Sunday during mass I dashed to look at her in the arms of her foster mother. She gave me the shivers. A pink silk ribbon was tied around her neck. Her head reared up like a cobra's, and she stared at people with her black eyes, gleaming like hot coals. As for Pisket, after her miscarriage, she disappeared for a while. I only saw her again the year after, when she came back to die in my arms. You won't like what I'm telling you, I know. But it's the truth. And the truth is hard to swallow."

Matthieu got the impression his brain was about to explode. Large drops of sweat rolled down his back. Years of research and speculation to arrive at this. All for nothing. At the end of the day Celanire was not Pisket's daughter. In despair he left.

To the east, along the rim of hills, Grande-Anse glowed red. At first he thought it was a figment of the fever that had set his mind ablaze. Then he realized the Fouques-Timbert plantation house was burning like tinder. At the very moment when Matthieu was watching in disbelief, the glow of flames had already reached as far as Antigua, dazzling the fishermen at Half Moon Bay, who hauled their boats up on the sand and, sensing some strange foreboding fell on their knees to recite the prayer for the dead. The flames could also be seen as far away as Nevis and Montserrat, whose inhabitants wondered where exactly could the fire be burning. Ever since a delegation led by Celanire had come to their rescue, they looked on the Guadeloupeans as their brothers and took an interest in their fate.

Agénor de Fouques-Timbert perished in the fire of his Great

House like a common mortal. Not only did he lose his life, but Ji, his concubine, his two illegitimate daughters, and six of his seven legitimate sons were also lost. Only the wildest and handsomest was spared, since as usual he had spent the night out, and was nicknamed Sanfoulanmò ever since, because he had defied death.

The incident deserves a closer look.

On April 26, the feast of Saint Alida, Agénor was waiting in his office at the Conseil Général for the director of a highway construction company to pay him his commission. He received 10 percent on all the contracts in the colony and demanded it in cash. He loved the smell of money. The filthier the bills, the more dog-eared they were, the greater his delight, since they reminded him of his own rotten life. The director had arrived at six on the dot, carrying the money in a wicker basket. The two men barely greeted each other. They had nothing to say. The money did the talking.

Agénor had then mounted Colibri and set off for Grande-Anse. On leaving Basse-Terre, shortly before passing through the Colchide neighborhood, he met a funeral procession. Some wretch was being hauled feetfirst in a miserable cart rigged out in black rags. A few musicians shuffled along in front, blowing their brass instruments, and a ragged group of mourners brought up the rear. And yet Agénor, who had everything—women, children, land, property, and political power—envied the deceased. *Lanmò*. Death. Eternal rest. He couldn't wait for Celanire to make up her mind. In his longing to see her in the flesh, he had gone to the carnival opening-night ball disguised as Nero, the emperor on whom he would have willingly modeled himself. Moreover, the crown of laurels and the Roman toga suited him. In his hands was a gilded wood lute, which he would have liked to fiddle as well.

Flanked by Ludivine, as sulky as ever, Celanire and Thomas were greeting their guests. Thomas was disguised as an Egyptian pasha, a costume that suited his paunch perfectly. Celanire was dressed as queen of the fairies, something out of *The Magic Flute*. It needed just a little imagination to guess the connection with her diaphanous, multicolored moiré dress, her golden crown, and the magic wand she brandished arrogantly like a whip. Agénor bent forward to kiss her hand, and when he looked up, he found himself level with her pair of eyes. There then followed a silent dialogue.

"What are you waiting for?" Agénor inquired. "If you want to take your revenge, take it."

"Revenge," retorted Celanire, "is a dish best eaten cold. Don't you know that?"

"But why are you so angry with me? It was nothing personal. For me, I couldn't put a face, a name, or even a sex to you. I simply needed a child. You'd do better to concentrate on your parents. Those two deliberately did you harm by handing you over to Madeska. You killed him, but he was only doing his job."

"Let's not get excited. Believe me, they've got it coming to them!"

Colibri, who knew the road by heart, didn't need to be whipped to gallop at breakneck speed to Grande-Anse, sniffing the air of the sea, which had already melted into the falling darkness. The Fouques-Timbert Great House stood on top of the Morne Reclus. It was an edifice built entirely of wood, surprisingly modest in appearance, since the family had never liked throwing money down the drain. Succeeding generations had added a drawing room here, a bedroom there, and even a washroom and a terrace. To house his seven sons, Agénor had added an attic divided into small bedrooms and a playroom.

Ji had been waiting in vain for Agénor for hours in the small drawing room. He used to love Asian girls and was one of the few white Creoles to frequent a tiny dance hall in Bélisaire, in the heart of the Chinese quarter. There the girls were as slender as lianas, and he would wrap them voluptuously around his body. After having desired Ji passionately, he now practically never looked at her. He had fallen out of love simply because a thousand signs indicated she was losing her youth. Her skin was wrinkling. Her flowing hair was thinning. Her joints, once supple, were now growing stiff. Familiarity made him impervious to her simpering airs of a Siamese cat, which once excited him, and he went upstairs to put away his 10 percent commission in the chest of drawers in his bedroom. This is where he stashed his money. He no longer trusted the banks ever since the Crédit Colonial had informed the police that his money had gone to help Pisket. It almost got him into serious trouble. After that he went down to the dining room, where the rest of the family joined him at table, and began handling his heavy silverware without uttering a word. His sons, who were frightened of him, lapped up their soup, heads lowered. Only Ji attempted to fill the silence with her chatter. Previously, her twittering amused him and prevented him from confronting his solitude and sadness alone. Now he could no longer bear it, and with one glance he silenced her. The meal lasted thirty minutes exactly by his pocket watch.

Agénor had never shared his bedroom with anyone. He made love to his women in an apartment on the second floor, then returned to his modest, poorly furnished bachelor quarters under the roof. For years, his nightmares kept him tossing and turning on his bed all night long, and the only way to get a little sleep was to get drunk.

His servant would set down beside the bed, next to the candle, which remained flickering until dawn, a box of cigars from Bahia, a goblet, and two carafes of rum. Apparently, that evening Agénor was unusually restless; he upset the carafes over the bed, soaking the sheets with rum. Then he dropped the candle. Hence the blaze. In a manner of speaking, the tragedy needed no explanation. It was the speed with which everything went up in flames that was inexplicable. In less than thirty minutes there was nothing left but a heap of ashes. In the time it took for the servants sleeping in the outbuildings to wake up, slip on some clothes over their nakedness, and start working the pump, absolutely nothing was left of a man, a family, and a Great House that had once commanded respect.

Agénor did not describe his final moments to anyone—and for good reason. So we shall never know what he saw at the last minute. Perhaps he didn't see anything at all and plunged headfirst into the void. We don't know either whether at the last moment he remembered Elodie or Ji, their consenting bodies pressed up against his, the cool breeze from the sea, or the taste of rum aged in oak casks. In short, we shall never know whether he left the here below with a heavy heart.

The whole of Guadeloupe, from Basse-Terre to La Pointe, was traumatized by the event, and crowds poured in for the wake. Death always takes you by surprise, but this one confounded people's imagination. A man they thought as solid as a locustwood tree and immortal as a *genippa* snuffed out in next to no time!

The female relatives transported whatever could be transported. They laid ten little sacks side by side in a single mahogany coffin, not knowing whether the ashes they had scooped up came really from the bodies or the furniture or perhaps something else, and Sanfoulanmò, the son who had been spared, led the mourners in tears. He had loved his family. His brothers. His half-sisters. His papa especially, however brutal he had been. Even Ji, whose hands had sometimes felt as soft as a mother's on his face. And then he found himself without any liquid assets, since all the money had gone up in smoke with Agénor. To cover the cost of the funeral he had had to mortgage two coffee plantations up at Vieux-Habitants. In his despair he contemplated selling the property and leaving for Brazil, where at least there was a future.

Agénor was too important a personality in the colony for the governor and his wife not to show their compassion.

So Thomas in full uniform and Celanire in a black taffeta dress showed up at the wake around midnight. Not a single jewel on her. Not even a pair of Creole earrings. As bare as a high altar during Lent. Around her neck a leather choker ornamented with guilloche hid you-know-what. She entered, head lowered under her black mantilla, and religiously knelt down. Yet anyone who had two eyes to see with, like Matthieu, was struck by her elated expression. They guessed that beneath that exterior she must have been in a festive mood. She had just laid her worst enemy to rest. When she looked at the coffin and its dismal contents, a fiery glow burned at the back of her eyes. You sensed she could burst out singing the Ninth Symphony's "Ode to Joy." She fought back a smile that was trying to curl up the corner of her lips. When she recited the prayers for the dead with the mourners, her voice rang out triumphant, despite herself. Matthieu was in agony. He realized that however hard he sniffed and snorted, snorted and sniffed, he would never prove Celanire's identity. The mystery would always remain unresolved. He would never be able to make more than assumptions

that everyone would poke fun at. He would never know what
drop of sperm had fertilized an egg to produce nine months later
a little girl who would bring so many trials and tribulations into
this world. He could say and do what he liked; this affair would
always make him look a perfect fool.

6

On July 14, 1909, Governor Thomas de Brabant and his wife
gave an unforgettable reception, one of the most grandiose they
had ever given, to celebrate Bastille Day and commemorate their
second year in Guadeloupe. Every guest mustered present for the
invitation. Yet it was whispered just about everywhere that the
governor was a dead loss. This one had made no major improvements—no roads, no bridges, no public works projects. If it
weren't for his wife, Guadeloupe could forget him, as she had
done for so many others. The wife's accomplishments, however,
were unparalleled, to say nothing of her intellectual activities
and her constant efforts to convince the Guadeloupeans that
they had a duty to defend their culture while opening up to the
rest of the world. Not to mention her charitable works—
orphanages, dispensaries, old people's homes, soup kitchens, and
shelters for the homeless. Despite this dazzling list of achieve-
ments, those who came into contact with her claimed she was
surprisingly bitter. Elissa de Kerdoré was the first to be driven to
despair. The vivacious, chattering Celanire, who was always prepared to fill your head with ideas and projects, had become taciturn. She had lost interest in everything. Nothing seemed to
amuse her—neither writing contests, plays, nor concerts of traditional or classical music. Some weekends Elissa would wait for

her in vain on the island of Fajoux. Once she had had to award the Prize for Creole Poetry without her. Even more serious, the sizzling Celanire had become lukewarm in love and reacted so little to any caresses that for a while Elissa wondered whether Amarante had not come back to take her away. On this point her spies had reassured her—Amarante had gone back up to the Wayanas and was composing music. Celanire never stopped sighing that she had got absolutely nowhere in Guadeloupe and had not achieved what she had come to do.

Elissa was not the only one to be worried. Thomas de Brabant was not insensitive to his wife's change of mood. So he set about arranging a grand tour for her in the New Year. As it also marked the fifth anniversary of their marriage, he was convinced it would do her a world of good. The plan was to travel through the countries of Latin America she had dreamed of visiting—the former empire of the Incas, Bolivia, Ecuador, and above all, Peru. She had become passionately interested in this far-off land while reading Flora Tristan. In her eyes, a few lines in *Peregrinations of a Pariah* marked the first link between sexism and racism, whereas the whole book was a powerful condemnation of slavery. Thomas had left nothing to chance. They would take the SS *Veracruz* from La Pointe to Caracas in Venezuela, then continue through the Andes by slowly and regally descending the rivers.

At the end of August, however, Celanire seemed to have regained her enthusiasm for life. She dashed from the governor's residence to the bishop's palace, and also paid frequent visits to the Sainte-Hyacinthe hospital, where she was allowed to consult the records. What could she be looking for day after day? One morning, in a frenzy, she begged Elissa to accompany her to Ravine-Vilaine. Ravine-Vilaine was a small village on the northern edge of the island that was fast becoming a place of pilgrimage. It would certainly have sunk into anonymity if it hadn't produced a saint who was causing a great deal of excitement all over the island. Not only had this Sister Tonine received the marks of stigmata, reliving the crucifixion of Our Lord Jesus Christ, but even after her death, she suffered little children to come unto her. By that was meant she gave a belly to sterile women who had dragged themselves through life on their knees to have kids. Some even went so far as to request she be canonized at Saint Peter's in Rome. She would be the first saint from the Caribbean, which, to be honest, was not exactly a region of saints.

Ravine-Vilaine was a very special place. Neither sugarcane nor coffee had ever been grown there. Not a sugar or coffee plantation house had ever been built there. No bell or siren had ever sounded noon for a population of slaves. To survive, the inhabitants felled trees from the forest, sawed them up, and made charcoal, which they sold once a month in the towns along the coast. Elissa expressed surprise. Why were they going to such a hole? Was Celanire, who had so mocked motherhood, now going to pray for a belly? Celanire launched into one of her usual explanations, which explained nothing at all. Elissa knew, like Thomas de Brabant, that Celanire never told the whole truth. She had come to accept her friend as a teller of tales who changed the contents of the story as she fancied, like a novelist writing her autobiography, adding, deleting, lengthening, eliminating such and such a chapter, and clarifying such and such a fact as the mood took her. Africa? Going by what she said, sometimes it was a barbaric land where the women languished from sexual discrimination, sometimes a victimized continent that the European predators had hacked to pieces. Thomas de Brabant? Sometimes she confessed that the orphan she was had married him out of necessity, tired of trudging along life's miserable path alone. Sometimes she claimed she adored him for his generosity and brilliant mind. He comforted her when her hopes had been dashed, for she had loved two men, two unsavory individuals who had scorned her. The first, whom she had revered as her master and creator, had denied her the affections of a father as well as the attentions of a lover. The second had held her heart and body in contempt.

Elissa, who let Celanire get away with anything, finally agreed to accompany her. They set off then on a long adventure. At Anse Médard they had to leave their carriage and hire the services of two guides in order to cross the pass of the Mulatière by mule, before descending deep into the valley and making their way through thick forest. The difficult journey had little effect on Celanire. On the contrary, she chattered away like a magpie and never stopped repeating that she had finally arrived at the end of the quest she had begun two years earlier. Quest? What quest? Elissa ventured. Celanire reminded her in no uncertain terms that she did not know who her biological parents were and that she was looking for them. Elissa, who had hated her own parents, especially her mother, and could not find peace with herself until she had put them far behind her, was ashamed of herself. Nobody can imagine what it's like not to know your family tree. Apparently Celanire did not hold Elissa's lack of understanding against her. She began to enthuse over the surrounding landscape: the intricate tangle of vegetation, the enormity of the trees, the size of the creepers, the vitality of the epiphytes, and the spears of sunlight that, in places, managed to pierce the forest canopy. When they arrived at Ravine-Vilaine, it was dark and raining—not those violent downpours common to the coastal regions, but a fine, misty rain that blurred the contours of the night.

Elissa was deep down a town dweller. She only put up with the island of Fajoux because of the sun's burst of laughter over the sea. She immediately hated this darkness, this dankness, this jail of foliage. However hard you craned your head, you could never see the sky, barricaded by devil trees, candlewood trees, and immortelles, in turn gnawed by the leaf of life creeper and the wild pineapple. Celanire had reserved a room with a woman she claimed to have known in Basse-Terre, a certain widow Poirier, whose husband had been lost at sea two seasons earlier, and who had done the cleaning at the bishop's palace. She was a handsome woman with teeth of pearl, and her verve was quite out of place in such surroundings. She told Celanire that some of the village women were waiting for her at the church. So without even opening their wicker baskets, Celanire dragged Elissa off down the main street—if we can attribute such a name to a path of beaten earth, a sort of forest track, which after winding a few yards among the guinea grass disappeared farther up. The huts along the way were all identical, a jumble of corrugated iron and wooden planks that looked as though they had been thrown together haphazardly. A group of poorly dressed women, as black as the charcoal they were selling, passionately kissed Celanire's hands and dragged her inside the church. Elissa remained outside, waiting for them. Religion was a constant bone of contention between the two friends. Elissa, who had read all the philosophers, especially Voltaire, professed to be a free thinker, whereas Celanire firmly believed not exactly in the Good Lord and his saints but rather in Satan, evil, and the invisible spirits. She even went so far as to claim they were constantly present in her dreams. Celanire and the women finally emerged. Then one of them took the lead and led the group along the path to the little cemetery under a grove of casuarinas. No mausoleums or family vaults here. A series of humble graves at ground level, mounds of earth edged with conch shells and marked here and there with a cross.

One of them bore these words in crude letters:

Here lies a saint
Sister Tonine
?–1905

What the Women Told Celanire

Nobody could say why God had chosen Sister Tonine as a recipient of His greater glory; sometimes He reveals himself in mysterious ways in the most humble, the most destitute of His creatures. Illiterate. Wretched. Licked by life.

Nobody remembers exactly the year she came to live in Ravine-Vilaine. She arrived unannounced and slipped into a wattle hut whose owner had died the year before and left vacant. She had no means of her own to build a home. She had roamed around for years. She had been out in the rain during the rainy season and exposed to the sun during the dry season. It was the birds who first signaled her presence. They flocked out of the woods, obscuring the sky with their feathers—wood pigeons, turtledoves, hummingbirds, sugar tits, and ortolans. Seagulls and cormorants also flew in from the ocean, carrying on their wings the smell of the sea. All of them settled on the roof of her hut like heralds bearing good tidings. Then the children came flocking in, the tiny tots crawling on all fours. Then the women. Finally, slower than the rest, the men—especially unsociable and suspicious because of the climate and hard labor they are sentenced to if they don't want to starve to death.

And yet they too ended up adopting Sister Tonine. They squabbled over who would bring her dasheen or yams from their vegetable patch, an agouti or a wild pig they had trapped. The reason for this infatuation was that you couldn't help loving the dear little woman. In her shapeless blue dress she was no taller or bigger than a ten-year-old. Black? Indian? Chinese? Rather a mixture of all three. Looking somewhat cracked, like those who have suffered no reprieve from life. In fact Sister Tonine sometimes sighed that the story of her life would break the heart of rocks, but she wouldn't say any more.

The years went by in a never-changing routine. Every morning she would sing with the children. In the afternoon she visited the sick and the bedridden, describing to the dying the wonders that awaited them. Then back home she would recite prayers or sing hymns with the women. She only stopped at nightfall, when she would begin to talk of God and the afterlife. No visions of the apocalypse or torrents of imprecations, but sweet-sounding words that compensated for our daily lot of suffering on this earth. Men and women alike never tired of listening to her depict the Garden of Eden planted with the tree of life in the very middle, the tree of the knowledge of good and evil, surrounded by a tangle of oleander and all sorts of sweet-smelling flowers. Every Maundy Thursday in the afternoon her torture began. On Good Friday, as she lay on her cot, the stigmata dug into her hands and feet, the wound pierced her left side, and the the crown of thorns lacerated her forehead with blood. She sweated, doubled up in pain, and sobbed all day Easter Saturday racked by unspeakable suffering. Then on

Easter Sunday she would rise up like our Lord Jesus Christ and, haggard and drawn from the pain, go and kneel outside to start singing the *Veni Creator.*

This happened Holy Week after Holy Week. After several years the prodigy came to the ears of folk from the neighboring villages of Saint-Esprit, Maraudeur, and Vieux-Habitants. They would begin flocking to Ravine-Vilaine on Palm Sunday, sleeping under the trees in the surrounding woods. On Easter Sunday they would file back home in a procession chanting hymns to the glory of God. One year, Sister Tonine began to perform miracles. It started with Madame Eudoxie, the doctor's wife from Saint-Esprit, whose novenas and husband's know-how had never been able to produce a child during their twelve years of marriage. On Easter Saturday Madame Eudoxie wiped the sweat from Sister Tonine's brow, begging her to intercede with the Almighty on her behalf, and one month later she missed her period. Nine months later she gave birth to a baby boy. The miracles continued with Madame Patient, the tax collector's wife from Cantilène, who gave birth to twins on the eve of her menopause. Soon there was a crush of well-to-do women who came looking for a cure for infertility, since this class of women is more susceptible to this kind of affliction.

Sister Tonine had but one enemy, the priest at Saint-Esprit who came up to say mass at Ravine-Vilaine on Sundays at eleven. In his words, a creature who claims to imitate the Son of God and openly flaunt His stigmata is guilty of the sin of pride. Sister Tonine was a dangerous crackpot. Suspicious, he launched an investigation and came up with quite a few revelations. According to him,

Sister Tonine was born at the other end of the island in the region of Port-Louis, which swarmed with mixed-bloods of every color as a result of the encounter of the three races of Europe, Africa, and Asia in the cane fields. While she was still a suckling, her parents had left her on the steps of the church, together with her brothers and sisters, and hung a sign around her neck with her name on it. Apparently the parents must have been Chinese or Indian, with a good deal of black blood, given the color of their offspring. Since the name wasn't Christian, the priest at Port-Louis baptized her before taking her to the orphanage. Tonine excelled by her good behavior, learning her catechism by heart and abiding by God's commandments. She served as an apprentice, then left for La Pointe. Then things took a turn for the worse. She met a shady character, a good-for-nothing, and from then on spent most of her time visiting him in jail. She followed him to Basse-Terre, where he must have been mixed up in some dirty business, and there it seems she had a baby girl who died at birth. She must have already been mentally deranged at this point, for she had trouble getting over the incident, which was certainly painful but nothing unusual in a place where hygiene left much to be desired and there was no neonatal medicine. She remained convinced that the child was alive, adopted by a well-to-do family, and insisted on getting her back. In fact, she saw the child everywhere. The priest managed to interrogate Dr. Médéric who on several occasions had treated her in his paupers' ward at the Sainte-Hyacinthe hospital. Breaking the Hippocratic oath, the doctor told him he believed Tonine was suffering from Kirschenfeld's disease, an ailment with symptoms of obsessions, halluci-

nations, fainting fits, and rashes. Armed with this information, the priest of Saint-Esprit didn't require much more to
gaily conclude that Sister Tonine was mad! He sent a report
to the bishop, asking him to intervene. In a diocese like
Guadeloupe there are so many problems to handle that the
letter remained unanswered. So he took justice into his
own hands and thundered against the poor woman from
his pulpit. He showered her with contempt, heaping on
insult to injury to such an extent that the villagers of
Ravine-Vilaine revolted. They in turn wrote to the bishop
and didn't desist until Bishop Chabot dispatched the unde-
sirable individual to France to purge his venom.

It was during the month of May that Sister Tonine fell
ill. That year the rainy season had been so wet that the
region, accustomed, however, to soaking up water, was
transformed into a quagmire. The villagers were up to their
knees in mud. If you didn't watch out, you risked being
sucked under. Frogs, toads, and snakes emerged from every
hole and wallowed in the thick sludge. Sister Tonine disre-
garded Father Albertini's advice. Come rain or shine she
continued to carry the word of God to those who needed
it. Not surprisingly, she caught a chill. She had never been
very sturdy. All at once she seemed to shrink, shrivel, grow
stooped, and become as gossamery as an angel. Her complexion was blemished by ashen streaks. A dry, persistent
cough tore at her chest. Sometimes she spat blood. But she
refused to take infusions or apply lotions and poultices and
repeated to those who begged her to take care of herself
that if the Good Lord had decided her time had come, she
should not have the audacity to disobey Him. Soon she
could no longer feed herself. In a panic the women sent

one of their boys to fetch the doctor in Saint-Esprit. Alas, he was slowed down by the spongy terrain, the buttress roots, the weeds, and the undergrowth that had sprung up from the rain. He had barely reached the pass of La Mulatière when Sister Tonine passed away.

At that time there were no cards announcing the funeral. Yet the news spread by word of mouth like wildfire. People came from every town, from every village, from every hamlet and every locality, weeping as if they had lost their mama. Before leaving those who had loved her so dearly, Sister Tonine sprinkled a few last miracles. She thus made a present of a son to Mama Célariée, who hadn't seen her blood for ten years and hadn't been with a man either during the same period of time. People were surprised at first, almost in shock. Then they recalled the affair of the Virgin Mary and said among themselves that the Holy Ghost blows wherever he likes.

When the women fell silent, Celanire, her face in tears, turned to ask Elissa:

"What do you think of all that?"

Elissa shrugged her shoulders. Not much; she didn't think much of the same old story she had heard a hundred times before. In Guadeloupe you could find a dozen stories, each one more surprising than the next, where ignorance, religion, and magic bickered with each other. At Vieux-Habitants a girl who had given birth to a baby boy on December 25 demanded he be called Jesus. At Calvaire, another preached with the voice of Our Lord Jesus Christ and was supposed to work miracles. She was said to have restored sight to a blind man and speech to a mute. A load of nonsense!

"But this woman really was a saint, don't you think?" Celanire insisted, trembling with emotion.

Elissa burst out laughing. A crackpot who thought she was Jesus Christ in person! Listening to this caustic answer, Celanire pulled a sour face. She seemed to think twice about letting her in on a secret and, turning to the women, began conversing with them in a low voice. They listened to her in raptures while Elissa tapped her foot in exasperation. Finally the group broke up.

Meanwhile the night had deepened. The tallow candles and oil lamps glowed in the huts, where the women served a thin soup to the children. In the rum shops, the men slapped down their dominos with such force, it sounded as though they wanted to smash the wooden tables. Elissa tried to keep up with Celanire's hurried strides. She sensed she had deeply hurt her, but she couldn't understand why. What had she said? What had she done? Surely, knowing her as well as she did, Celanire couldn't possibly hold it against her that she had not swallowed the gullible women's tale and their ramblings about Sister Tonine's sainthood.

They arrived back at the widow Poirier's, where a hearty dinner was waiting for them. Celanire lingered in the dining room to chat with the widow Poirier while Elissa went to bed, tortured by troublesome thoughts. She had alienated her friend. But why? Emboldened by the dark, the rain was now stamping angrily on the zinc roof. The smell of humus and leaves from deep in the woods and the moans of wild animals in heat seeped in through the shutters. Suddenly the wind veered toward Montserrat.

Two days later in Basse-Terre, Celanire turned her back on Elissa. Both the doors to the governor's residence and the Gai Rossignol were closed to her. The letters pleading for an explanation went unanswered. Up till then Elissa had never been abandoned, and had never been disappointed in love. Her epistles therefore were tinged with anger and hurt pride. She would perhaps have accepted matters if another had taken her place in Celanire's favors. But her spies were adamant. The only person she saw in a tête-à-tête was Bishop Chabot. To find out what was going on, therefore, Elissa defiantly turned up at the Gai Rossignol and, catching Celanire unawares, locked herself up with her in her office for four long hours. What the two friends talked about never leaked out. Some pupils claimed they heard Elissa crying. What we do know for sure is that as a result of this conversation, the two friends were reconciled, and from that moment on Elissa attended every meeting with Bishop Chabot. The three of them studied plans for a mausoleum that Celanire wanted for Sister Tonine. As bold as ever, she had drawn an edifice of white marble inspired by the Taj Mahal. Bishop Chabot, however, had little liking for these pagan monuments. He preferred the tombs of the kings of France in the basilica at Saint-Denis. As for Elissa, she had no opinion. Celanire, Bishop Chabot, and Elissa, however, all agreed on the cathedral that should replace the humble log church at Ravine-Vilaine. The stones for the facade would come from the banks of the river Moustique. The high altar would be designed by a wrought-iron craftsman from Grande-Anse. The frescoes would be painted by a cousin of Elissa's, a mulatto from Capesterre with the looks of an Inca. All this was to be financed by donations. Alas, despite the public display of devotion for Sister Tonine, this was not enough. Then something extraordinary happened: the governor levied a special "solidarity" tax that allowed the work to begin.

To supervise the building site, Celanire and Elissa left Basse-Terre and moved in with the widow Poirier, whom we have already met. Strange how the presence of Celanire wherever she went caused a commotion. It was as if she were back in Bingerville with Tanella and the widow Desrussie, where she was the only topic of conversation. The inhabitants of Ravine-Vilaine, at first well disposed toward her—Wasn't she a firm believer in Sister Tonine's sainthood? Wasn't she turning their village into one of the jewels of Guadeloupe?—soon turned against her. A girl who cleaned for the widow Poirier declared that the three women were as intimate as husband and wife. Three Zanmis! Something unheard of in these parts! They spent their nights and siestas under the same mosquito net. They bathed together in the same tub, scouring each other's backs with kisses. All day long it was a litany of sweet talk and brazen lovemaking.

Then something else cropped up! A hunter who had gone into the woods to catch thrushes and ortolans claimed that just before dawn he had come across Celanire apparently waiting, sitting under a wild cherry tree, her lips smeared with blood. At first he hadn't recognized her and just stood there looking at her. Then it was only his presence of mind that saved him. With Celanire in hot pursuit, he had climbed to the top of an ebony tree. Apparently, she didn't know how to climb trees and had paced up and down below in her rage. This little game lasted until the sun came up, when she scampered off back to Ravine-Vilaine.

Up against such gossip, the good that Celanire was doing went unnoticed. Yet she opened a kind of dispensary where, assisted by Elissa and the widow Poirier buttoned up in white-and-green-striped overalls (let us not forget Celanire likes uniforms!), she distributed basic medication free of charge such as asafetida, tincture of arnica, and paregoric elixir, and recommended infusions and poultices made from local plants. She also began evening classes for the women. She taught these women, whom society had forgotten, how to read, write, and count, and generally educated them, hammering into their heads her favorite slogan: "There's more to life than serving a man like a slave." She also taught them to sing Vivaldi a cappella.

In next to no time the cathedral in Ravine-Vilaine was completed. One had to admit it was an edifice fit to rival the most grandiose buildings on the island, and even in Martinique. In an exceptional gesture, Bishop Chabot, in all his pomp, left Basse-Terre on Advent Sunday, followed by a considerable crowd, to say mass there. He also chose this particular day to proclaim loud and clear the name of the new building: the cathedral of Sainte-Antonine, which popular belief soon transformed into Saint-Sister-Tonine. While Celanire sobbed in the front pew, her head on Elissa's shoulder, her hand in widow Poirier's, the bishop climbed up into the pulpit and delivered a poignant homily on the subject—death is a snare that only afflicts the unbeliever. The Providence and Goodness of the Lord are boundless. Likewise God gave His only Son to save the world, so He took Sister Tonine, but gave her daughter to save the wretched of Guadeloupe.

He didn't say any more. And left everyone guessing what he meant!

In early February Celanire, Thomas, and Ludivine embarked on the SS *Veracruz* for their journey through the empire of the Incas. Elissa insisted on coming with them. She too had read the *Peregrinations of a Pariah* and greatly admired Flora Tristan. Moreover, she could speak Spanish. But Celanire absolutely refused. On the day of departure, under a floppy, wide-brimmed hat she wore a cream-colored wild silk ensemble and a burgundy fichu on which lay a heavy gold chain necklace weighing at least five hundred grams.

Ludivine, at the difficult age of fifteen, had momentarily lost her beauty. Only a pair of dark, velvety eyes remained that never took their gaze off her stepmother. Her hatred toward her had never relented. She told herself it might take her years, but she didn't care, one day she would uncover the truth.

When the ship's siren announced that visitors should disembark, Celanire and Elissa embraced, clearly demonstrating their passion for each other. Thomas looked at them tenderly and benevolently, like a father looking at his daughters, priding himself on their beauty. And it's true they were beautiful, forming a perfect contrast, one black-black, the other almost white, one tall and the other short, both of them lithe and slender.

Ludivine, who considered Thomas to be a spineless individual, despised him for being so accommodating.

Peru

1910

1

Sometimes Yang Ting thought of Guadeloupe as a woman he had loved but had given him nothing in return. He compared her to Paruera, the place where he lived, to Arequipa, the nearby town, and thought her fairer than anything around him. Neither the deep valley of the river Chili, nor the sparkling cone of the Misti volcano, nor the surrounding rim of snow-capped mountains, in his eyes could match the sweltering heat of Grande-Terre, the sugarcane plantations, the raging rivers, the banana groves, and the life-giving rain hammering on the zinc roofs at night. Ah! If only it were more tolerant, more open to others, that island would be a Garden of Eden! On the days he went into town, he didn't look twice at the seventeenth-century cathedral, the University of San Augustin, the Monastery of Santa Catalina, and all the Inca ruins that were the pride of Arequipa. The entire journey, in fact, had been based on a misunderstanding. After the death of Pisket, Kung Fui had remained stricken by grief. He had adored his twin sister, and she felt exactly the same way about him. Now that she was gone, life had lost its meaning, and nothing mattered anymore. Ever since the aborted sacrifice, Yang Ting had only one thing in mind—put as many miles as possible between himself and Grande-Anse. Nothing now was to prevent the crafty little devils in the police, headed by Dieudonné Pylône, from snooping around the Blanc Galop and discovering the contract entered into with Madeska. While Pisket was alive, any escape had been impossible. She had been in no condition to leave Grande-Anse to begin a new life elsewhere! Once she was dead and buried, everything had changed. Taking advantage of Kung Fui's pitiful state, he had decided to take control. He had been beguiled by a certain Aloysius, a braggart of a Frenchman, who worked out of La Pointe and offered contracts for Panama or land in Peru in the Colca Valley. Aloysius strongly advised him to go to Peru because of its large Chinese population. And, moreover, according to him, the Colca Valley was an extraordinary place. Cotton grew like a weed and you only had to bend over, pick it, and bag it to become rich.

But all that had been a scam. Nobody grew cotton any longer in this region of Peru. Finally liberated from slavery, the blacks had deserted the fields as they had everywhere else and were determined to have a good time in town. At Paruera, nature had reclaimed its empire, and all that the two companions had acquired with their inheritance was a hacienda in ruins under a roof of missing Spanish tiles standing desolate on barren terrain, spiked here and there with silk cotton and rubber trees. Furthermore, the nearest Chinese lived at least four hundred miles away. Kung Fui had very quickly sunk deeper into despair. At first, when he was not weeping for his beloved Pisket, he managed to put all his energy into clumsily wielding a pair of pruning shears and a machete alongside Yang Ting. After a few months, however, he no longer ventured out of doors. Soon he no longer left his room, no longer got out of bed, and remained addicted to his opium pipe. Left to his own devices, Yang Ting remembered the region of Port Louis where he had grown up.

Refusing to give in, he set out to grow sugarcane instead of cotton. But he never managed to achieve his aim. On the haciendas of Peru, as on the plantations of Guadeloupe, the Chinese were feared and hated. The Indians didn't want him as boss. They wanted a white boss, a white with *sangre azul* who spoke Spanish. He was nothing on this earth. With the help of some day laborers hired for the job, Yang Ting was reduced to growing cassava, corn, a little rice from the Andes, and raising sheep and fowl that he sold in the market at Arequipa, squatting among the Indians, looking like one of them under his dirty poncho. On weekdays Artemisa, the mulatto woman, cooked for him, patched up his clothes, and occasionally warmed his bed. As long as he had been in good health, life had been bearable. But age plus the icy winds blowing down from the mountains began to wreak havoc and misery on his body. Finally he sold the hacienda for next to nothing. Then he piled all his belongings as well as what remained of Kung Fui into a cart and left for Lima.

Whereas at first the colonizers were only interested in gold and precious metals from the Andes, their designs gradually shifted to the coast, once a barren strip of land squeezed between sea and mountains. Lima embodied the heart of this transformation. In some ways the capital was a welcome relief for Yang Ting. In Paruera his few contacts had been with the Indians, who seemed to be in perpetual mourning, whereas here the noisy crowds of blacks, Chinese, and mixed-bloods reminded him of his hometown in Guadeloupe. There wasn't a single white family's house where people of color didn't rule as cooks, launderers, and gardeners. Huddled around the Plaza de Armas were the blacksmiths' workshops owned by the mulattos whose reputation ran the whole length of the coast, while the streets echoed with the cries of the *aguadores,* the water carriers, straight from the land of Africa. In the evening around the glow of oil lamps black women sold tamales, *anticuchos,* and a host of spicy foods of a dubious nature. But on the whole the city disappointed him. As a result of numerous earthquakes, there were few reminders of a time when it was once called the Ciudad de los Reyes. He found himself in a small town shivering and muffled up in every season in layers of fog. An icy drizzle constantly seeped in from the ocean, soaking the cobblestones, the hordes of stray dogs, and the baroque facades of the few colonial dwellings. Two steps from the Puente de Piedra, in a blind alley of the mestizo neighborhood they called a *callejón,* he bought a modest little shack with no windows and one door for an opening. It was built of clay and straw and covered with a traditional tin roof. He also purchased two dozen donkeys for transporting lime and bricks to building sites, and hired by the month two gangly *arrieros* who drove them along, whip in hand, cigar in mouth. He had lost his delusions of grandeur. What mattered was survival, and this trade, however wretched it seemed, was a lucrative one. Nevertheless, he felt even lonelier than before and at a total loose end. Gone was the time when he was up before dawn, laboring with his day workers, plowing, sowing, harvesting, as well as taking care of the animals. In Lima, while Kung Fui was killing himself with opium, he had all the time in the world to kill. In his idleness he developed a liking for bullfights. Every Saturday he went to cheer the fledgling black *capeadores* and fervently applaud the exploits of the black toreador, Rafaël Martinez. He also regularly attended cockfights and concerts. Several times a week he used to go as far as the ports of Chorillos and El Callao to gaze at that lifeless gray expanse that had the nerve to call itself a sea. Behind his back, beyond that mass of black mountains, lay another sea, this one warm and welcoming, whose spray had solidified to give birth to his native land. Above all he got into the habit of spending hours and hours in the taverns, drinking *chicha*. His favorite was La Wiracocha, because of the singers who came in at midnight and captured the desperation of his heart with their gravelly voices. It was constantly filled with blacks and Chinese, driven half insane by alcohol and nostalgia for the lost paradise of their childhood homelands, those wicked stepmothers who had sent their children into slavery. Yang Ting, however, did not like talking about his early days. In Guadeloupe people had always treated him as an outcast from an orphanage and had never accepted the fact that his color made him just as much a Guadeloupean as the blackest of them. He spoke Kréyol, believed in people in league with the devil, and danced the *gwo-ka*. So where was the problem? In their opinion, Guadeloupeans could only be of African descent. He had been designated Chinese and as a result excluded once and for all! Leaving him behind like a bundle of dirty clothes, his papa and *maman* had vanished God knows where. He owed his life to the Christian charity of Madame Charmène Elysée. Madame Charmène Elysée was a vivacious mulatto woman who was not satisfied with taking care of her husband and twelve children. With the considerable fortune her white Creole papa had left her, she had opened an orphanage, which she poetically called the Drop of Milk. There she took in the countless fatherless and motherless infants picked up on the steps of churches, in streams, and at crossroads, yelling their hunger. It was among the litter of starved, abandoned, and wild little things who crowded into the refuge that he had got to know the twins Kung Fui and Pisket, as well as their little sister Soumathi. Helpers at the Drop of Milk were volunteers, well-to-do matrons, women friends devoted to Madame Charmène Elysée. Although they were quick to hand out punishment, they were also kindhearted and proved to be acceptable stepmothers. Among their protégés, however, they had singled out Kung Fui and Pisket as their whipping boys, a couple of depraved, dirty little vermin. Hadn't they caught them at such a tender age doing filthy things in bed together! They preferred, by far, Soumathi, gentle and obedient, who had been quietly baptized Antonine, or Tonine. Although there was some truth in what they said about Pisket, who was a disagreeable, taciturn, and selfish child, giving off a smell to upset the boldest of noses, Kung Fui, on the other hand, was a most attractive young boy, full of brazen and comical ideas. He had quickly realized that sugarcane had been the black man's burden and downfall, and he had no intention ending up the same way. So at the age of fifteen he left Port-Louis and tried a number of trades at La Pointe. Housepainter, laundryman, bricklayer, hawker, powder monkey, carnival *moko zombie,* and kitchen boy. Each time people made it clear they didn't like his looks. As a result he went underground. He formed a gang with the ironical name of the Yellow Hand, which stopped at nothing in the way of robberies and even murder. It specialized in burning plantations. The blacks had sworn to bring the remaining white plantation owners to their knees and made lucrative deals with those who gave them a helping hand. Their method had been perfected down to the last detail. They waited for a moonless night. At eleven in the evening, when the countryside was fast asleep, they would invade the cane fields, pile heaps of straw in a number of different places, and set light to them. The flames would leap up in every corner, and bundles of sparks would explode in the darkness. Soon an orangey wall rose up to the sky, and no sight was more sublime. Obviously, the police thought otherwise, and Kung Fui as well as Ying Tang spent a good deal of their time in jail. Finally they decided to make themselves scarce and went into hiding at Grande-Anse. There, Pisket, who had no other talent, found work in a bordello. After three months of hanging around half-dressed girls and their body odors, Yang Ting had had enough and went back to La Pointe.

Yang Ting couldn't help thinking of Soumathi—Tonine, if you prefer—as someone he had hurt. What had become of her? Gone crazy, probably. She had always been a bit cracked. She had accompanied him to the foot of the gangplank of the steamship *Tourville,* crying her heart out, pretending to take his promises at face value. Of course he'd soon send her the money for the fare, and then she would come and join them.

Soumathi—Tonine!

She had completely escaped his memory when at the age of twenty he bumped into her at a place called La Rose de Sable, a den for society's outcasts situated on the Morne Miquel, where they smoked opium, drank rum, and the desperate gambled in the hopes of winning their way out of a life of hell. Tonine was no longer the little sister victimized by her siblings, sniveling and skinny as a stray cat. She was hardworking and well behaved, an apprentice to a seamstress. Her virtue did him the world of good. Furthermore, she worshipped him like the Holy Sacrament and confessed that she had always kept a place for him in her heart ever since their time at the Drop of Milk. Flattered by her confession, he soon moved in with her in a tenement yard on the Morne La Loge. But he was not made to live on love alone in a shack! As soon as Kung Fui called him back to Grande-Anse, he realized this juicy contract was their chance of a lifetime. Agénor de Fouques-Timbert was loaded. They weren't going to relieve him of just a few crumbs of his fortune. They would get out of him enough to last for the rest of their lives. Tonine pleaded with him. The farther away they kept from sorcerers, diviners, and mischief makers, the better off they would be! Those people had formidable powers! And then she was a sentimental type. Selling, sacrificing your own baby, an innocent newborn! Yet another great idea of those two villains for whom jail was not good enough. Finally, when he threatened to leave without her, she had been so much in love with him that she followed him. As soon as they arrived at Bélisaire, he realized his mistake. Pisket and Kung Fui did absolutely nothing but spend their time lying in bed, drifting amid the smoke of their opium pipes. As for the money paid by Agénor de Fouques-Timbert, nobody ever saw the color of it. Pisket had locked it in a safe at the bank. All the work at the Blanc Galop fell on them. They had to soak, soap, and scrub the laundry, starch it, hang it out to whiten, and iron it. What's more, it was poor Tonine who had to run around with a heavy tray on her head, making the deliveries. Not a minute's rest! What kept Tonine going were the prospects for her child. If they ever got their share of the cake, they wouldn't have to worry about his future. For she too had become pregnant. Yang Ting, however, was far from being delighted and looked moodily at the calabash of her belly under her shapeless dresses. Why did they have to saddle themselves with another stone around their necks when they already lived so miserably? For the first time during their life together she stood up to him. Even if Kung Fui did break his word and didn't give them what he had promised, *tété pa jin two lou pou lestonmak*. The breasts are never too heavy for the stomach. She wouldn't ask anything from anybody and would expect nothing from anyone. She would work hard for her boy—for it would be a boy; she could feel it—and give him the instruction and education she never had.

But he had betrayed her.

One evening at La Wiracocha he had just sat down with his

drinking companions when a waitress brought him his glass. He was about to down it without another thought when he changed his mind and looked up. He got the impression he had been kicked full in the chest. Reeling from the shock, his teeth chattering, he stood up, gasping for breath, and stammered in his poor Spanish, "For Christ's sake, where did you come from?"

The girl quietly explained she was a *china-chola* from Urubamba, come to seek her fortune in the capital. She couldn't have been more than sixteen. Petite, slender, yet well built, with pretty curves exactly where they should be. A shiny black skin. Slit eyes. Her hair, a stream of silk. Since he had left Guadeloupe, Yang Ting had given up womanizing. Artemisa, the mulatto woman, had done more than half the work in seducing him. Suddenly his member vigorously reminded him of its presence. Burning with the desire of a sixteen-year-old, he dashed over to the owner, who was casually keeping an eye on the rum guzzlers from the bar.

"Jesus, is she yours?"

Jesus shrugged his shoulders.

"Who? Amparo? She's not my type!"

All these years of solitude had changed Yang Ting's character. He was no longer what he used to be. His own desire scared him. He dared not approach Amparo, struck by her staggering resemblance to Tonine—minus her gentleness and vulnerability, of course. This girl looked as though she had guts, knew what she wanted and what she was doing. He watched her pirouette across the noisy, smoke-filled room, carrying her tray on her shoulder, wipe the tables with one sweep of her cloth, laugh, joke, and firmly extricate herself from the groping hands of the rum guzzlers. Occasionally he got the impression she turned toward him with a little half smile and encouraged him. Then he got hold of himself. What could an old bag of bones like himself be possibly imagining?

Around two in the morning, he got up and left. He had never seen such a night. Black as the ass of a Kongo slave. Up above, a wretched little crescent of a moon illuminated next to nothing. He slogged through the dark to his neighborhood *callejón*. When he reached home, a scream that made his blood run cold sobered him up on the spot and made him dash inside with all the energy he could muster. Kung Fui, usually nailed to his bed in a perpetual stupor, lost in his dreams, was lying on the floor, as dead as he possibly could be. There was no sign of a wound. His features had been contorted in terror that only some terrible aggressor could have caused. Yang Ting grabbed a machete. But however hard he searched the four corners of the house, tore outside, and paced up and down the neighboring streets, nothing moved in the funereal darkness.

Yang Ting wept bitterly.

Kung Fui may have become a mindless, apathetic, and blind deadweight, but he represented Yang Ting's last link with the land of his past, his deepest, inner self. It was his entire childhood, his youth, his dreams, and his hopes that were about to be buried. He had admired him, worshipped him, served him like a slave, and never been able to refuse him anything. Not a thing.

One night, a few months after arriving in Bélisaire, Kung Fui had hammered on the door of the room he shared with Tonine and dragged him to his quarters. What a sight! The musty room stank of urine and excrement. Pisket, lying half unconscious on the filthy bed, was losing her blood in great gobs. A miscarriage! Fearful of indiscreet gossip, Kung Fui had called neither doctor nor midwife and was stifling his sister's moans with a pillow. In the dawn's early hours she finally ejected her fetus. Then for some unknown reason she stopped bleeding. Kung Fui looked as though he would go crazy. He wept, stammered, and fumed. All his grand plans had been shattered. An individual like Madeska would not let them off lightly. Kung Fui would have to reimburse him his money, which meant slipping back on the dog collar of misery. Unless . . . unless . . . Suddenly an idea germinated in his highly imaginative mind, and he looked up. Unless they chanced upon a surrogate belly! Since Yang Ting looked puzzled, hoping he hadn't heard right, Kung Fui went on to explain: a belly for sale, for God's sake! So many girls forced into an unwanted pregnancy would be only too willing to get rid of their bun in the oven on the cheap. So the two accomplices began scouring the bordellos of Grande-Anse but came up empty-handed, plagued by bad luck. And Madeska was beginning to suspect something! It was then that Kung Fui pleaded with him. Tonine was going to give birth in a month or two, wasn't that so? They would tell Madeska some story or other. Who can predict exactly when a woman gives birth? Yang Ting, knowing that Tonine would never accept such a scheme, laid down his terms. They wouldn't tell her anything. They would make her believe the baby had died soon after it was born. And the deal was made!

Madeska, the diviner, divined nothing. Likewise, the hell-hound of a midwife he dispatched for the occasion. When she arrived, Yang Ting claimed the premature birth had taken them by surprise and that the baby, a girl, had popped out on her own to see the world for herself. They handed the infant over to her, wrapped in a rag, and the dirty trick was done. Tonine took it quite differently, however. She did not believe a single deceitful word of the tale they were spouting and realized straightaway they had handed her baby over to Madeska as a substitute for Pisket's. Beside herself with anger, she threatened to go to the police. After so many years her screams still echoed in his head— "Assassins! Scoundrels! Thugs!" He had called her a nut-case, punched her, then abruptly showered her with kisses.

At three in the morning the remains of Kung Fui began to give off a foul stench. From a waxy yellow his pockmarked, swollen face changed to gray while thick sooty streaks streamed over the sheets. At noon, unable to bear it any longer, Yang Ting went to look for some wood to make a coffin. The few *zambos* he managed to muster recoiled from the stench. Soon he was all alone assembling and nailing the planks. But the afternoon heat made the stench unbearable. It was as if the coffin were porous and the smell of decay seeped out through a thousand invisible cracks. Yang Ting gave up the idea of a wake. At four in the afternoon he decided to get it over with and asked his *arrieros* to carry his companion to the graveyard. No flowers or wreaths, please. The funeral cortege was composed of half a dozen veiled women clothed in black, mouthing prayers, who never miss an opportunity to woo death.

Shortly after having buried Kung Fui, Yang Ting, who had never had trouble sleeping, found it impossible to get his sleep back. He began to have the same grisly dream. Kung Fui wrenched him awake with a hand as cold as death's. Gripped by an eerie anguish, Yang Ting followed him across a barren land-scape dotted with meteorites, lit meagerly by a sliver of a moon. At the end of their journey a wide-open coffin was waiting for them. He went up behind Kung Fui and looked inside. On a bed of unspeakable filth strewn with rotting livers, gizzards, and intestines lay a baby, a little girl, with her throat slashed.

Until then Yang Ting hadn't given a thought to the infant he had surrendered to the mischief maker's knife. His very own child? Unlike Tonine, he had never wanted her and consequently felt no responsibility whatsoever toward her. Suddenly he sensed he had committed two crimes—one against Tonine, whose motherhood had been stolen, the other against the innocent victim, who had not asked to come into this world and who had been martyrized as soon as she opened her eyes. Incapable of falling asleep in the blackness of the night, he argued with himself, spent hours endeavoring to justify his behavior, as if he were facing a tribunal. Okay, he had acted wrongly. Yet his act, however dark it had been, had ended happily. The police had picked up his little girl, and then Dr. Pinceau had rescued and adopted her. At the present time she couldn't be lacking for anything. She was surely enjoying a better life than she would have with impoverished parents like Tonine and himself. But however hard he repeated this argument to himself over and over again, he finally realized he was atoning for his dual crime with a life of failure and solitude. The money it had procured him was cursed, and he would never stand to gain from it.

As a result, he was now a regular visitor to La Wiracocha, downing more and more glasses of *chicha* to chase away the bitter taste of his life. As a rule, when he arrived, the tavern was still deserted except for a few blacks gambling illegally. He would sit down in a corner and systematically get drunk. One afternoon when Amparo set down the *chicha* in front of him, her expression was unmistakable. Despite his decrepitude, the young girl had taken a liking to him.

People in Lima still talk about it to this day. If you go in for a drink at Juanito's in Barranca or at the Brisas del Titicaca near the Plaza Bolognesi, they'll tell you about it, adding numerous unverifiable details. They will tell you a storm was raging the evening Amparo left with Yang Ting. Frightened by the wind, which had already uprooted the centuries-old mahogany trees in the plazas, the inhabitants of Lima's poor neighborhoods never gave up nailing down their doors and windows. They will tell you that the waves of the ocean swept away the homeless sleeping on the sidewalks and flooded the second floors of the houses along the *malecón*. They will tell you the heavens opened and poured gallons of water over the streets and pavements.

The regulars had always been suspicious of Amparo, who had suddenly turned up out of the blue at La Wiracocha. In answer to their questions, she said she came from far away, from Urubamba, which explained why nobody had heard of her family. But her sly looks and cheeky smile did not go down well, and nobody appreciated her sharp tongue, especially from a waitress. Soon all the men boasted they had slept with her, whereas in fact nobody had.

That evening thirty pairs of eyes saw her untie her apron and walk out arm in arm with Yang Ting around ten o'clock. Behind their backs, tongues began to wag. Some of the regulars wondered whether Yang Ting had heard of the incident in the valley of Canete, when over a thousand Chinese had been massacred in a single day because one of them had dared lay hands on a *zamba*. Others had no scruples making offensive comparisons between the sexual performance of the Chinese and the blacks, who were more hot-blooded, more virile. And others recalled that the Chinese were nasty pieces of work, making up whole battalions in the Chilean army.

At dawn Yang Ting's *arrieros,* who had come to pick up their instructions for the day, were surprised to find the doors and windows of their boss's house smashed in. The modest dwelling sitting under its cluster of trees could not possibly hide any treasure likely to attract *bandoleros*. With machetes handy, they cautiously walked around the house before going in. Yang Ting's bedroom was a vision out of hell. It was as if a furious battle had been waged. The walls and floor were smeared red with blood. The blankets and bedsheets were in shreds. Yang Ting's body was naked, covered with bite marks, deep gashes, scratches, and bruises. But the horror was capped by the sight of his male member, which had been ripped off and stuffed into his half-open mouth like a cigar. The regulars from La Wiracocha crowded into the police station to make their statements, and the police ran around looking for Amparo, who was probably the last person to see Yang Ting alive. To their amazement nobody with this name lived at the address she had given—Jirón Paruro 394. Although they repeated her description over and over again to the men, women, and even the children, none of the *callejón*'s inhabitants had ever seen the likes of her. They looked for her in vain throughout the city of Lima, going through the labyrinth of its shacks with a fine-toothed comb. A court summons was then issued the length and breadth of Peru, and the police in Chiquian, Pisco, Ica, Ayacucho, and Cuzco were put on high alert. After a year they reluctantly closed the matter. She must have slipped into Chile or Bolivia, whose borders with Peru were wide open. In order to recuperate the cost of burying Yang Ting, even though he had been thrown like a dog into a common grave, the municipality of Lima helped themselves to his house. They did it up very cheaply and rented it out to some Chinese railroad employees who cleared out in fright after only one week. Every midnight a terrible racket broke out in the two bedrooms—moans, screams, groans, and the sounds of a struggle. The next tenants did not stay longer for the same reasons. Neither did the next. Soon the rumor spread, and nobody wanted to live there. The house finally fell into ruin, and it came to be known in the neighborhood as the Casa de Los Espíritus, the House of the Spirits. During the daytime people quickened their step along its sidewalk. At night they made a wide detour by the Calle Las Dallias to avoid it.

In our countries, where imagination reigns supreme, popular curiosity is not satisfied with a mystery. Everything has to have an explanation, preferably supernatural. Mama Justa, a black woman from the region of Ica on the south coast known for the clairvoyance of its seers, soon furnished one. After having drunk a cup of worm-grass tea, which sharpens the vision, she fell asleep and had a dream in which she saw Yang Ting as a young man on his island, unrecognizable with a full head of hair and a perfect set of teeth. The life of shame he had led there was revealed to her, and when she awoke, the whole matter became crystal clear. She then told his story to anyone who cared to listen. The young Yang Ting had committed a crime against two women—a terrible, unspeakable crime, worse than a robbery or a murder, which has a motive and never fails to have extenuating circumstances; one of those crimes which nobody can forgive, not even the most generous-hearted. He thought he was safe in Peru, where he had been hiding for fifteen years, turning into an old bag of bones. But that was an illusion! You can run and hide wherever you like; the earth is not big enough, God's justice has eyes like a hawk, you can never escape your sins.

One of the victims on whom he had wreaked so much harm had taken the shape of Amparo and got her revenge.

2

This voyage to South America that Thomas de Brabant had counted on to change his wife's mood was not the success he had hoped for, since it was dramatically cut short by illness.

In order to satisfy a last-minute whim by Celanire, Thomas had to completely rearrange the order of things, and the journey had started with Peru instead of ending there. Given such short notice, he had quickly studied the country's three major regions—northern, central, and southern Andes. In Lima they stayed at the Hotel Raimondi, one of the capital's most luxurious establishments, famous for its azulejos as well as its carved, gilded ceilings. Very quickly it became obvious that Celanire's interest in Peru was extremely limited. She seemed to forget all about Flora Tristan. She never as much as glanced at the travel accounts or historical narratives Thomas had obtained, nor even leafed through a magnificent work of art entitled *The Andes: From Prehistoric Times to the Incas.* Thomas endeavored in vain to arouse her interest in a minority of African descent in Peru that was as dynamic and fascinating as other such communities of the Americas in Brazil, Colombia, Cuba, and Haiti. His life with Celanire had, in fact, completely transformed him, and he had become an ardent defender of black cultures. He had so much to tell her about Peru after reading the major work by Enrique León García called *Las razas en Lima: Estudio demográfico* with the abundant help of a dictionary. Alas! She paid no attention whatsoever to what he was saying.

So what in fact did she do?

She disappeared for days on end and even a good part of the night. It was as if she were looking for someone. She was seen scouring the working-class neighborhoods situated on the other side of the Puente de Piedra. She bought nothing during her endless rambles, and apparently had little liking for all those trivial knickknacks tourists are so fond of, such as altarpieces, miniature clay churches, poker-worked calabashes, and gold or silver filigree jewelry, for every evening she returned to the hotel empty-handed. Only once did she make a purchase, bringing back a dog-eared little book for which she said she had paid a small fortune—*La bruja de Ica*. It was the extraordinary tale of an eighty-year-old black witch, Jesús Valle, a slave belonging to the former marquis of Campocumeno, who had great trouble preventing the workers of a hacienda from transforming her into a living torch.

Forsaken and abandoned by his wife, Thomas came to detest Lima, and his mood turned morose. Compared to the blazing sun of Guadeloupe, the *garúa* became unbearable, and Thomas remained holed up all day long under the gilded ceiling of his room, reading grammar book after grammar book with the aim of improving his Spanish. A maniac for organization, he also began preparing the next step of the journey. So much for Bolivia! It was too far south! After Peru they would head north, traveling via Ecuador and Colombia. To get there they would take a horse-drawn carriage as far as Pucallpa. There they would embark on the Rio Ucayali, then the Rio Marañón, and finally the royal Amazon. He had been assured that throughout the journey the landscape would take their breath away, not only his but his entire family's. As a result, he filled Ludivine's head over the dinner table with a description of the dazzling sights they would soon be seeing. After passing a spectacular landscape of fields rising in terraced rows up the sides of the mountains in the manner of the Incas, their boat would sail between sheer walls of granite, masked here and there by the thick foliage of the tropical forest. Thomas could embellish these descriptions as much as he liked; Ludivine, who thought him a terrible bore, did not listen to a single word. She was bored by Lima—at her age they are bored by everything—and sulked in front of her *ceviche de camarones,* a speciality that the chef was particularly proud of. Deep down, Thomas wondered why Celanire had insisted on bringing her along. She completely neglected the teenager in Lima, and the girl was left to her own devices for days on end. Only once had she taken her to mass in the cathedral and had her admire its collection of gold-embroidered chasubles. To him such behavior seemed quite out of line.

The day before they were due to leave for Pucallpa, Thomas had Ludivine stay behind in the dining room and tried to get her interested in the Paracas and Nazca cultures. He was telling her how in the sixth century the whole of Peru had been the scene of a major upheaval when Celanire came and joined them. She was unrecognizable—almost frightening to look at. Her complexion had turned sallow. Her eyes, usually so sparkling, had glazed over, circled by octopus-colored rings as big as a hand. Her cheeks were sunken, her walk unsteady. It was as if she had just waged a battle that had completely drained her. She collapsed onto a chair and contorted her face into a smile for Ludivine. She seemed incapable of uttering a single word. Her hands were shaking, and the precious anthropomorphic clay jar that Thomas wanted her to admire slipped from her grasp. She sat staring stupidly at the pieces scattered over the floor. After a while, still without uttering a sound, she withdrew to her room. One of the most striking features of Thomas's character, like that of so many men, was his obstinacy. A few minutes later, when he went up to his room to find Celanire collapsed on the bed, as if felled by an invisible hand, it did not occur to him to change their plans. Celanire spent a bad night. In her sleep he could hear her moan and cry out even, and had great trouble waking her up.

Around five in the morning the de Brabant family finally managed to leave the Hotel Raimondi and was seen off by a host of bellhops already up and about. Outside was total darkness. A sliver of a moon slumbered on its back above the rooftops, which were flattened like pancakes. The carriage quickly drove through the outskirts, left the city behind, and, turning its back to the sea, galloped toward the mountains in the shape of upturned funnels. A bitter wind frayed the blankets of fog unfurled against the black sky.

After they had journeyed for an hour in a subterranean darkness, the mountaintops began to turn pink, and gradually the tiny silhouettes of peasants appeared in the distance. Some of them scampered down the steep slopes as if in child's play, bent double by their enormous loads. They were probably on their way to sell their corn and beans in the nearby markets. Others emerged as dots on the immense patchwork of fields, driving their oxen in front of them. Farther on miniature herds of sheep and cows gamboled, chased by dogs and children wielding sticks. Her left hand tucked into Thomas's paw, Celanire seemed to be fighting to keep her eyes open and wore a mask of extreme drowsiness. Thomas carried blindly on as if he were oblivious to her condition, and in the glow of a lantern read to her a poem dedicated to Pachamama translated from Quechua:

> Calling your name,
> I crawl toward you, Mother Earth,
> On bloody knees,
> Here I am, Mother Earth,
> Scattering flowers of "panti,"
> I bow to you, Mother Earth,
> Golden nugget, rainbow robe,
> Star flower, Mother Earth.

When he had finished, she managed to murmur a few words of admiration. Then she curled up in a corner, immediately fell asleep, and began to snore. Thomas had no other choice but to continue reading in silence. In the meantime Ludivine was passing the time as best she could with a card game. One of the waiters at the hotel had taught her the secrets of a game of patience, and she was annoyed she could never get it right.

They hardly ever drove through a village. As far as the eye could see stretched the mosaic of fields. Around one in the afternoon the coachmen drew to a halt in the small town of La Oroya. They were taken to an inn called the Blue Ceiling, a peculiar name, since the place was whitewashed. In spite of its elegant appellation it was nothing but a dusty, unswept tavern. Celanire, who usually surprised everyone by wolfing down tons of cakes, whole chickens, and platters of red meat, while remaining as slim and lithe as a gazelle, did not touch a thing. She pushed her plate away with a tired hand and dolefully asked for a glass of milk. Just as the grouchy mulatto waitress slammed it down in front of her, Celanire slipped off her chair and collapsed on the earthen floor. It was all over in a few minutes. In the time it took for Thomas to stand up in a fright and for the mulatta to grab a bottle of *chichi* and skillfully pour a few drops between her clenched teeth, Celanire had already opened her eyes again. But what eyes! Two bottomless holes devoid of any gleam of life. Her brow was covered in sweat, and her body was as limp as a rag doll. The waiters hurriedly carried her behind a curtain into a room crawling with flies adjoining the restaurant while one of them ran to fetch the only doctor in the place. Through the window Ludivine could see people walking to and fro on the sidewalk, oblivious to the fact that Celanire was so sick.

Around four in the afternoon, when Thomas was beside himself with waiting, the doctor, an Indian half-caste strapped in a military-style riding habit, arrived, clutching his black leather bag. Thomas antagonized him considerably by throwing himself on him, babbling in French, and forgetting every word of Spanish he had ever learned. By way of an answer the doctor articulated every syllable of his Spanish, signifying clearly that *he* was not French-speaking. Finally the two men found themselves on common ground, speaking a sort of pidgin English. The doctor was categorical. Celanire's asthenia was a complete mystery to him, and he had never seen such a serious case, except in instances of dysentery when the patient drains herself from top to bottom. The only thing he could think of was to give her a shot of camphorated oil so that her heart did not give out. It was obvious she couldn't continue such a risky journey, and he advised them to return straightaway to Lima to consult with a specialist.

To her dying day Ludivine would never forget the return journey over unfamiliar roads in a carriage suddenly transformed into a hearse. Daylight was fast dwindling. An icy wind blew down from the encircling mountains, which became increasingly oppressive. The horses galloped on, snorting and whinnying like mad, and flocks of buzzards flapped along the branches of the trees, shivering as they huddled against each other. Celanire seemed dislocated. At the same time she had never looked so beautiful as her husband hugged her in his arms, as fragile as a cameo. Suddenly Ludivine realized how much Celanire meant to her. She wondered whether her feelings toward her weren't to a large extent tinged with tenderness. She had always imagined she hated this woman, who perhaps had killed her mother. But she had been constantly wrapped in her affection. From an early age it was Celanire who had taken care of her when she was ill, dried her tears, calmed her tantrums, who had given her the taste for a certain type of music, a certain type of poetry, and taught her it was not a curse to be born a woman. What would become of her if she lost her? If she lost too that overriding obsession to unmask her identity and bring about her punishment? What meaning would there be to life if there was nothing left to do but drink, eat, sleep, get married, and have children? Surprised at herself, she began to cry as she hadn't cried for ages.

Finally the horses arrived on the sprawling outskirts of Lima, where the wretched of every color were crammed together. The din of their hooves woke the roosters, who, thinking it morning, began to crow. Once they had crossed the Puente de Piedra, there was a sudden crackling of fireworks, and yellow and silver streaks zigzagged across the sky. Our weary travelers realized that this third Saturday in February was also the first day of Carnival, and that the population of Lima was jumping for joy. Dancers disguised as devils dressed in extravagant costumes adorned with hawks' feathers, bulls' horns, and snake tails cavorted around their carriage. On the Plaza de Armas, groups of black musicians played the *tejoleta*. Amid a general outburst of commiseration, Thomas found his suite again at the Hotel Raimondi. Clutching Celanire like a baby, an old black servant climbed the grand staircase and carried her up to the second floor while another went to fetch the best doctor in town. Ludivine lay down on a corner sofa. Exhausted, she very quickly fell asleep. But her sleep was disturbed by repeated images of bloody piles of dead fowl lying plucked and eviscerated in a cockpit. She finally opened her eyes and saw a man with oily hair and a conceited look in deep conversation with her father. Dr. Iago Lamella seldom paid house calls, especially after eight in the evening. But when he heard it was a Frenchman, he made an exception, because he had studied in France, was a frequent visitor to Paris, and had great admiration for the birthplace of the Rights of Man. And then his governess had been French. He was explaining to Thomas in a laboriously refined French that after having examined Celanire, he remained extremely perplexed. He could diagnose no illness. The liver, the kidneys, the heart and the lungs, every organ in the body, was in perfect working order. The blood and the lymph were circulating freely. It was simply as if the patient had lost all her strength. All her vital functions had slowed down, and if this continued, the outcome was anyone's guess. He suggested massive doses of cod-liver oil and shots of camphorated oil in order to reactivate the organs.

However improbable such a treatment may seem, it had an effect. Around midnight Celanire emerged from her wasting disease. She opened her eyes as distant as stars and in a tiny voice clearly said:

"Thomas, take me back to Guadeloupe. I have nothing more to do here."

The port of Lima is called El Callao, and it isn't much to look at.

Fishermen's boats bob on the milky, melancholic sea next to a few old steamships whose hulls are eaten away with rust. Thomas had had the good fortune to find two first-class cabins de luxe on board the SS *Pachacamac* leaving for Esmeraldas in Ecuador. From there he hoped to continue on to Cartagena in Colombia by land, then sail to Caracas in Venezuela, and finally find his way through the Caribbean to Guadeloupe. At dawn they set sail out of the harbor, and all the passengers assembled on the shiny wooden decks to gaze at the sinister Fronton jail, where during the wars with Chile so many enemy soldiers had been tortured. Then the open sea began to parley with the ship's prow as it tore through its belly. Traveling first-class on the SS *Pachacamac*, you rubbed shoulders with the usual crowd of tropical aristocrats,

owners of haciendas and fincas who had made their fortune from
sugarcane, cotton, and coffee, and who all had their hands
stained with the blood of black slaves. Their black or mestiza
nurses accompanied them in fourth class but came up to join
them at six in the morning to look after their spoiled, pasty-faced
children. There were also a few priests traveling to Rome and
some retired generals. The news that the wife of a senior French
civil servant, confined to her cabin, needed constant nursing,
quickly spread around the ship. As a result numerous good souls
came to offer Thomas their help, although he had never asked
anyone for anything. He received them in the small sitting room
adjoining the cabin so that he could keep an eye at the same time
on the lifeless shape that was his wife. He agreed to Madame
Eusebio because no sooner had she entered the cabin than
Celanire aroused herself out of her comatose state, propped herself up against her pillows, and held out her arms, smiling like a
child who finds a familiar face waiting for her after school.
Madame Eusebio looked like nobody on this earth. She was from
Borbón, a small town in Ecuador at the mouth of the Rio Caya-
pas inhabited mainly by descendants of African slaves. In Quito
she had looked after the five children of a Peruvian diplomat,
who had been so satisfied with her services he had taken her with
him to Lima. Suffering from homesickness, she had saved up
enough money and was now returning home.

Quite frankly, she was ugly, but nevertheless she possessed a
piquant sort of charm. Her teeth, perhaps a little too large, were
of an impeccable ivory; her cheeks were dotted with warts, much
like birthmarks, and her bulging eyes emitted a powerful mag-
netism. While she hugged Celanire passionately up against her,
whispering words of Spanish in her ear, Thomas stood staring at
them, hopping from one foot to another in astonishment.

Where had the two women first met? By way of explanation Madame Eusebio peremptorily indicated he should leave. Dumbfounded, he closed the door behind him and went to join Ludivine, slumped in a chaise longue on the deck. To while away the time Ludivine was making an effort to read, but *Madame Bovary, Eugénie Grandet,* and *Le Père Goriot,* all those books her father had recommended as masterpieces, made her yawn, and she sat there blinking and staring at the dazzling lid of the Pacific clapped over the ocean depths.

Today ocean travel is coming back into fashion. People pay a fortune to cruise slowly from one point of the globe to another. But at that time travel by ship was boring, and everyone dreamed of a faster mode of transportation. On board there were very few distractions. During the day the men played endless games of billiards. In the evening they sat down to poker before crowding into the bar to wet their mustaches in the crushed ice of their cocktail glasses. The women badmouthed each other behind their backs and rivaled in elegance at dinnertime, which was occasionally followed by a cotillion that alone broke the monotony of the journey. Every Saturday they danced the waltz or the foxtrot. At night they huddled under their blankets on chaise longues and peered into the dark for the sign of a light on the coast. The farther north they sailed, the greater the number of birds that flocked slowly across the sky. But nobody looked up in that direction. These landlubbers felt they had been tossed by the waves from time immemorial and had lost touch forever with their familiar surroundings. They imagined they would never get rid of the peppery, bitter smell of the sea, which irritated their nostrils.

From that moment on Madame Eusebio never left Celanire's cabin. From morning to night it was filled with the smoke from the mysterious plants she burned. She barred Thomas from entering, and he was reduced to wandering the deck at all hours of the day, lighting up Havana after Havana in the smoking room and downing glasses of port in the bar. Sometimes the captain took pity on him and invited him to his table for meals. But Thomas never failed to launch into endless tirades against the conquistadors who had devastated the Amerindian cultures. He also extolled the merits of Simón Bolívar and regretted that his dream of building the Gran Colombia had never been realized. Moreover, he meddled in politics, daring to criticize President Eloy Alfaro and saying it served him right if the crowd had recently torched him like a carnival puppet. Blathering away in this fashion, he appeared to forget that his traveling companions possessed the courtesy of the Spanish and that his Gallic outspokenness risked offending them. In short, the captain ended up leaving him to lap up his soup all alone in his corner. At night he went and slept on a mattress in his daughter's cabin that the stewards had laid out on the floor. He quickly realized that here again his conversation bored Ludivine to tears, and he took comfort in his beloved poems translated from Quechua. Since he had lost his sleep worrying over Celanire's condition and read until dawn, he wrapped the only lamp in the cabin with a green shawl so as not to disturb the young girl. In the early hours of the morning, while she was still asleep, he slipped on his clothes without washing.

We don't know whether Madame Eusebio treated Celanire with the medication recommended by Dr. Iago Lamella. Cod-liver oil? Shots of camphorated oil ? It's highly unlikely! She did exactly whatever came into her head. We do know with certainty, almost down to the last detail, the diet she had her follow. Twice a day she went down into the heat of the kitchens, tied an apron around her waist, and began preparing her patient's food tray. The most incredible stories began to circulate about her behavior, spread by the chefs and kitchen boys. For them there was no doubt Madame Eusebio was a *bruja,* worthy of those witches from the southern coast of Peru. More than milk, she needed blood and more blood, a never-ending request for blood. Sometimes she curdled it with rock salt, sliced it, then steamed it in a pan sprinkled with chopped parsley. Other times she filled vials of it, which she wrapped in her mantilla as a precaution against prying eyes. She searched for offal, liver, hearts, and brains and above all, filet steaks, which she cut into fine strips like carpaccio. Despite his aversion for Madame Eusebio, Thomas very quickly ascertained the results of such a treatment. In a few days' time, Celanire emerged from her drowsiness. In the morning she would leaf through some illustrated magazines and in the afternoon appear on deck, leaning on the arm of her nurse. She would shuffle over to the railings, close her eyes, letting the ocean breeze caress her face, then totter back and lie down on a chaise longue. While Madame Eusebio wrapped her legs in a plaid rug, she would exchange a few words, which got less laborious by the day, with her husband and stepdaughter. Her interest in her traveling companions and for life on board returned. What music did they dance to at last night's cotillion? What was Ludivine reading? Had she managed to play her Beethoven on the piano in the smoking room? Then she went back inside her cabin as soon as the wind freshened. The entire first class waited for these moments, however short they were. Although the women turned their noses up at her color, the men lathered themselves up into a frenzy over the contours of her breasts, the curve of her hips, and a glimpse of her ankle, seized once more by their age-old fascination for the *morena.* Of course there was always that wretched kerchief tied around her neck. What did it hide? Thereupon the most outlandish stories began to circulate. At the age of sixteen Celanire had been doused with acid by a lover she had scorned. Aiming for her eyes, his hand had trembled with rage, and he had drenched her throat. This had occurred somewhere in Africa, a few years before she married Thomas. The latter had used his influence as governor and had the guy shipped to a penal colony. He was probably still there. Or else they claimed that as a child she had almost ripped her head off with a skipping rope and had been patched up by the best surgeon in Guadeloupe, who had then raped her. And so on and so on . . . But the one thing that emerged from all this gossip, where bits of truth had been crudely stitched on to bits of legend, was that Celanire was a woman best not to meddle with. In her time, as the Peruvians say, she had waltzed with Lucifer and danced the polka with Marshal Castilla. They pitied Thomas, regarding him simply as the incarnation of the perfect cuckold.

Celanire improved every day during the two-week voyage. Once they reached the coast of Ecuador, she was fully cured.

Perhaps it was the effect of the illness, but from that date on Celanire's character radically changed. Up till then she had been the life and soul of the party, full of energy, always on the move, a little person whose company, after all, was somewhat tiresome. She slowed down, wrapped herself in thought, and became languorous. Her eyes lost their sparkle and deepened. She let others express their opinions and listened to them. She seemed to be constantly hiding inside her things, which were giving her food for thought. Her language too became more moderate, reflecting her new mood. She began to repeat that she needed a new aim in life to continue, a new reason for living.

At Esmeraldas Celanire and Madame Eusebio wept greatly at the moment of separation when Madame Eusebio set off in the direction of Borbón. Yet once again Ludivine couldn't help noticing what she called her stepmother's indifference, even her hypocrisy. The carriage that bore Madame Eusebio away had no sooner turned the corner of the Avenida La Floresta than Celanire stretched like a cat, grinning in seventh heaven at regaining her health.

Guadeloupe
The Same Year

When they landed at the Lardenoy wharf in La Pointe, all the lychee trees on the island, from Matouba to Montebello, from Cocoyer to Trois-Rivières, were loaded with fruit, a good three months ahead of time, and it was as though clusters of tiny Chinese lanterns had been lit among the thick foliage. The lychee is a miserly and secretive tree. It only bears a few bunches at a time, and even then only every seven years. What then did such an abundance herald? A series of catastrophes, no doubt. Since March was not the hurricane season, some people peered at La Soufrière. It was true that for some weeks now it had been emitting gas and smoke again, as nauseous as somebody breaking wind. Others remembered it was the tenth anniversary of an earthquake that had devastated La Pointe from top to bottom. Afterward they had lost count of the number of dead and homeless. Other conflicting voices claimed that on the contrary, the lychees were a sign of good fortune. Good fortune, however, was something the folks in Guadeloupe were not used to seeing, and nobody paid them any attention.

Elissa de Kerdoré was waiting for Celanire at the foot of the gangway with members of the Lucioles association, clutching bouquets of arum lilies. Celanire accepted the flowers. Oddly enough, she refused to return Elissa's outpouring of emotion and gave her a reluctant peck, as if suddenly she was embarrassed by their relationship. As for the Lucioles members, she scarcely greeted them. She eluded Elissa's questions about the journey, explaining merely that in Lima she had fallen seriously ill. She had almost lost her life, in fact. As a result she had seen nothing of what travelers enthuse over—the *selva,* the *páramo,* the pyramids of the Incas and their temples of worship. She hadn't visited Machu Picchu. No, she hadn't made a pilgrimage to Arequipa in the footsteps of Flora Tristan. No, she hadn't been interested in the condition of the Amerindian women. Thereupon she turned her back on the crowd of inquisitive women and headed for the carriage, whose horses were stamping impatiently over a mountain of manure.

The journey from La Pointe to Basse-Terre lasted the entire day.

Comfortably propped against the cushions, Thomas and Celanire constantly dozed off. As for Ludivine, she never tired of gazing at her surroundings. She had forgotten the splendor of her adopted island. They drove through a series of landscapes, each one more impressive than the next—from the formidable mangrove swamps around La Pointe and the cane fields of Petit-Bourg, bristling with their shaftlike flowers, to the banana groves at Capesterre, each tree bent double from the weight of its cluster of fruit, and the foothills of the volcano flecked with fleecy clouds. After Gourbeyre, they made a sharp turn, and the horses seemed to gallop straight for the blue gulf of the ocean. Then they swerved suddenly to the right and entered Basse-Terre.

It was barely dark. But with shutters lowered, the houses were already asleep. At the governor's residence the servants, making believe they were glad to see their masters back, served a light supper. Ludivine's nurse went into raptures: how she had grown in such a short time! How could she possibly talk to her like a little girl now and tell her bedtime stories! Then everyone retired to their quarters. Thomas and Celanire had been sleeping in separate bedrooms for some time now, and night visits to each other were rare. Once he had drunk his laudanum, Thomas was about to drop off when he heard the door creak open. He opened his eyes and to his surprise saw his wife appear, her hair falling loose, wearing a white silk negligee over a nightdress of the same color, a lace ribbon around her neck.

She came and lay down next to him in bed, and he caressed her tenderly, surprised by her mysterious, preoccupied expression.

"What's the matter, my little pet?"

She curled up against him. He loved her fresh smell of the rain forest.

"Do you remember what Montaigne said: 'The soul which has no set aim is lost'?"

He burst out laughing.

"I thought you hated Montaigne. Since when have you been reading the *Essais?*"

She turned to face him.

"I want a child!"

"A child?" he repeated, flabbergasted, almost frightened.

He doubted he was capable, but miraculously, he felt his member stiffen. Meanwhile, she was clasping him in her arms as she used to do and whispering in his ear:

"Please, Thomas! All I can do now is be a good mother."

Reading Group Guide
Who Slashed Celanire's Throat?

1. *Who Slashed Celanire's Throat?* opens with the Reverend Father Hutchard gazing at Celanire while giving us a brief introduction into her character. How does this initial introduction of our heroine differ from the character we've come to know in the end? Describe the development of Celanire's character.

2. We are told in chapter 4 (pg. 45) about Hakim's hatred of the French (". . . and anti-French dreams") which seems to be a sentiment held by many members of the community. For Hakim and those who share his views, what do the French represent?

3. Celanire's arrival at Adjame-Santey coincided with the beginnings of an influx of French influence over African tradition. Discuss the role of Imperialism in the novel. What kind of an impact did all of the changes brought about by imperialism have on the quality of life of the natives? How much of a role did Celanire play in the introduction of these changes and how much of it revolved around her? How much did she stand to benefit from them? In this vein discuss the differences and similarities between Celanire and Thomas De Brabant's first wife, Charlotte. How much of their differences are based on their cultural upbringing?

4. While resisting Celanire's advances in chapter 6 (pg. 60) Hakim ponders about Betti Bouah, "Didn't he realize that once the Africans had hoisted themselves up level with the whites, they would prove to be even more wicked?" Compare and contrast Celanire's behavior and activities toward the people of Bingerville to that of the French imperialists. Considering Celanire's actions, do you agree or disagree with Hakim's statement?

5. We are told in chapter 6 (pg. 68), "At that time homosexuality was considered a repulsive vice," and while doing time in Cayenne (pg. 119) Condé gives us more insight into Hakim's personality: "He would never be cured of what he carried inside him. He would never be anything else but what he was." Discuss Hakim's sentiments toward his own sexuality. How much of an asset was Hakim's homosexuality in resisting the charm and advances of Celanire? Would you consider his resistance successful or futile? Compare and contrast the community's response to male homosexuality as opposed to lesbianism.

6. Celanire can be seen as both an asset and a threat to the community. Discuss this duality. What is your impression of Celanire and what motivates her?

7. The title *Who Slashed Celanire's Throat?* implies a murder mystery, and throughout the story we are led in an investigation into the true origins and intentions of Celanire. Although the novel is narrated by an omniscient narrator, the stories of the various characters are what lead us in uncovering the truth in our investigation. What effect does this have on your reactions to the events? Whose point of view seems the most reliable and why?

8. While magic and superstition are a common practice and belief in various countries including Africa, it is probably unfamiliar territory for most readers. In what ways might this affect the reader's response to the novel? How much of an explanation does the occult provide for the activities in this novel? Discuss the possibilities of other more concrete explanations for the bizarre activities that surround Celanire.

9. On page 94 of *Who Slashed Celanire's Throat?* Dr. Pinceau tells us how he yearned to make a creation like Dr. Frankenstein did in Mary Shelley's *Frankenstein*. Comparing the theme and structure of *Frankenstein* to that of *Who Slashed Celanire's Throat?*, what is Maryse Condé saying about the consequences of this form of scientific experimentation? Discuss the ethical implications. Are there similarities between Dr. Frankenstein's monster and that of Dr. Pinceau? Discuss the role of religion in this novel.

10. The happenings upon which the novel is based took place in 1995, yet Maryse Condé sets the novel during the turn of the century. Discuss the differences and similarities between Guadeloupe's, Bingerville's, and Peru's society in the 1900s and the society of these countries in 1995. Discuss the ways in which these differences and similarities may affect the structure and development of the story.

11. Much of the novel dealt with the different roles men and women play in African society. The men are allowed a certain amount of freedom that is not a privilege for the women, i.e., polygamy, visiting prostitutes, etc. How do the behaviors and expectations made on the two sexes differ in this culture? How does the introduction of French culture affect the ways in which the African culture normally views the role of men and women? Discuss the ways in which Celanire defies the traditional role of a woman in African society.

LaVergne, TN USA
20 April 2010
179818LV00002B/6/P